BLOODY PAWS

A Kim Jansen Detective Novel – 1

BRUCE LEWIS

Black Rose Writing | Texas

Second printing

ISBN: 978-1-68433-815-3
PUBLISHED BY BLACK ROSE WRITING
www.blackrosewriting.com

Printed in the United States of America
Suggested Retail Price (SRP) $18.95

Bloody Paws is printed in Garamond

Dedicated to my wife, Gerry, who listened to endless struggles
and knew exactly how to challenge me to continue
through seemingly endless rewrites.

A Special Thanks to My Supporters

Mike Bander, life-long friend and first draft reader, for giving me the good, bad, and ugly.

William Watson, MD, friend and retired psychiatrist, who analyzed my protagonist and made him more real. And for listening to endless complaints about the process.

Cousin Charles Lewis, who spurred me to a major (fourth) rewrite with a simple comment: "Your characters are all too nice."

Sheila Craven, friend and professional editor, who volunteered her time for a line-by-line edit—and still takes my calls.

Bruce Connors, friend and brilliant retired attorney, who advised on legal and ethical issues, offering positive feedback throughout the creation process.

Novelists Susan Clayton Goldner, author of the award-winning *Tormented*, and Martha Pound Miller, author of *Devil's Child*, for their guidance and moral support.

Mary Ellen Bramwell, author of *In Search of Sisters*, and editor extraordinaire, who fixed my timeline and so many other mistakes. She made everything better.

Reagan Rothe, founder and publisher of Black Rose Writing, for taking a chance on my first novel.

Black Rose Writing's creative team: Social Media Jedi Chris Miller for his book promotion ideas, Design Director David King for his amazing cover and book layout, and Sales Director Justin Weeks for smoothing the production process.

12/30/21

BLOODY PAWS

To Dr Twaites,
for keeping me
healthy so I can keep
writing!

[illegible signature]

PROLOGUE

The unconscious is not just evil by nature, it is also the source of the highest good: not only dark but also light, not only bestial, semi-human, and demonic but superhuman, spiritual, and, in the classical sense of the word, divine."—Carl Jung.

August 7, 2019

The group stood bunched together behind the soundproof window, looking at each other in nervous anticipation of what was about to happen. A detective, a street cop, and a friend. Not an unlikely line-up for a prison execution.

On the other side of the glass, a killer sat facing them, an intravenous tube taped to an arm, awaiting the lethal injection. They wanted to pick up a remote and put their lives on pause. It was happening so fast—and yet in slow motion. It was the sensation people get when they hear skidding tires behind them, look in the mirror—a car coming too fast to stop—and wait for the impact, their fate sealed. Time stands still. They cannot process the information fast enough to react. Now, death is coming like a freight train—at full speed—with no engineer.

The condemned had written some final words with a fat, black marker, on a one-foot square of cardboard—the kind Portland's homeless flash at passersby to solicit handouts: "I'm sorry. I love you guys." The observers' minds screamed a collective "NO!" but nothing came out of their mouths. They let out a gasp as the killing dose of barbiturate disappeared, the injection complete. A few fleeting seconds later, the figure slumped, death nearly instantaneous. Tears flowed down the cop's face. He had just witnessed a tragedy from which he would never recover.

CHAPTER ONE

May 23, 2019

The black-clad woman clipped her iPhone onto the dash of the van and gave a command. “Siri, play the Moody Blues album Days of Future Past.”

“Sure, here are the Moody Blues, just for you.” A moment later, the London Festival Orchestra exploded with *Morning Glory*, an uplifting overture which brightened the dark night. The woman turned up the sound and pulled away from the curb, heading across town. Bars had just closed and the streets in Portland, Oregon’s Pearl District Neighborhood were already empty. Street lighting, competing with a waxing moon, barely lit the roadway.

As the cacophony of instrumental sounds faded, an ominous voice spoke—rather than sang—the lyrics:

Cold-hearted orb that rules the night
Removes the colors from our sight
Red is gray and yellow, white
But we decide which is right
And which is an illusion

Tonight, Helen had no illusions. She saw no colors or shades of gray, just black and white. She would decide what was right.

A mile later, she steered the van to the curb, turned off the engine, slid open a side door, and stepped onto the sidewalk. Helen pulled her knit cap over her ears and rubbed her arms. She did not know if she was shivering from the cold or her mission. Helen left the van door cracked, rather than close it and disturb a half dozen homeless campers scattered along the sidewalks and patches of grass under the 405 Freeway. She did not know why she would try to be quiet. The endless flow of traffic above drowned out any noise she might make. Helen looked up through a 10-foot gap in the north and southbound lanes of the freeway, her eyes fixed on the rising moon. She closed her eyes and listened. Odd how the rhythm of the freeway traffic matched the rhythm of the sea, her mind filling with images of giant waves pounding the Oregon Coast.

When Helen opened her eyes, the bleak coldness of space surrounding the moon sent another chill down her spine. "Vengeance is a dish best served cold," she thought. She zipped up her sweatshirt and snugged the hood around her face. She remembered the phrase from her college French class, which meant revenge is more satisfying if exacted when unexpected, long after the original grievance. Her grievance against Jerry Hoffman was fresh in her mind—only weeks old. But her revenge would be unexpected.

She turned her gaze from the sky to a dome tent pitched inches from a freeway support column with a No Camping sign visible. The sign did not say camping Prohibited. The city's sign maker figured his readers were at such a low grade level they might not understand Prohibited, but would comprehend the word, No. Well, apparently not. The homeless offer a big middle finger to anyone trying to reign in their anti-social behavior.

Helen waded through sticker-filled weeds, discarded paper cups, plastic bags, and broken glass until she was standing outside the offending camper's tent.

"Jerry, are you there?" A growl greeted her. She recognized the sound of Pirate Pete, Jerry Hoffman's one-eyed Beagle.

"Get the fuck out of here or my dog's going to rip you a new one," came a muffled warning from inside the tent.

"Jerry, it's me, Doc Helen. I'm here to give you your vitamin shot."

"I would love a snot," said Jerry, his alcohol-lazy tongue unable to pronounce the word.

"Shot, not snot," Helen said, then stopped. She knew there was no sense lecturing him. His daily fifth of cheap whiskey left him permanently dazed and confused.

"Jerry, how about coming over and getting into my van for your shot? I have hot coffee and donuts for you and doggie treats for Pete." Hoffman did not question why he would get a "snot" in the middle of the night. After a few minutes of moans, grunts, and swearing, the tent zipper slid open. A head of greasy, matted hair—partly singed from a fire—and a gray beard poked through the opening with food bits clinging to its whiskers. Hoffman climbed out of the tent, followed by Pete. The 6-foot-2, 270-pound man with narrow shoulders, enormous belly, and too-thin legs looked like a pear on Popsicle sticks. He swayed back and forth and then fell on his butt.

"Let me help you," Helen said. At 5-feet-10 and 150 pounds, she was no lightweight but struggled with the big man's weight as she slipped under his arm to provide support. Hoffman's body dipped several times on the short walk, his legs nearly buckling under his weight. When they got to the van, Helen helped him onto a 7-foot-long stainless steel procedure table. The workspace had been designed as a mobile care unit for dogs. Helen slammed the van door shut, unconcerned about the loud clank.

"Lay down and relax while I prepare your snot," she said, mocking the man. He did not notice. His head swung from left to right and back, trying to bring the world into focus a moment before he passed out. When Jerry woke up, she was holding a syringe.

"I need to take a piss," said Jerry, his speech clearer, attempting to lean forward, but unable to sit up. "What the fuck," he said, realizing someone had tied down his arms and legs. Despite the man's size and residual strength from his long-past days as a dockworker, the canine surgery ties locked him in place.

"Do you recognize me, Jerry?"

"You are Doc Helen. You work with Dr. Briggs, who has been caring for Pete. I'm getting a vitamin shot," duct tape over his mouth muffling the words.

"Look again, Jerry. Yes, I'm the Doc. I'm also the woman you left for dead in the park last month. Well, guess what? I'm alive and well and here to deliver you a special shot. But this won't be any shot, Jerry. It's a one-way ticket to Hell." Jerry Hoffman was blank. He did not understand a word she said.

"I gotta pee," he repeated, squirming as much as the restraints would allow. Ignoring his plea, Helen slipped the needle into his vein and held her finger over the plunger. Jerry mumbled something through the duct tape that sounded like, "Oh my god, no."

"Did I hear 'I'm sorry'? Do you feel any remorse?" Tears flowed down the man's face. He shook his head. Helen could not tell if he was trying to apologize or clear his head.

"I can't hear you, Jerry," she said, and ripped the duct tape off his mouth. Jerry yelped as the tape pulled out a section of mustache, and he took a massive gulp of air. "That's good, Jerry. Take a deep breath. It's going to be your last."

"I'm sorry, so sorry," he said. "It was Little Bobby's fault. I was drunk. He gave us the pills, cheered us on."

"Yes, you were drunk, and you were full of Viagra, and you were full of violence. And now you're full of shit. Take responsibility, you miserable bastard. You and your pals attacked me when I was drunk, half passed out, and helpless." The anger she had been swallowing came up, her hand forming a fist like a hammer that smashed Jerry's nose. Blood spurted across his torn, stained t-shirt. Hoffman howled in pain. Pirate Pete let loose with his own piercing howl, his mournful tone matching Jerry's. "It's okay, Pete," she said, offering a treat to settle him down and patting him on the head. Finally, she pulled the syringe from Jerry's vein, blood seeping from the puncture, and held it inches from Jerry's face—so close his eyes crossed. "Yell. Scream. Beg. Say whatever you like. No one can hear you." Jerry gulped more air through his mouth, his nose closed from blood.

"Hey, Siri, let's play a special song for Jerry. Play Fiona Apple's song about the ocean."

"I'm sorry, I don't know who Jerry is," Siri answered.

"Siri, sometimes you're useless."

"I've been told that," Apple's intelligent assistant responded.

"Play Fiona Apple's song, *Container*. Listen closely, Jerry, this is your swan song."

I was screaming into the canyon
At the moment of my death
The echo I created
Outlasted my last breath…

Hoffman turned his head toward the sound. When it finished, Hoffman looked like he was going to ask what it meant. Before he could open his mouth to object, Helen re-inserted the needle into a vein and pushed in the plunger. The clear liquid disappeared into Hoffman's vein. He tried to grab his chest, forgetting she had tied his hands. A crushing weight pushed out all the air in his lungs as the massive dose of barbiturate paralyzed his breathing, then slowed and stopped his heart.

He bucked, shook, and twisted from the pain for 30 seconds more before he lay still. In death, his bulging eyes remained open. Unlike the dozens of dogs she had euthanized—a two-shot process—she had left out the Propofol, an anesthetic that would have rendered Hoffman unconscious and pain-free when he received the second killing shot. Inflicting the maximum pain was her goal. She broke off the needle tip and deposited the syringe in a hazard disposal box on the wall. She rolled Jerry's body off the table into the refrigerated box used for transportation of dog corpses. When she had secured his body and closed the lid, she turned to Pete.

"Pete, do you want to join Jerry?" Wouldn't Pete be better dead than trying to survive on garbage and the goodness of another homeless scofflaw? Instead of preparing another shot, she removed Pete's tracking collar, opened the van door, and gently placed him on the ground. "Good luck, Pete. The streets might be better than Hell, where Jerry is going." Pete looked at her and ran off. She closed the door and climbed into the driver's seat. She started the engine, cranked up Love Me by She Wants Revenge, and pulled away from the curb and into the night.

***

With a Portland Police Bureau officer in tow for security, Elton Hobson and Gail Muncie moved cautiously toward the dome tent pitched next to a city "No Camping" sign. Across the street, the homeless were packing up and scattering. They knew they needed to leave the area or risk losing their prized possessions: grocery carts filled with cardboard, empty cans, plastic containers, ragged clothing, and discarded small appliances. Why someone with no access to electricity would lug around a banged-up bread maker or electric blender is anyone's guess. More often than not, their carts were bright red—hostages from the Target store downtown. At other stores, if you tried to roll the carts more than a few yards from the front door, all four wheels would lock up.

Wearing N-95 masks, rubber gloves, goggles, heavy leather shoes, and overalls, Hobson and Muncie were ready for anything, including a decaying body. Hobson has seen more than Muncie, who at the tender age of 36, with only 10 years under her belt as a City of Portland Parks maintenance worker, had only stumbled on one rotting corpse. One was enough for a lifetime. Although the masks beat back some smells, an odor of cigarette smoke, body order, wet dog, and something rotten broke through and assaulted their noses, escaping from the thin tent wall in front of them.

"Anyone home?" Hobson yelled over the freeway sound. He tried again and got no answer. Didn't mean a thing. A night of partying on a 12-pack of PBR tall boys, 16 ounces for a buck—or a drug overdose—would smother a response.

"Muncie, you go first," Hobson ordered.

Muncie frowned. "Yoo-hoo, anybody home?" she called out.

Hobson smiled and said, "You sound like Aunt Bea on the Andy Griffith Show coming to drop off an apple pie to a neighbor."

"Elton, you're dating yourself. The last episode aired in 1968. You must be older than you look." Hobson's resisted a comeback, his mouth forming a tight line.

"I've watched all 249 episodes," Muncie admitted.

"Enough nostalgia," said Bill Blaise, the Portland cop accompanying them. The homeless did not like having their so-called treasures and household items carted away. Some got violent. "I've got better things to do than babysit you two all morning."

With their metal pick up sticks thrust in front of them like bayonets, they moved closer to the unzipped tent opening. Muncie used her stick to push open the door enough to look in. As she poked her head through, another wave of rot struck her and she pulled back. "Oh God, that's bad," she said. Dobson squeezed his eyes shut, grimacing under his mask.

"Is it a body?"

"Where the hell do these people go?" Muncie wondered, ignoring Hobson's question. Although her job was routine, incidents that required calling the police, being interviewed by detectives, and filling out endless paperwork, were unnerving. This time she and Hobson got lucky. No one was home. Muncie pushed her way into the tent—on her hands and knees because of the low ceiling—and crawled forward until she was inside. She sat down and looked around.

The former occupant had placed a bowl of kibble in one corner and an assortment of mismatched clothes in another. Moving the lice-ridden pile with her stick, Muncie spotted a tattered cloth wallet under the clothing. She grabbed it with the pickup stick, then thrust it through the tent opening. Hobson jumped back like a soldier on a battlefield about to be stabbed.

"Check this out, Elton."

He grabbed the wallet, opened it. Inside was a welfare identification card for Gerald Hoffman. A photo showed a red-faced man with a gray-streaked, scraggly beard and overlong hair pushed back behind his ears. It looked like a jail booking photo. One more thing she found odd: in a Ziploc bag was a pair of women's lace underwear. She put down her stick, opened the bag and pulled them out. They appeared to be clean, almost new. The label was Agent Provocateur. "I've found something odd," Muncie called out.

"Are you going to keep me in suspense?" said Hobson.

"Hang on, I need to check out something." Muncie pulled her cell phone from her overalls, Googled the brand website, and pulled up a similar pair selling for more than $150. "Christ," she said, "a hundred and fifty fucking dollars for panties." Her own underwear from Walmart came three to a pack for $7.99.

"What the hell are you talking about?" said Hobson. She did not answer.

"Hey Hobson, this guy has a pair of high-class women's panties. I just looked them up on the Web. They cost what we make in a day. I think we should package them with the I.D. Might interest the cops." City protocols required them to turn in all pieces of identification and any other personal items that could identify a missing person.

"Whatever, Muncie. Let's get this crap cleaned up and move onto the next shit-pile.

"I'm done here," said Muncie, crawling out of the tent and removing her mask for some fresh air.

Hobson pushed the wallet and panties toward Officer Blaise. "No way," he said. "I'm not doing your paperwork for you. I am here to observe only and provide security." Hobson would turn in the I.D. card to their boss, along with a report of Hoffman's few belongings. They would leave out details of the detritus going into large plastic bags. Their boss would pass their report along the bureaucratic chain to the Portland Police Bureau. Hobson was tempted to toss the I.D. in the trash because of the dreaded red tape it started. Besides, he did not know Gerald Hoffman, and he did not enjoy cleaning up Hoffman's mess. Did anyone care whether this homeless man lived or died? Either way, chances were he was never coming back to claim his so-called treasures, including the panties.

"We should wait to see if the occupant returns before dragging this stuff away," Muncie said. "He may have taken his dog for a walk."

"Are you going soft in the head," Hobson snapped. "We don't wait when a person sets up house-keeping under a No Camping sign. Everything goes, and it goes now. You know the rules." Muncie was pushing Hobson's button. Many of her coworkers had been fired when they were caught tossing personal items and identifications in the trash to avoid paperwork. Muncie could not afford to lose her job. While Hobson may have 18 months until retirement, she was a single mom with two college-bound high school students to support. Her pension was not due for another 15 years.

"Let's do it, Hobson," Muncie said.

"I thought I was giving the orders," Hobson shot back.

"Come on, guys," Officer Blaise said. "Let's get this crap packed up."

With the identification card and other personal effects secured in the glove compartment, Hobson and Muncie loaded the last evidence of Gerald Hoffman's life into the back of their truck. It would be one more load that added to the 2.6 million pounds of trash picked up annually from abandoned homeless camps in Portland.

CHAPTER TWO

February 12, 2019–When it all Began

At six-feet-six inches tall, Jim Briggs towered over his colleagues.

"We're going to miss you, big guy," said Bill Merchant, raising a glass to Briggs. Everyone cheered. Merchant, the founding partner of PawsCare, a booming dog-only veterinary clinic and surgery center in Chicago's Gold Coast neighborhood, said, "We still can't figure out why you're leaving."

"Are you ready for the truth? I'm not sure you can handle the truth," said Briggs, folding his arms. He pursed his lips, put a hand over his mouth, rubbed his chin, and shook his head as he made eye contact with each of the ten people in the room. He was playing the role of disappointed teacher, ashamed of his students for not knowing the answer. His audience unconsciously began swaying from foot to foot, some gulping champagne in anticipation of his answer.

"It's too damn cold here," he said and smiled. "Look outside. Ice is everywhere, and the temperature is minus 20." The room let out a group gasp of relief and then burst out laughing. Jim Briggs' journey from veterinary school to mobile pet care provider was a long, winding road that began in the Midwest. A week after Briggs graduated from Carlson College of Veterinary Medicine at Oregon State University, he flew to Chicago for an internship in the middle of an economic downturn. When he arrived, he found himself on the front line of Chicago's Pet Wars.

With fewer dollars available for pet care, veterinary emergency rooms began offering more services and longer hours, cutting into local veterinarians' income.

The fur flew, so to speak, with accusations and threats hurled back and forth. Reduced income meant staff layoffs. A few veterinarians more than normal committed suicide. And they were already known to have the highest suicide rate among professionals, caused by the stress of caring for sick or injured animals while trying to comfort their worried owners. Others abandoned the Pet Wars battlefield altogether, taking jobs as cab drivers with the same hours but less overhead and stress.

Six years later, Briggs stood in the middle of his fellow veterinarians, who were all partners in PawsCare. "Some of you know I've always wanted to launch a mobile pet care service. And, yes, Portland can be rainy and cold, but we only get snow for a day or two a year. Compared with Chicago winters, it's like Palm Springs in the summer." Briggs took a sip of champagne and continued. A big part of my love for Portland: it's absolutely canine crazy. It's a place where nothing is too good for your dog. Money is no object."

Briggs did his best to explain the appeal, describing how one pet store offers a goat-milk cappuccino, a Puppuccino, and sells marijuana products to ease canine anxiety and pain. "Portland also has 33 dog parks, more per capita than any city in the nation," Brings said.

"I get it," his colleague Stuart Smith said with raised eyebrows. "Portland has cannabis on every corner, so the dogs and vets are all stoned. They are all nice and relaxed. Give some pot to the dog owner and you'd be in veterinary Utopia." The group cracked up.

"On my trip to visit my mother a few months ago, I did a lot of walking and bike riding around the city. On one walk, I saw Noah's Arf doggie daycare, PAWco's Taco Wagon, and Fetch Eyewear, an optometry/frame shop (for humans) which donates 100% of its profits to animal rescue." What drew sniggers from his Midwestern colleagues was his description of the Sniff Hotel. "That's no joke," Briggs assured them. "Picture this: the three-story yellow and black building fills half a block. On the bottom floor is a separate entrance for the puppy nursery. A few doors down is a pet store. Around the corner is a cocktail lounge/pub where owners and their dogs can hang out. They even serve special non-alcoholic drinks for the pups."

"You're making this up," Merchant called out.

"No, it would blow you away. They rent a ten-by-ten canine hotel room with a picture window for $63 a day. On the roof is a play area," he said, adding, "That's where I will house any of you who come for a visit." More laughter.

"One more reason I'm leaving." Again, they stopped to listen. Some were smiling in anticipation of another joke. Without warning, he shifted to a serious topic: his mother's failing health. "My mom has advanced COPD and has been going downhill fast. I want to spend more time with her, help make life a little easier if I can."

The group wished him good luck, gave him a last toast, then left. "Stay in touch," said Bill. "I'll leave it to you to lock up." Briggs grabbed Bill, hugged him, and then let go. "I don't want to be mushy, but I love you, Bill. You took me on when I was fresh out of college, when the Chicago vet business was in turmoil, and you nurtured my career. You're a good man. I won't ever forget."

"My pleasure," said Bill, who added. "I'm glad you've forgotten how I worked your ass off for low wages for so many years. I believe I got the long end of the stick." They shook hands and Bill gave Briggs a little punch in the arm as he left.

Jenny Morrison stayed after the others had left, her time with Briggs running out.

Morrison, a veterinarian partner like Briggs, was saddest to see him leave. She and Briggs had been best friends and lovers. They arrived in the clinic nearly the same day as fresh-faced interns and had been together ever since.

When it came time for Briggs to leave Chicago, he urged Jenny to join him in Oregon, even suggested taking their relationship to the next level. They talked about having kids and forming a veterinarian partnership in Portland. The night before the send-off party, after making love, Jenny said, "I want to be with you Jimmy, but I just can't leave my mom and dad. I need my brothers and sisters, the big family dinners. I want my kids to know their grandparents and their aunts, uncles, and cousins."

Briggs would have one more chance to change her mind. He had a month-long break from work before his move and planned to spend it with her in Bermuda.

***

The next day, Briggs and Jenny packed up for the trip. As they looked forward through the windshield, about to head to the airport and to an uncertain future—and the possibility of losing one another—they held hands. Briggs looked over and smiled at Jenny. "Let's see where this trip leads." She offered a weak smile. Before he could put the car in gear, Briggs's phone rang. "Dr. Briggs, this is Jim Connell, your mother's pulmonologist. Ruby Joyce is on life support and, doesn't have much time left. If you want to see her before she passes, you need to come now."

"If I can get a direct flight to Portland tonight, I can be there in the morning," said Briggs.

Briggs explained the situation to Jenny.

"I heard him, Jimmy. You've got to go. You'll just have to come back out in the fall or next year for our trip."

That's not what he wanted to hear. He could see his chances of a life with Jenny slipping away.

***

When the elevator door opened, Jim Briggs ducked under the metal door frame, surveyed the room and walked toward the nurse's station. Six nurses, their faces lit up by computer screens, snapped to attention. Coming toward them was a mass of red: a red Hawaiian shirt, a man with long red hair pulled back in a ponytail, a close-cropped red beard, and pale, reddish skin.

A nurse stood up to greet him and blurted, "How tall are you?"

"Ginny!" a second, older nurse, scolded.

"Hi, I'm Nancy Morgan. You must be Ruby Joyce Briggs' son. I've cared for your mom several times during her stays over the past year. She's a ball of fire. I'm her day-shift nurse."

"She's full of piss and vinegar," Briggs added.

"That too," Morgan acknowledged. Morgan, at five-feet-two, had to bend her neck back at an uncomfortable angle to take in the man in front of her.

"Yes, I'm Ruby's son. I'm Jim Briggs." Looking down at Ginny, who returned to her computer after her embarrassing outburst, Briggs smiled and said, "I'm six-feet-six in my stocking feet."

"Sorry," she mouthed.

"No problem, it's not the first time someone has asked."

Briggs got the question in restaurants, from patients bringing their dogs in for care, and passersby on the street. He had not expected it when he stepped into the critical care unit at Providence Hospital, where he would give approval to remove his mother from life support.

Briggs was feeling self-conscious about the Hawaiian shirt. He could not help wonder if the nurses thought he had gotten lost on the way to a luau. Were the nurses conditioned to the odd way people act when faced with the death of a loved one? Were they only dreaming of their own escape, perhaps a tropical vacation. The shirt was Ruby's last present to her only son, a Christmas gift to brighten his winters in Chicago.

"Mr. Briggs, Ruby Joyce is straight ahead, first door on the right. Take as much time as you like. I'll check on you in a few minutes."

"Thanks for coming to visit," said Ginny, the young nurse, intent on making amends for her initial faux pas.

"It's Valentine's Day, why wouldn't I visit my mother?" Briggs said, cocking his head as if waiting for an answer. Ginny turned red. Briggs smiled.

Nurse Morgan interceded. "Call me if you need me. Use the button clipped to your mom's bed."

Briggs turned, took five long steps, and was at the door. He pushed it open a crack to see if Ruby was awake, trying to avoid disturbing her—if it were possible to wake someone in a coma near death. He went in, stood in the room entrance, took a quick look around in the semi-darkness, and closed the door behind him. Briggs walked to the window, passing his mother's bed without looking at her, and pulled open the shade.

The sky was a mixture of dark and light, covered with clouds. Sun poked through in several spots, illuminating the trees in the neighborhood fourteen stories below.

Briggs did not want to turn around, face the moment.

Experience as a veterinarian-surgeon, and a stint as an emergency medical technician during college, should have better prepared him.

"*Hey, Jimbo, get on with it. It' s only life. She' ll be better off where she is going.*"

Briggs closed his eyes and slapped the top of his head several times, trying to silence the ever-present voice in his head.

But there was no escape, even on a day like today, in a place like this. He called the voice DIME, the Devil in My Ear. And DIME referred to him as Jimbo, like his mother did when he was a kid and she had been unhappy with him.

Ruby confessed to Briggs later in life that it was her formula for "toughening you up, making you a man after your dad died." Jim Sr, a newspaper reporter, who suffered a massive heart attack on deadline and died, was 44. Jim Jr, 12. Mom was 29.

"I'm the only parent you've got, Jimbo, so buck up; don't be a crybaby," she told him when he broke his arm in a touch football game. She was relentless. What might have seemed like a good idea at the time—and he credited her for his never-give-up determination—implanted a dark code in his brain; always negative, countering the best side of him. A girlfriend he confided in referred to his positive, optimistic side as his 'Happy Half.'

Ruby never let up on the "Jimbo, you can do better, swim faster, find a cuter girl, get better grades theme"—even if the girl was class president and his grades were A's or A-minuses.

When Briggs turned around, he shivered, the cold reality of his mother's death closing around him like a coffin. He watched Ruby Joyce's chest rise and fall to the rhythm of the ventilator while an incessant beeping sound signaled that the end of life was a heartbeat away.

For a moment, he had no feelings at all. Then a second later tears rolled poured down his face. He sank into a chair by her bed and sobbed.

"Damn you, you never listened to anyone." She did not respond. "I love you, but if you had only quit smoking…." In the end, COPD and lung cancer had killed her. Almost.

Ruby Joyce responded to none of his sobs. Her half-open eyes were unblinking.

Briggs wiped away the tears and grabbed a tissue from a nearby box to wipe his nose.

As he sat on the bed, holding her hand, he talked to her. He told her he was wearing the Hawaiian shirt she gave him.

He described his Chicago farewell party and shared his dream for the future, a future that would not include her.

"What I have wanted for a long time is my own business. I plan to save my money, buy a van, stock it with supplies, and offer mobile dog care to clients in northwest Portland." She did not answer, not even a squeeze of the hand that might signal her recognition or approval.

After a half-hour, nurse Nancy Morgan walked into the room, explained the procedure for disconnecting his mother from life support, then waited for him to sign the consent form. He thought about telling her he was a doctor of veterinarian medicine and knew all about ending a life. For his mother, they would turn up the morphine to eliminate any possibility of pain, then turn off the ventilator, and wait for the heart rate monitor to turn from beeps to a continuous tone.

Nurse Morgan reviewed his signature and began the process for hastening Ruby Joyce's end of life.

Death was quicker for a dog, first anesthetizing it, then stopping its heart, a 30-second, two-shot procedure. Mom would die from natural causes, the morphine only palliative care.

Briggs leaned over and whispered in Ruby's ear, "You could be annoying, but I love you, Mom. I'll miss you."

An instant later, her head flew off the pillow, her eyes bulging with terror inches from Brigg's face. He jumped back. Then just as quickly she lay back down, as inert as before. He had seen his dog rally at the last second when he was a kid before the vet administered the killing shot. That left a scar. His mother's reaction—he guessed the moment her spirit exited her body—created a rip in his soul.

CHAPTER THREE

March 1, 2019

Jim Briggs had scattered his mother's cremated remains into Devils Churn at Cape Perpetua, on the Oregon Coast. Now, he was sitting in the office of his mother's attorney, waiting for the will reading and the next phase of his life.

"You're a lucky young man," said Miriam Wilson, 63, Ruby Joyce Briggs' attorney, as she reviewed a 30-page stack of legal-size paper, the details of Ruby Joyce Briggs' will.

Although Jim Briggs was an only child, Briggs expected some aunts, uncles, and cousins would also be beneficiaries. He had never discussed inheritance with his mother.

"You know your mom and I were best friends."

"I did. She said she loved you."

Wilson smiled, and said, "We traveled together, had girls' nights out, and lots more—stuff I won't bore you with. But nothing boring about Ruby Joyce." Nothing boring about Miriam Wilson either, judging by walls full of photos with celebrities and politicians. "The good news is that Ruby left everything to you, an estate worth more than $2.5 million," Wilson said. "Her estate includes $1.3 million in investments and a 2,500-square-foot, 3-bedroom, 3-bath condominium in the Portland Pearl District worth another $1.2 million. She bought the condo a few months ago. With her failing health, I imagine she had little time to unpack boxes."

Briggs gasped at the numbers. Although he had rarely visited his mother while working in Chicago, he knew she had invested in real estate and had always lived in moderately priced homes. That she had amassed so much wealth amazed him.

Although she had helped him with some veterinary school costs, he still owed $150,000 after six years of payments. Given his new millionaire status, he felt he had to apologize for his everyday dress: a Hawaiian shirt, shorts with his red hair-covered legs protruding, and Keen Sandals.

"You look fine," Wilson said, noticing that Briggs was suddenly looking at his clothes and squirming in his seat.

"Ready for me to read the will? It's short."

"I won't try to control you from the grave," Ruby had written. "But I want you to use some money to launch the mobile business you've been dreaming about. When you do, help the homeless by caring for their dogs for free. That should be easy enough since you're a veterinarian. And Portland has plenty of homeless to choose from. Trust me, you will benefit far more than you give."

"Regardless of what you decide," her letter continued, "I will always be proud of what you have accomplished."

"That's the end," Wilson said, handing the letter to Briggs.

Briggs' eyes filled with tears after he read the last line to verify Ruby's parting words. He would miss her, even if she often had been overbearing and occasionally outrageous, like his 21st birthday when she brought pot (he did not smoke) and a cake with a penis and vagina made of icing (which embarrassed him). The words on the cake: "Have a Happy Fucking Birthday, Love Mom." Add five tumultuous marriages to alcoholics to the family dynamic and it was easy to see how he and his mother had a complicated relationship. Her annual oyster parties, with oysters she had shipped from New Orleans, were wildly popular with her eclectic coterie of friends. Invitees might include a judge, a doctor, a convicted burglar, a call girl, and the owner of a wig shop. In the studio above the wig shop, Ruby Joyce offered illegal silicone breast enhancement injections, administered by the sales representative for the silicone manufacturer. For Ruby, the decision to get her breasts enhanced led to a total mastectomy thirty years later. Who knows how many others suffered the same fate.

At the beginning of each party, Ruby would say, "Jimmy, please don't call me mother in front of my friends. Makes me sound old." *Old* was all of 30.

That Mom's will stated she was "proud" shook him. It was something she would never say while alive because it might have blunted her "try harder, Jimbo, you can do better" mantra throughout his life. No matter how much he accomplished, it was never enough. At the end of her life, she had yielded a bit, using "proud" as a punch line to her life and their relationship.

"She never, ever said she was proud of what I had accomplished," said Briggs, wiping his tears with his arm.

Wilson handed him a tissue and said, “She was. She talked about you all the time. She was very proud.”

“It would have been nice for her to say it to me when she was alive—even once,” Briggs said. Wilson looked up in surprise and frowned. The frown was sympathetic rather than a sign of disgust.

“I will transfer the money and other assets to you,” she said, Briggs recovered.

Wilson got up and walked to the door, opened it, and told her assistant, “Please help Dr. Briggs with the final paperwork.”

“Sorry about my meltdown, Miriam. My mother and I had a complicated relationship after my dad died.” Wilson did not ask questions. She understood and had experienced Ruby’s bipolar personality more than once. Relieved that they had completed the reading and paperwork, Briggs was ready to launch Have Paws—Will Travel.

***

“Close your eyes, Jim. I have something to show you,” Marketing whiz Brittany Connors said, as she took Briggs by the arm and led him toward GoodTime Mobile Media’s finishing area. The entrance was 10-feet tall, so Briggs did not need to duck when walking through the door.

“Okay, open your eyes.”

Briggs’ face lit up.

He walked around his newly painted Freightliner 2500 Sprinter, a long, wide van used by delivery services. It would be the home of his new veterinary business.

A week after his mother died, he had given Brittany a hand-drawn plan for interior features, colors, and a business name. She had quickly pulled together vendors necessary to make Briggs’ dream a reality.

On the side of the forest green van was a line of one-foot-high dog paws. It appeared a dog had stepped in white paint and walked across the surface. Above, the white paws were the words, Have Paws—Will Travel, the name a tribute to his great grandfather, Joe Briggs. Every Sunday, Grandpa Joe sat in a big, leather-bound chair with Briggs at his feet. For hours, they watched reruns of *Have Gun—Will Travel*, a black-and-white TV western with a dapper hero vigilante named Palladin. Printed under the new company name was Loving Mobile

Canine Care and James Allen Briggs, D.V.M. "Brittany, the new van looks fantastic," said Briggs, completing the walk-around.

"For a guy your size, I think the proportions are just right," said Brittany. "I knew you would like it." She was a 30-something with black hair and deep blue eyes, a striking attribute of people with Black Irish heritage. "Wait until you see the inside." Briggs slid open the side door and looked in. Scanning the interior, he went through a mental checklist, like a pilot before take-off. Seven-foot-long stainless steel worktable / bed. A refrigeration unit for canine bodies. A bike with saddlebags attached to the wall would be perfect for helping the dogs of homeless in places unreachable by van. Briggs also had designed cabinets for veterinary supplies, and a space for a refrigerator for perishable medications to maximize storage.

"Is it all there?" Brittany asked.

"Better than I had imagined," said Briggs, running his hands over every surface, confirming it was real; his dream had come true. Brittany's expert team had not come cheap: Briggs had to pay an extra $10,000 in overtime hours and rush charges to meet his timeline for the business launch. "It was worth every penny," Briggs assured Brittany. She smiled.

Besides her work on the van, Brittany had launched a marketing campaign that included recruiting dog-owner clients from the web community, Next Door. She had filled 25 client slots with a waiting list of ten more. Briggs would have his hands full, offering 24-hour response for emergency and routine care for $500/month, plus expenses. Best of all, Brittany had set up electronic payments for the new clients, and each had paid upfront for three months. It seemed money was no object for wealthy and upper-middle-class dog owners in Portland's Nob Hill, Alphabet District, and Pearl neighborhoods.

"Here's the invitation list," said Brittany when they returned to a conference room to review additional marketing plans. "We are targeting about a dozen vet clinics and animal hospitals in the area. They are all potential clients; they will want to use your services, like euthanasia, when a client can't bring a dog into the clinic or the vet doesn't want to handle home calls at night. You'll want to use their surgery facilities in emergencies. We've rented the roof of the Sniff Hotel for the business debut and will supply food along with Oregon wines and local craft beer."

"Any luck recruiting the homeless with dogs?" Brittany asked.

She had devised a plan that would allow Briggs to record contacts with the homeless and then maintain a connection by using a dog collar with a GPS tracking collar that worked with the PupFinder App.

"It's been hit-and-miss, but I think I've latched onto at least a dozen homeless and their dogs."

***

Briggs then closed his eyes and shook his head, as if trying to shake out some painful memories of his initial contacts with Portland's unsheltered citizens. He was still reeling from an encounter the day before with a homeless man dodging cars on a freeway to collect cash from passing motorists.

He was certain the man was about to commit suicide and take his dog with him. And there was nothing he could do to prevent it. Traffic was coming too fast. The driver of one oncoming car spotted the hazard, swerved slightly, jammed on the brakes, and then laid on the horn. He gave the homeless man the finger and raced on.

As another bunch of cars approached, Briggs wanted to turn away. A Land Rover in one lane and a Tesla in another raced toward the man, who was straddling a six-inch-wide cement barrier, with his terrier balanced on top. One false step would add the man's name to next week's pedestrian death toll.

Just then, the light changed to red on the freeway offramp and the cars came to a screeching halt. The man pulled out a piece of cardboard begging for money with a "God Bless" added to the end. No one rolled down a window to offer money.

When the light turned green, the cars raced off with man and dog facing down the cars, their lives at the mercy of luck. The man's homeless female companion observed from the sidewalk 10 feet away with no sign of concern.

"Sir, please get out of the street," Briggs, standing on the corner, yelled over the traffic. "It's dangerous. You and your dog could get killed."

"Fuck you, man. Mind your own business." Apparently, cash for his next meal was more valuable than his life. The man's hair was hanging in greasy tangles, his once red sweatshirt, now faded to pink, covered the top of oversized pants. A piece of clothesline held up his jeans, ripped knees and all.

When the cars stopped for the next red light, Briggs crossed the street to where the woman was standing. The traffic again started up with rush-hour commuters racing by, eager for drinks at a local pub, or headed for dinner at home. Or a Monday night football game.

When Briggs started talking to the woman, the man jumped between oncoming cars, onto the sidewalk, and demanded to know what Briggs was doing. "Are you hitting on Sally, my woman?" His tiny dog, still balancing in the middle of the offramp, looked confused, but did not budge from the top of the mid-lane barrier.

Even though Briggs towered over the man, he did not back away. He moved in closer, his stinky breath enough to make Briggs' knees buckle.

Despite the threatening tone, Briggs stuck out his hand and introduced himself. "I'm veterinarian Jim Briggs. I recently launched a mobile dog care business and looking for clients."

"Baby, this boy is crazier than a bedbug," he said to Sally. When the traffic stopped again, the dog jumped off the barrier and ran over to watch the interaction. Despite the man's raised voice, he seemed relaxed. "We don't have shit to pay for vet care, right Barney," the man said, turning to his dog for acknowledgment.

"The care is free to anyone with a dog who does not have a permanent home." Briggs had learned not to call them street people or homeless. Looking at Sally, the man said, "What do you think?"

"I'd say if it's free, we gotta have it. Maybe the good doctor can patch us up, too," she said, raising her arm to display a three-inch-long gash on her hand that looked fresh. "Those jagged tuna can tops are like razors. Hardly worth the trouble since there was only a bite of tuna left."

"Okay, Dr. Briggs, you and Sally can talk. I've got to get back to work." With that, he waited for the light to halt traffic, then limped to his spot, one leg stiff from an injury. Except for the ragged clothes, he could have been the flagman at the start of a NASCAR race. What gave him away—besides the clothes—was his cardboard sign with the message written with a black marker: "Please give to a good cause. Three mouths to feed. God bless."

"Eric is all bark and no bite," Sally said, describing her significant other.

"I understand," said Briggs. "In the meantime, I've got a collar for Barney that allows me to keep track of him. It's called PupFinder. I'll be able to find you tomorrow, bring some food for Barney, and give him a check-up."

"And I'll patch up the hand," Briggs said to Sally. "I'll give you a tetanus shot, too."

Eric, Sally, and Barney were typical of Portland's 4,000 homeless: angry, hungry, and worn down trying to survive on the streets. The perfect clients.

Jimbo, your mother might even approve.

That voice in his head again. Was he dizzy from all the doubts running through his head, or the speed of his new life. His mother had died in mid-February, he spent March getting his van ready and recruiting clients, and now April Fools' Day was approaching. "It's no joke," he told himself. He always wanted a mobile care service and now he had it. After several not-so-pleasant interactions dealing with the homeless and their dogs, he was not sure he wanted them as clients. Yet, that was part of the deal his mother made in her will in exchange for leaving him everything.

CHAPTER FOUR

April 1, 2019

Charles "Chuck" Grayson walked in the door of his home, threw the keys to his Prius in a bowl, and collapsed in an overstuffed chair. His French Bulldog, Mellow, jumped into his lap.

"You miss mommy, don't you," Chuck said to Mellow. "I miss her, too. It's just you and me now." He told Mellow the same sad story every night. "Not sure how much longer I can do this." Mellow, his late wife's dog, cocked her head. She did not understand what Chuck said, but sensed something was not right. Widowed only three months since Mattie lost her two-year-long battle with breast cancer, feeding and walking Mellow was the only thing that got Grayson out of bed. Along with fresh news for his blog.

Chuck walked to the cupboard, pulled out a can of dog food, opened it with a struggle, and dropped the contents into Mellow's dish. Then he walked over to a table to look at the growing stack of unopened mail. When Grayson looked up, the image in the mirror caused him to jerk away. Red veins covered his nose. Bags had ballooned under the eyes. Hair was sprouting uncontrollably from his nose, ears, and head. The belt that once fit his 34-inch waist perfectly was now four inches too long, matching his silver hair which hung three inches over a dirty shirt collar. Scuffed black shoes and socks with holes covered unclipped toenails. None of it was surprising, given the stress he was suffering and his poor diet: most of his calories came from alcohol. Besides several glasses of box wine each night, he lived on cereal and frozen macaroni and cheese dinners. Which he also often had at lunch. Otherwise, he picked up junk food on the go.

"Pitiful," Grayson said to the emaciated man looking back at him.

His 30-year career as a crime reporter came to a crashing halt a year before Mattie's death when he refused to switch from writing for the print edition to online only. The collapse of print journalism was too painful. No way he was going to give tacit approval to this downward trend by moving to the Web. Plenty of 30-year-olds would gladly fill the spot for half the money—no byline required. The urge to continue covering the news left him with no choice. After struggling with what was supposed to be idiot-proof website building technology, he successfully launched the blog UrbanStreetPDX. Calling in a favor from the public information officer in the Portland Police Bureau, he secured a new press pass.

To get his mind off the urge to drink wine, he sat down at his computer, logged onto his blog, and begin working on a post about the day's events. Finally, he could not resist the wine. Forty minutes and two glasses of wine later, he posted a story about a homeless woman who was high on drugs running amok in the morning rush-hour traffic.

***

Cops Save Homeless Meth Addict Pleading for Death–It was No Joke

By Chuck Grayson, Editor, UrbanStreetPDX.

April 1, 2019—Today is April Fool's Day, but this story is no joke. It's becoming too common of a tale in Portland. Yesterday, the city witnessed the meltdown of a homeless woman pleading for death. She wasn't the first. And, sadly, won't be the last. As usual, local police came to the rescue.

According to the officers at the scene, Maxine Dorothy Reid went off the rails on a drug trip. Naked, screaming, and spinning in the middle of the street, she was working hard to become the city's latest fatality. Maxine might as well have been screaming into a canyon because the roar of the freeway overpass nearly drowned out her calls for help.

With rush-hour traffic swirling around the homeless woman, Portland Patrol Bureau Sergeant Mark Larson and Officer Kim Jansen worked quickly to corral and transport her to a nearby hospital emergency room.

"I got a call from a 9-1-1 dispatcher, requesting on-scene support because a dog was barking frantically and snapping at officers," said local veterinarian James Allen Briggs, III, DVM. Briggs is the owner of the mobile canine care service, Have Paws—Will Travel. He also has a city contract to pick up sick, injured, or deceased animals, and assist the police as needed.

In her latest brush with the law, according to the police report, Maxine had stripped off her clothes and stood in rain, while screeching, "I give up. God, please take me."

One observer at the scene said, "Her body was a shapeless skeleton of abuse and neglect. Her breasts were dollar-size pancake flaps, hanging from a bony chest."

Apparently, God was not listening to Maxine Reid. Unless you believe Portland cops are angels. On this wind-whipped 38-degree morning under the freeway, sainthood was not the mission of Officers Larson and Jansen. Their job was to prevent a rush-hour traffic jam and stop Maxine from hurting herself.

This was not Maxine's first brush with the law. Cops refer to her as their *arrest champ.* Charges have included methamphetamine possession, public intoxication, indecency for urinating and defecating in public and disturbing the peace: 21 arrests in 12 months. In most cases, they have booked Maxine at the county jail, and she was back on the street in less than 24 hours. How long they locked her up after an arrest hinged on the availability of hospital beds and her general mental state. Once Maxine came down from a drug high, she could tell you who she was, the date—and yes—the name of the U.S. President.

Frustrated judges repeatedly have sentenced her to rehabilitation instead of jail, hoping to reverse her downward spiral. That bit of mercy usually has only worked for a week or two. After releasing herself before completing the voluntary rehab program, public records show, Maxine has been right back in her old neighborhood of fellow addicted homeless helping her get high.

"I've thrown up my hands. I've tried and tried, and nothing works with her," said one of the social workers assigned to work her cases. "She is what we call terminally homeless because we know that in a year or two, she will end up dying on the streets, like dozens of other homeless each year. I know it sounds harsh, but it's the truth. Call it a failure of the system, but her end won't be pretty."

"Like 200 other Oregon residents with no next-of-kin, the state will pay for the disposition of Maxine's remains through the Indigent Burial Fund," another former social worker predicted. "May her restless soul be at peace."

Please comment below.

"Sadly, I fear this poor woman will soon become another victim of Portland's mean streets." — T. Morris

"Maxine is a scourge on society. Police need to lock her up and throw away the key."—W. Frank.

"With all the tax funds voters have approved for low-cost housing, you would think someone could find some solutions. Throwing money at the problem isn't working."—L.M. Milton, Jr.

***

With Maxine bundled in a blanket and cuffed with plastic ties in the back of the police car, Officer Jansen walked over to Jim Briggs, who had corralled Maxine's dog, Buster.

"Hi, I'm Kim Jansen."

Her adrenaline pumping from the morning chaos, Jansen extended a hand and squeezed harder than intended.

Briggs winced at the power of Jansen's grip. "Sorry," she said. At 5-feet-10 and 145 pounds, she was strong.

The clarity of her ice-blue eyes slightly stunned him. "I'm James Allen Briggs, DVM." He was not sure why he felt it was necessary to reveal his full name and professional credential. It just tumbled out. "Call me Jim," he quickly added.

"My friends call me Kim." For an extra moment, they made direct eye contact and said nothing. Jansen's shoulders relaxed, and she smiled. Briggs could not help smiling back. An invisible cauldron of chemistry was boiling over.

Briggs, suddenly self-conscious, broke the trance.

"What happens to Maxine now?" asked Briggs.

"We'll take her to the hospital where they will hold her overnight for observation. Routine police work," said Jansen. "It's becoming too routine. The latest Portland crime report may have shocked the community but didn't surprise us: fifty percent of all police calls and arrests are homeless related."

"I saw a news item on it," said Briggs. "I was as surprised at the amount of police involvement. And I work with the homeless every day. Most of them are on their best behavior when I'm around because I'm patching up their dogs for free."

"Jansen, let's go." Larson yelled over the traffic. "We need to drop off Maxine and clock out. Our shift has been over for an hour. Sergeant Harrison will fry our asses if we put in for overtime." Bull Harrison was one of the Portland Police Bureau's patrol sergeants. He was a tough, play-by-the-book former Marine drill sergeant who would not put up with sloppiness or bending the rules.

"Hey, relax, Larson. You're a hotshot now. We all heard your detective shield came through, and you're about to leave the lowly ranks of police who work for a living. You're the new golden boy."

Larson gave her the finger.

"Love you, man," she fired back with a smile.

"Larson, come over here and meet Jim Briggs. He's a local veterinarian and our go-to guy for Code 10-11 canine control issues."

Larson, three inches shorter than Briggs, but beefier from weight workouts, stuck out this hand, and Briggs shook it. "Dr. Briggs, you can't imagine how much paperwork you're saving us. Thanks for your service. Let's meet in the next couple of weeks for beer. You, Kim, and I can get acquainted and exchange some homeless horror stories."

"Sounds good to me," said Briggs, who thought the scene he had just witnessed with Maxine was enough horror story for a lifetime.

When Mark turned and headed for the patrol car, Kim unbuttoned her uniform breast pocket and pulled out a notebook where she scribbled a phone number and handed it to Briggs.

"Call me," she said. "We can set up something."

Again, her ice-blue eyes locked on Briggs. He wondered if she was suggesting a date night or if her "Call me" command was merely an effort to get the three of them together.

Before Briggs could ask, Jansen turned and headed back to her patrol car, on the way to the hospital to deposit Maxine.

Right, Jimbo, I think you can do better than Jansen, don't you? Isn't that what your mom used to say? Blue-eyed blondes are a dime a dozen. How about a redhead with green eyes and a perfect smile? With all your red hair, think of how many redheaded kids you could produce.

Briggs wanted to choke the voice in his head.

CHAPTER FIVE

April 2, 2019

The day after Maxine's meltdown, Jim Briggs was re-thinking his mission to help the homeless. The size of the problem was overwhelming, with no solutions in sight.

To clear his head, he planned a lunch walk to get away from his mobile office. He knew just the place.

He packed gouda, wheat crackers, trail mix, and an apple into his messenger bag and headed for Portland's International Rose Test Garden. With 10,000 rose bushes, you could find lots of places to hide out in the 4.5 acres, especially mid-week when there were fewer visitors. Best of all, he had seen none of the homeless there.

His first stop on his three-mile round-trip walk would be SugarBurst donuts on 23rd Avenue for dessert. He had his sights on two donuts: a Cointreau crème brûlée and a Meyer's Lemon.

He was a block from his condo when he got the first of his dose of daily homeless horror.

Near Sisters Coffee, Dirty Harry (Briggs 'nickname for him) was darting between the coffee shop and Safeway, a filthy sleeping bag draped over his shoulders like a King's cape. The ratty sandals he wore did not match his outfit.

A half-mile later, Rashad, a well-groomed African American man in his twenties, was selling Street Roots, a newspaper focused on homelessness and social justice. The vendors bought them for fifty cents and sold them for a dollar, more if their customers were feeling generous. The proceeds helped them earn money toward a permanent home. Briggs handed the man a $10 bill. Excited for the big donation, Rashad handed Briggs two books: one of poetry written by the homeless and the second a resource guide listing over 300 agencies with services for those living on the streets. Based on the chronic homeless population, Briggs observed, they delivered few services.

When he arrived at SugarBurst, a homeless U.S. Navy Veteran, Kenny, was perched on a milk crate, a yellow umbrella shielding him from the sun.

"Hey Kenny, it's Dr. Briggs. Remember me. I volunteered to be Bella's veterinarian."

"At no cost to you," Briggs added.

"I remember. Thanks. We're doing fine right now. But you better get inside if you want any good donuts because a group of southern ladies at the counter appear ready to buy the entire inventory."

"Okay, I'll get my donuts and come back out to talk to you."

Briggs ducked under the open door in time to overhear one woman squeal in a Texas drawl: "I love Mexican Hot Chocolate donuts." The woman saw Briggs out of the corner of her eye, turned around, and faced him, scanning him from head to foot. She looked at him as if she were a butcher inspecting a hog hanging from a hook at a meatpacking plant.

"Hey young man, you're a big drink of bourbon," she said. A compliment, Briggs figured. Better if she had said, "Big Drink of Texas Blue Corn Bourbon." Bourbon was Briggs' favorite whiskey.

"Go ahead of us. We're just hanging out while our husbands are in town for a law conference. These donuts look so good you just eat them with your eyes." Briggs moved to the head of the line to pick out his favorites, then carefully placed the donuts in his messenger bag and walked outside. He handed Kenny a $20 bill. "This will get you some coffee and a donut or two, or lunch."

"Oh, I never eat junk food," Kenny said. "I'm a vegetarian. I'll go to Whole Bowl, that food cart down the street." A whole bowl was a container of warm beans, brown rice, cheese, salsa, avocado, olives, sour cream, and cilantro. It was the last meal Briggs would expect Kenny to eat. Most homeless, he had observed, were omnivores, like bears: they ate whatever they could find. The $8.95 price tag for even the smaller bambino bowl seemed like a barrier.

Briggs knelt on the sidewalk and called Bella. Bella cautiously walked over and let Briggs scratch her behind the ears and rub her belly. She did not object when Briggs lifted her into his lap for an examination.

"Kenny, Bella looks pretty good. Her skin is dry, but some better food would help with that."

"I do what I can," said Kenny.

"I'll come back later with some food and a collar. No cost to you."

"Great Doc, thanks. I'm not sure how long I'll be here, but this is my regular corner so you can catch me some time."

Briggs got up, pulled his messenger bag over his head, and continued on his mission. He was only two blocks closer to the park when he saw a man talking to himself. The man, dressed in a mishmash of clothes, with no other belongings evident, was digging in a trashcan, licking paper, pouring crumbs in this mouth from pastry bags, and drinking the last swallow or two from soda cups.

Briggs pulled a $20 from his wallet and offered it to the man, who took it, said nothing, and went right back to dumpster diving.

Briggs suddenly lost his appetite, turned around, and headed home.

Yeah, Jimbo, these losers would make me lose my appetite, too.

Briggs tried to ignore the babble in his head. But DIME was right. The misery was endless. And no one seemed to care.

He'd go home, get his bike with medical supplies, and continue his effort to sign up homeless clients. He could help their dogs and patch them up. That was worth something, wasn't it?

***

The bright spring sun peeking over the horizon awakened Jim Briggs. He opened his eyes and sat up. Looking through floor-to-ceiling picture windows, his eyes swept across the Broadway Bridge and Willamette River, settling on Mt. Hood. The once-active volcano, a crisp image 60 miles distant, was white with heavy winter snow.

Briggs had slept little. His brain had wrestled with two visions: Kim Jansen's blue eyes and smile and Maxine's cringe-worthy nakedness. Her plea for God to take her—a simple desire to die and escape her miserable life on the street—sent a chill down his spine. Briggs had been having flashbacks since witnessing Maxine's meltdown, like someone with PTSD. The Maxine experience, combined with the increasing number of negative interactions with the homeless, was a recipe for recurring nightmares. Homelessness was a boil on Portland's backside. Unable to go back to sleep, Briggs grabbed his iPad and connected with OPB, the local PBS station.

As the news broadcast started, he heard the horn blast from a train arriving at nearby Union Station. Opened in 1896, the station had earned a mention in the registry of historic places, while still serving as an intermediate stop along

Amtrak's Cascade and Coast Starlight routes. Briggs loved the sound. Some days he could imagine himself climbing into the train car's upper deck, where he could open a window and feel the rush of air taking him to parts unknown—some place where homelessness did not exist. A long blast of the horn pulled him out of his daydream.

Jimbo, don't forget the homeless camp right next to the station. Maybe they can join you on the trip.

Briggs pushed away from the negative thought. He listened to the morning news report, which included a story on the latest City of Portland scheme to ease homelessness and the ongoing confrontations between the cops and the city's unsheltered citizens. The report filled up a full five-minute segment of the broadcast. The mayor had created a short-lived policy to let the homeless sleep wherever they wanted, as long as they packed up and moved on by 8 a.m. the next morning. A legion of park workers and street cleaners, backed up by the Portland Police Bureau, was tasked with enforcing the policy, cleaning up the mayor's mess.

The homeless, normally self-isolating along freeways or beneath overpasses, were everywhere. So many tents filled the parks and lined sidewalks, you might have guessed a Boy Scout Jamboree was in town. Everyone hated the policy, from the business community to the homeless to social justice advocates. Two weeks after the mayor's misguided sleep-anywhere edict, he reversed himself with no alternative to offer.

An aside to the PBS report was a note by the morning broadcaster calling attention to the latest coroner's report with an undetermined number of people disappearing without a trace. How many of the missing were homeless, no one knew.

Jimbo, what're a few more homeless names added to the list of those who vanished?

Briggs had no answer for his constant companion. He sat up and read his email. One was from Kim Jansen, and several were from clients with routine requests for dog care.

He added up the client requests, looked at his time, and figured he should get moving. First, he needed a hot shower. He turned on the water, let the steam fill the space, and then stood under the pounding spray for five minutes. Just warming up, his eyes closed, he heard a familiar whiny voice.

Jimbo, you heard the guy on the radio. What more do you need? Homelessness is a scourge in Portland, and it's not going away soon. It was bad 10 years ago, and it is still bad. Lots of smoke and no fire for cleansing the unwashed from city streets.

Briggs moved his mind away from the negative babble and back to his upcoming date with Kim.

Why can't we handle stray humans, the way we handle stray dogs, DIME persisted, barely audible above the shower spray?

"What the hell," Briggs thought. "Humans as strays." A black hole of thought, DIME giving voice to the unthinkable. Yet Briggs felt a pull toward the words.

DIME left it there for a minute.

Where did that ugly, negative voice come from? Briggs wondered.

Listening more closely, even though the thoughts were in his own head, he heard DIME say,

"*Jimbo, what do we do with stray dogs?"*

"We euthanize them," answered Briggs reflexively, talking to himself. "One point four million annually." He knew the figure because he was among the nation's veterinarians tasked each year with humanely putting down strays never adopted from the no-kill shelters. No-kill shelters were America's dirty little secret that the public either ignored or refused to believe, even if they heard the magnitude of the death toll.

"You're not suggesting," Briggs pushed back.

I'm not suggesting. I'm telling you, Jimbo. The hell with the homeless living on the street, using sidewalks and gardens for toilets, panhandling everywhere with their cardboard signs telling pitiful stories. Not to mention harassing visitors and locals.

"It's a sad state of affairs," Briggs' Happy Half countered. "Everyone deserves a home, hope, and dignity."

The humanitarian side of Briggs' brain kicked in. An epidemic of societal indifference left the working-poor living in cars, created a national epidemic of evictions that leads to homelessness, and abandoned the mentally ill to 72-hour crisis lockup. The drug-addicted, the panhandlers, and hoboes were all on their own.

A final sad category of neglect was the terminally homeless—those likely to die prematurely on the street—their bodies carted away to a pauper's grave, nothing more than depleted bones and wasted flesh in a bag, a mere statistic for the coroner's report. Some homeless had recently begun disappearing. The authorities did not know where they came from or where they went. And it seemed no one cared. Not even the police who had become society's de facto social service agents in the absence of any real mental health system.

Sure, Jimbo, we could round them up, force them into shelters and off the streets. Just say no to the misguided notion they should be able to wander like free-range chickens.

"Harsh words, hateful words," Briggs' Happy Half countered, a little angered and frustrated by DIME's negative vibe.

So, Jimbo, what are we going to do about the homeless problem?

Briggs ignored the interruption.

DIME persisted: *You know what we do with strays and sick animals, right Jimbo? You do. You're killing poor Ginger, the Teller Family's border collie, this week.*

"I'm euthanizing Ginger," Briggs said. "We euthanize dogs. Families think of it as putting them to sleep."

We won't be putting them to sleep, Jimbo. We will KILL, Bill—fill' em with a syringe of pure death.

Briggs shook his head. Such a sinister thought.

Jimbo tries to ignore me, shake out his ugly ideas. But I know I've planted a little piece of dark code in his neural network, spreading like an ugly viral tweet.

Briggs turned off the shower, grabbed his towel from a warming rack, and buried his face in the plush cotton. Warm, soft, and soothing.

Refreshed, Briggs decided: No one would die. Not Maxine. Not any of his new homeless clients. Not at his hands, at least.

Stepping out of the shower, he wrapped a towel around his waist and grabbed a razor out of the medicine cabinet. He kept his beard trimmed with an electric but loved a hand razor lubricated by warm shave cream to clean up his face and neck. His every-day shave cream was fragrant-free. On a day like this, when he wanted to replace his ugly thoughts with something uplifting, he would recall the image of his grandfather applying Old Spice shaving cream. It amazed him how deftly Grandpa Joe swirled a razor around his face with only an occasional nick. Joe was his hero, dead for nearly 20 years. Old Spice was a time machine propelling him back to warm memories.

As Briggs shaved, he had an idea. He would use the free databases at the public library to track down the families of the homeless and, hopefully, reunite them. If he could encourage the interaction between even one homeless person and his or her estranged loved ones, then Briggs could offer support rather than death. As an incentive, Briggs thought he might offer money to relatives of the homeless, a few hundred dollars a month for six to twelve months.

Jimbo, why would you waste money on one of these losers when a syringe filled with $10 worth of death would be so much more permanent?

Briggs punched right back through the DIME's twisted reasoning. He began thinking about the dozens of homeless and their dogs he cared for who might be candidates for his cash-for-shelter idea. If not cash, then maybe he could find a family with a little compassion for a down-on-their-luck relative to help.

Jimbo, why would you do that?

"Because it is the right thing to do."

CHAPTER SIX

April 7, 2019

Ray and Mary Johnson were showing signs of senior spread from eating too much meat and potatoes and not enough vegetables. Each was 20 pounds overweight, the extra pounds nicely disguised by their oversized Heavenly Considerations sweatshirts. The image of a dog in angel wings standing at the Pearly Gates adorned the shirt fronts. The couple wore matching jeans and tennis shoes.

Sitting in front of the Johnsons was an assortment of donuts—a chocolate bar, two glazed, three jellies, two apple fritters, and a powdered—and two cups of coffee. Between the donuts with sprinkles and the bright logos of their t-shirts, they were a riot of color.

When Briggs entered the donut shop, they leaped from their seats like over-anxious puppies. Powder sugar covered Ray's lips. Mary wiped jelly off the corner of her mouth with a napkin.

Even before Briggs met the Johnsons, he had decided to buy their pet cremation business, pending reviews of health permits and financials by his lawyer and his accountant.

Worldwide, the pet funeral business, including cremations, generated a profit of more than $100 million annually. Although a dog cremation averaged $200, some were extravagant. The most expensive on record was for a Tibetan Mastiff in China. Cost: $733,000. It included a jade coffin and a plot of land at the foot of a mountain range.

Briggs wanted a piece of the lucrative market for cremating dog remains and returning them in an attractive box or urn to veterinary clinics and hospitals. He figured he could easily double his income. The extra money would help him realize his goal to give back to the community, especially to the dogs of the homeless, without depleting his nest egg his mother left him.

"Order a coffee drink for yourself," Mary and Ray offered, stepping forward at the same time to shake Jim's hand. After ordering a latte, he sat down across from the Johnsons, who had settled onto an over soft sofa that sank under their weight. They both leaned forward, on the edge of their seats, as if they did not want to miss a word Briggs had to say.

Briggs' latte arrived, and he was just about to take a sip when Ray exploded with recognition. "We thought your name sounded familiar when you responded to our advertisement, but we didn't associate you with the green van with the white paws on the side."

"That's me," said Briggs, amused by the Johnson's Chihuahua-like enthusiasm and energy.

"So Dr. Briggs, we're delighted you came. Can we call you Jim?"

"Absolutely," said Briggs.

"I don't want to B.S. you, Jim, so we are going to be upfront about our business. We are making plenty of money and have for the past 10 years. More and more people, as you know, want their pet's ashes returned to them. A way to keep their little companions alive, at least in their minds. Veterinarians love the service because it bonds them to their clients. Cops, firefighters, and animal control officers love us because we take dead animals and dispose of them, under a long-term contract, at a very competitive rate. And the animal shelters love us because we help them move the unadoptable pets out of their shelters to make room for new residents."

Before Briggs could ask the obvious question, Mary jumped in. "We both had health scares this year. I had a triple bypass and Ray had prostate cancer."

"Sorry to hear that," Briggs offered.

"No need to be sorry," Mary continued. "We're both fine. We have more medications to take, but part of that is getting older. Anyway, it got us to thinking. We've got plenty of money. Yes, we could make more and wait until age 65 to retire. But why?"

"Exactly," Ray said, adding an exclamation point to Mary's statement. "Why wait!"

"Sounds like you've made an excellent decision," said Briggs. "I'm definitely interested in Heavenly Considerations. It would complement my mobile care business."

"Let's make this easy for everyone," said Mary. "We will show you and your accountant the books, then discuss a price, and move forward. We would be willing finance the deal and take a monthly payment as retirement income."

Briggs reached down and picked up a custard-filled maple bar and took a bite, then lifted the donut-filled box toward the Johnsons. The Johnsons selected jelly donuts. "Here's to discovering new horizons and celebrating the best of what life offers," they said in unison, raising the donuts like they were glasses of champagne.

Hey Jimbo, we have the perfect resting place for strays, don't we?

The voice brought Briggs' thoughts back to the nuts and bolts of the pet cremation business: basic equipment included a cremation unit—a giant industrial furnace—and a cremulator to pulverize bone and tooth fragments into fine dust. Once the two-part process finished, you could not tell the difference between a human or a dog. DNA ceased to exist.

Later that day, Briggs urged his lawyer and accountant to complete their business reviews. In less than a week, Briggs had struck a deal with the Johnsons. They agreed to consult with him as part of the business transfer until he felt comfortable running the operation alone.

After a few days with the Johnsons, he knew he could not manage the business alone. He needed help, and he needed it fast.

CHAPTER SEVEN

April 15, 2019

Have Paws—Will Travel had been open and on the road a short time, but Jim Briggs' plate was already full. He had a long list of paying clients and an expanding list of homeless with dogs he would doctor for free. While the wealthy, paying clients were already generating profits to pay off his investment in equipment and marketing, the homeless' dogs were mostly in poor condition, in need of lots of extra care, offsetting his gains.

One potential homeless client he could not get out of his head was Maxine Dorothy Reid. When police had taken her to the hospital for observation, Briggs agreed to drop off her dog, Buster, at the Humane Society until she could pick him up. When he checked, he discovered that the Humane Society had released Buster to Maxine and was back on the street. A few days later, as he was making his rounds to homeless camps, Briggs spotted Maxine and her dog, Buster, in a grassy area under the freeway. With her shanty camp in view, he parked the van, got out, and walked over to her tent. Buster ran over and tried to jump up on Briggs.

"Hey, little guy, how are you?"

Maxine saw Buster jumping on this big man and yelled, "Get the hell away from that guy before I smack you."

"It's okay, Briggs said.

"Who are you?" she demanded.

"I'm Jim Briggs. I'm the veterinarian who helped Buster two weeks ago when the cops pulled you out of the traffic." Not surprisingly, she didn't know him since the time "they met" Maxine was in another world having a mental meltdown—naked and screaming in the middle of rush-hour traffic. "Can I call you Max?"

She looked at him blankly, then her face turned red. "It's not Max. It's M-A-X-I-N-E. That spells Maxine, you idiot. Do you get it? People are always trying to shorten my name without asking. I fucking hate it."

She scowled, her face red from screaming.

Was she about to slip into another methamphetamine meltdown?

"Sorry," Briggs offered.

Briggs wondered if Maxine felt shortening her name, even by three letters, devalued her. Coin collecting came to mind, his favorite hobby as a kid. The fewer minted in the best condition were the most valuable. Maxine appeared to be a worn-out penny.

And both will get melted down, right Jimbo: the penny into a mass of metal used to produce shiny, new coins. Maxine will just get melted into a pile of ash and bone fragments.

"I not buying your babble about killing and cremating Maxine or other homeless until I give my plan a chance," Briggs argued. "I'm determined to find homes for them. If I don't help, who will?"

So, the name Maxine had weight, even if Maxine, the woman standing in front of Briggs, did not. At 4-10 and 85 pounds, the six layers of multi-color clothes she wore added little bulk to her bird bones. He had seen how fragile she was as she ran naked while cops tried to corral her a few weeks before. Maxine was 45 going on 70—ravaged, Briggs judged, by drugs and her life on the street.

When Briggs reached out to shake her hand, she did not pull away. Her hands were rough like sandpaper, but her touch so light it was like a chickadee landing on your palm. Her hand disappeared into his massive paw a second before he felt a sharp jab like a needle prick. Not surprising, since her fingernails were cracked and jagged—no doubt from tearing them off with her teeth. The nails were black, like most people living on the street with no access to toilets or showers and, as a result, little interest in personal hygiene.

"Thanks for helping Buster," she said, her voice quieter after Briggs reminded her of the circumstances. She barely looked up, too embarrassed that she didn't have more to offer.

"Maxine, let me give Buster a collar and a leash. No charge. They come with a unique identification code, which I can register under your name in case he gets lost." He did not mention the GPS chip that would allow him to track her and Buster using the PupFinder app his marketing consultant set up for him.

Maxine pulled out a slightly bent cigarette stub, lit it with a throwaway lighter, and cackled, "Lost! We have both been lost for a long time. I don't want to lose this little guy. He's all I have." Her voice was a smoker's raspy croak.

Buster was all she had unless you counted her household goods, all tightly packed in a stolen grocery cart. Her possessions included tarps, clothes, cups, string, a radio with a broken antenna, spoons, knives, and forks. Personal items included a pair of slippers with a hole in the bottom. Other treasures: a sack of cans and bottles, a tent, and a lump of cloth that appeared to be a sleeping bag. At least the cans and bottles were worth a dime apiece.

A disability check no doubt paid for her cigarettes and a cell phone. Besides an occasional two-for-one burger at McDonald's, most meals were at the nearest restaurant or supermarket—in the dumpster out back.

To boost her income, Maxine could play-act like the best of the homeless panhandlers. When a potential donor appeared, she would look down, feigning humility. Her cardboard sign pleaded for $18 cash to buy a room for the night and concluded with a "God Bless."

"How would you like me to record your name in Buster's record?" Briggs asked, careful trip another angry response from Maxine.

"I'm Maxine Dorothy Reid from Prince Edward Island, Canada," she said, chin thrust forward, proclaiming herself a proud member of the Reid Clan.

"Okay, I will list Buster's owner as Maxine D. Reid, Prince Edward Island."

"No, no, no," she said, again angry that Briggs wanted to shorten her name. "List my home as Johnson Street. That's where we hang most nights. And don't be abbreviating. I thought I made that clear. Looks like you're more brawn than brain. It's Dorothy, not D with a period, not Dee. Not Dottie."

He said, "Okay, got it. It is Dorothy, D-O-R-O-T-H-Y." He was losing patience with the woman and her continuing assault.

"The Doc can spell, how about that Buster?"

"Maxine, one more thing I can do for Buster. I can inject a chip into him the size of a rice grain. He won't know it is there. If the collar comes off or is stolen, whoever finds Buster can get him scanned and reunite the two of you."

"You mean like those supermarket scanners?"

"Something like that. Inserting the chip only takes a minute and is painless. Oh, it's also free, something I do as a community service for all Have Paws—Will Travel clients."

"Client, huh? Imagine, Maxine Dorothy Reid is now a client. Isn't that fancy. Okay, go ahead."

The interaction with Maxine lasted less than 15 minutes. But Briggs knew he would see more of her over the months ahead. And, somehow, he knew she was a stray who would never find a home other than a patch of weedy grass under the freeway.

"I gotta go, Doc. Got to earn some money for Buster and me," said Maxine.

Briggs dug in his wallet and pulled out two twenties.

Here's your first contribution for the day," said Briggs, handing her $40. "Remember, anytime Buster has a problem, you can flag me down." Maxine did not respond. Instead, she turned, gave him an over-the-shoulder glance, the remnants of a cigarette pinched between the fingers as she waved goodbye.

"Come on Buster, you've got to put your cute little nose by the donation jar and earn your keep."

No doubt she would settle down in front of a supermarket or popular tourist spot downtown. A cardboard sign would appeal for food for her and Buster, and would end with God Bless, as if God's blessings came cheap—for a little loose change. Or for a donation of a quarter or fifty cents, God's light would shine on you.

Jimbo, if such divine light ever existed, it had dimmed a long time ago for Maxine.

"I think her light is dimming for sure," said Briggs.

He had added a PupFinder GPS chip to Buster's collar so he could find them for his next wellness check. The GPS was also the only way to keep track of a nomad like Maxine.

Jimbo, now you've tagged Maxine, it's time to bag her.

"A monstrous idea," Briggs countered, his thoughts about the homeless getting darker and more distressing by the minute.

"She seems like a nice lady," he said to no one. "Surely, someone will take her in."

CHAPTER EIGHT

April 15, 2019

Helen Williams rolled out of bed, stood up, and giggled when Rod patted her on the bottom.

"That was nice, Babe," he said, closing his eyes as he enjoyed the glow of their lovemaking.

"The best," Helen answered, pushing his hand away.

She walked to the shower, turned on the water, and waited for it to heat before stepping in.

As the water cascaded over her head and down her body, her mind slipped into a daydream of a vacation snorkeling with Rod in a warm Bali lagoon. With the sunlight illuminating the azure blue water around them, they touched hands, closed their eyes, and became one in the gentle ocean current.

Helen opened her eyes and was back home. She turned up the shower temperature. She and Rod had left Boston for new jobs out west. They settled into a townhouse in Northwest Portland with sweeping views of the city.

Since Helen had lost a baby three months into a pregnancy, she and Rod had been struggling. Rod wanted to try again immediately. Helen pleaded for more time. As a result, intimacy had eluded them. Then something happened this morning: lights switched back on in their marriage.

As she was waking up, Rod's fingers had settled on her lower back, then drifted under her panties. He took his time. She reached out in kind. Over the next 45 minutes, there was an explosion of pent up emotion. The passion they felt before the miscarriage had returned. It was like that feeling you get when the cylinders line up on a slot machine: pure joy—evidence you're one of life's winners. As she bathed in the warm glow of the morning, Rod stepped into the shower. They moved in for a kiss and were carried away in a second wave of passion.

***

Helen was reading the New York Times on her iPad with one hand and eating a piece of toast with the other when Rod walked in the room. He was wearing shorts, tennis shoes, and a sweatshirt. "Are you running to work, sweetheart?" Helen asked.

"Yes, I'll do a five-mile loop, check out Pioneer Square to see if tents are going up for this weekend's beer festival, then head into the office." Rod had taken the job at MoneyOne as manager of the new internet cafes that offered banking, coffee, and use of conference rooms and web connections for business meetings. He would shower, shave, and change in the employees' locker room.

"How about you, Babe?"

"Working on a promising leukemia drug trial."

"Helen, I can't believe they treat dogs for leukemia, let alone conduct drug trials. Is there anything Canine Therapeutics isn't developing?" She had worked at the pet drug research company for only a few months but had settled in. She and her boss, Susan Llewelyn, had become best friends. Helen finished the last bite of toast, put down her iPad, and walked over to Rod. She put her arms around his neck and pulled him toward her. "I love you, Rod."

"I love you, too," he said, and they kissed. They were back in sync, standing together, looking forward toward a brighter day. They would make a new baby. And soon. Maybe they just did.

"One more thing," said Rod.

"Another kiss?" Helen asked.

"Of course, but would you mind dropping off our federal incomes taxes at the post office? The filing deadline is today."

"Give me that kiss, and I'll make that a priority before I head to the office." They kissed, parted, and Rod headed out the door for his run. It was the last time she would see him.

***

Helen's boss and friend Susan Llewelyn, executive vice president of research at Canine Therapeutics, waved to Helen as she walked into the lab.

"Helen, come to my office," said Susan, who was looking down at the floor. She closed the shades to screen them from her colleagues in the lab.

"Okay, sure. Is something wrong?"

"Sit down," Susan said abruptly, then quieter, "Please."

"Honey, I'm sorry to tell you this, but I just got a call. There has been in an accident. Oh god, I'm so, so sorry."

"What are you talking about?" said Helen, wringing her hands and twisting her wedding ring, panic rising in her chest.

Susan put it out there: "The Portland Police Bureau called and said they tried to get in touch with you but called me instead when they could not get through."

Helen pulled out her phone and looked. "I forgot to turn it on. I was running a little late, grabbed it, and ran out the door."

Helen grimaced and leaned forward. "Tell me."

"Rod is dead," said Susan.

Helen's mouth opened, but nothing came out. Her eyes went wide as if she had seen a ghost.

"How is that possible? I just saw him. We made love this morning for the first time in months. We kissed. Everything in our lives was coming back together after I lost the baby."

Susan knew all about Helen's difficulties over the baby and Rod. They had shared several girls' nights out and intimate details of their lives after several glasses of wine.

"What did the police say? How did it happen?"

"The officer who called—Kim Jansen—said witnesses saw Rod step into traffic to avoid tripping on a homeless woman sprawled asleep on the sidewalk. Officer Jansen said a passing Max Train hit him. Death was instantaneous, she said."

"He got hit by a train?" she repeated the words, then began sobbing. "No, no, no. It can't be," said she, squeezing out the words.

Susan stepped out of her office to give Helen some privacy.

As Susan exited the office, Helen's sobs and then screams of agony pierced the walls of the soundproof room. Others in the lab area looked up with questioning looks.

"Helen just found out her husband, Rod, died an hour ago," Llewelyn said in a stage whisper. "An accident. Run over by a Max Train down by Pioneer Square."

The room went silent. Eyes went back to their computers.

CHAPTER NINE

April 23, 2019

Someone was shaking her.

"Helen, Helen. Are you okay? Wake up, Helen." The voice was soft and warm. It sounded like her boss, Susan.

When Helen opened her eyes, the world tilted 45 degrees. The lower part of her body was planted in a chair. Her head was horizontal, one eye closed. She raised her head, a pain jabbing her between her eyebrows. She felt something slimy on her face. She tried to right herself, grasping the sides of her desk to keep from falling onto the floor. The sight of vomit covering her desk and a stack of papers made her stomach flip.

"What have you done, Helen," Susan asked, surveying the mess. "I should have made you take time off. It's only a week since Rod's death and you're spiraling out of control."

Helen picked up a flask on the corner of her desk and shook it. Empty.

"Too much of this. Or what was in here: Rod's 30-year-old single malt scotch. Maybe 16 ounces."

"For Christ's sake," Susan exclaimed, "Hang on, I'll get some paper towels."

Since Rod's death, Helen Williams had been going downhill. First, she was late for work. Then she would fall asleep in the middle of the day. Then she drank so much—like last night—that she just passed out and slept at her desk.

This was the first time, however, Susan had found a mess like this after one of Helen's alcohol binges.

"Helen, I hate to do this to you when you're so down, but I'm putting you on notice. Go talk to someone, get your drinking under control, give yourself time to grieve, then come back. If you do that, I will keep your job open for you."

"Please don't make me take time off," Helen begged. "I can't stand being alone."

"I have no other choice. The lives of thousands of dogs and millions of investment dollars depend on our work. I can't jeopardize that."

Susan used the paper towels to do a quick wipe of Helen's face, then helped her to the restroom to clean her up.

"Helen, I'm going to call an Uber. Don't worry about your car. It will be secure in our campus lot. When you need it, I'll give you a ride."

"I understand," said Helen. "You're a great pal. Thanks for not firing me."

Susan escorted Helen out of the building into the waiting car.

Helen thought she had hit rock bottom trying to cope with Rod's death. Not even close; she had tumbled halfway down a deep canyon with a long way to fall.

***

It had been a week since Helen's boss, Susan, had escorted her out the door of Canine Therapeutics, Inc. Although she had promised Susan she would clean up her act, her cycle of drinking and passing out at night, continued.

When the 7 a.m. alarm on her iPad sounded, Helen slapped at the screen, attempting to halt the noise amplifying the pounding in her head. Her mouth felt like it cotton. Her bladder was screaming.

She could also hear the not unpleasant burbling of her coffee maker. The French Roast was calling to her. Strong coffee might revive her—if she could hold it down.

Her eyes were still closed as she turned over and reached out to Rod. All she got was air. Where Rod had been was a bitter-sweet memory. She groaned in pain at his absence, while feeling connected to his soul. Before the loss of the baby and their intimacy, 7 am was a special time: they would touch feet. She would put her hand on his hip as they drifted in and out of the last dreams of night. Some mornings, she would wake up and let her hand drift down to Rod's crotch, moving her fingers until he responded. He said she had magic hands. When he could not stand the intense feeling any longer, he would turn over and enter her from behind and reach around with his own magic touch.

Instead of ecstasy, with Rod gone, there was nothing but agony. And she knew she had a long, agonizing road ahead. Conventional wisdom proclaims, "it only gets better with time." Helen did not believe it. She could see no end in sight.

Helen forced herself to get up, staggered to the bathroom to relieve herself, and turned on the shower. Steam filled the room. Just as well, Helen thought, because she did not want to see herself in the mirror. Everything was softer, quieter in the fog. Even her headache.

"Today is a new day," Helen thought. "No more alcohol. I'll get help. I'll start the grieving process."

Instead of reaching for a bottle of scotch, like she had most mornings, she poured a cup of coffee. Helen added a touch of half and half, then moved over to her kitchen counter where she set up her iPad to read the latest news on OregonLive, the online edition of the Oregonian, Portland's daily newspaper.

The news reports were much the same every day: Democrats and Republicans slugging it out over immigration, a spreading wildfire near a horse ranch in Eastern Oregon, and an attack by a homeless man on a college student. The student challenged the man over bags of rotting trash the man had brought onboard a Portland streetcar.

Helen laughed at Pearls Before Swine, her favorite comic strip. It was her first laugh since Rod's death. The feeling was like your first gulp of air after coming up from the deep end of a swimming pool. You feel alive, renewed.

As she scanned the news, an advertisement for an administrative manager for Heavenly Considerations, a pet crematory, caught her eye. The advertisement referred her to a website for a detailed list of job qualification must-haves and wants. When she saw the words "someone with veterinary experience" a plus, she knew she had a chance.

CHAPTER TEN

May 1, 2019

Helen opened her laptop and double-clicked on the application for Heavenly Considerations, a pet crematory looking for administrative support. She spent an hour reviewing the application, then emailed the completed form to the online address listed.

Walking over to the coffeemaker, she passed a mirror and looked at her face. Two days without drinking had transformed her from a puffy-face hag with red rings around her eyes to someone she could recognize.

If she were honest with herself, she would admit she had not stopped drinking, just returned to her normal consumption: two glasses of wine, instead of eight ounces of Scotch. Helen's iPhone came to life with the sound of a train arriving at a station. That was her boss, Susan, checking in.

"Hi Susan," Helen said, her voice clear and upbeat.

"You sound so much better," Susan offered.

"I feel better. My head is clear when I'm not sobbing over Rod. I go between feeling sorry for myself and feeling optimistic about the future."

"You'll always have a future with us," Susan assured her.

"You're the best, Sue. Your friendship means the world to me."

"Now I'm about to cry," said Susan. "When you feel like some girl-talk, any time of the day or night, just call. And stay away from the office for the next two weeks to give yourself more time to get over the initial shock."

"Thanks Sue, you're the best."

"Gotta go, Helen. I've got a meeting. See you soon."

Susan's phone call made her think life would be okay again. Then the nightmare of Rod being struck by a train engulfed her.

"Oh God, what am I going to do. I can't live without him," she wailed. Ten minutes later, she was all cried out. She walked into the bathroom, washed her face, and applied fresh makeup. "Tonight I'm going to LeJoyeux for dinner," Helen proclaimed to the fresh-faced woman in the mirror. "I'll have my favorite:

a savory crepe, with a mixture of roasted chicken, thyme, garlic, tomato, green onion, gruyere, and goat cheese. And maybe a bottle of Blanc Fume to wash it down." She smiled and the woman in the mirror smiled back.

***

Knowing she would have a sweet crepe to top off her dinner and wine at LeJoyeux, a restaurant a half-mile from her 14th-floor apartment in the Pearl District, Helen had a veggie salad for lunch. She washed it down with a glass of white wine, convinced her newfound semi-sobriety would keep her emotions even, avoiding highs and lows. The wine did just the opposite, freeing a torrent of tears. When she was not crying, she kept herself busy working on home improvement projects and texting friends in Boston.

She spent her day responding to their good wishes, online sympathy cards, and polite inquiries into what had happened. They could not believe the circumstances of Rod's death. Helen waited until 6 p.m. for her second glass of wine of the day. She uncorked a bottle of Kendall Jackson Chardonnay, then put it back in the refrigerator. Better would be a sip of Rod's single malt Scotch, its familiar warmth and earthiness matching the day's early spring warmth.

Tonight would be a turning point, she knew. LeJoyeux would be a placeholder for the next chapter in her life. To celebrate the moment, Helen walked to a drawer and pulled out a pair of Agent Provocateur panties Rod had bought her for Valentine's Day. Over the panties and a matching bra—she pulled on a gauzy dress, with white and yellow flowers that had an ethereal quality to them—like a Henri Matisse painting. Her mood was light. She closed her eyes and recalled a similar feeling she got when she and Rod had spent two weeks in Villefranche-sur-Mer on the French Riviera.

When she opened her eyes, her brain jolted her back to reality. Her head spun, either from the stress of the moment or the Scotch.

When the wave of dizziness passed, she grabbed her purse and headed out to dinner.

"Nothing is going to keep me down," she thought. "I deserve to be happy."

Fifteen minutes later she walked into LeJoyeux. She ordered a bottle of Blanc Fume and her favorite crepe. About halfway through dinner, LeJoyeux's owner, Alain, who doubled as a server, walked over to Helen's table and asked her if everything was okay. She had been sitting and staring into space, sipping her wine, but otherwise, had not been her usual chatty self. He recognized her but was not used to seeing her alone.

"Hi Helen, how are you? You seem down."

"I'm fine," she said, and let her declaration sit for a moment while grinding her teeth and clenching her jaw. "Well, maybe not. I just lost my husband. A train hit and killed him last month." Talking at three nearby tables stopped and their occupants looked her way. A woman at one table mouthed, "Sorry." Helen nodded her thanks.

"Oh my gosh, I read about that. That was Rod? The reporter on the news said a homeless woman was sleeping on the sidewalk and forced him to step into the street. I'm so sorry."

"Me, too," she said.

"However, I've determined I am going to be happy again," Helen mumbled, forcing a half-smile. "LeJoyeux seemed like a good place to start." Another woman, listening to the conversation in the small space, which held six tables, patted her heart.

"We are always glad to have you," the owner said, "Shall I put the rest of the wine in a bag?"

"Please, and I'm ready for my bill."

The owner leaned in and said, "I want to be part of your new beginning on your road to happiness, so the dinner tonight is on me."

"Thanks so much," she said, offering a weak smile. "I already feel better."

A few minutes later, she was back on the street heading to her empty home and a bottle of scotch, her evening companion.

***

Helen was halfway home on her eight-block walk when she came to a community garden under the freeway. A black iron fence enclosed it, squeezed between a parking lot and 16th Avenue, a busy, one-way street with little traffic after rush-hour. She heard talking, laughs, and whoops coming from the garden's interior. She opened the gate and glanced at a canvas sign wired to the fence: "Welcome to a Peaceful Urban Space."

"My day can't get any better," Helen thought, closing the gate and walking toward the voices. She was inside when a pack of dogs ran toward her, baying, barking, and yapping, then surrounding her. When she went down on one knee to greet them, they went quiet and sniffed her. They did not know she was a veterinarian but must have sensed she was a friend, someone who liked dogs.

Helen stood up and continued walking toward the voices, faces visible ahead, as the dogs—now her pack—followed her, like the Pied Piper.

A little guy walked forward and said, "Well, well, who do we have here, crashing our little party? From the looks of your dress and shoes, I'm guessing you are not homeless." Helen shook her head. "No, I'm husband less. He died last week."

"No shit," said Gerald Hoffman, who overheard the conversation.

"I'm Bobby, what's your name?"

Intimidated by the little man, she blurted out, "I'm Nancy." A fake name seemed safer.

"No, I'm not homeless. Just passing by. I was out for dinner."

"Hey everyone, Nancy's been out to dinner. The wine bag in her hand says LeJoyeux. Let me guess: you just had a nice savory crepe and washed it down with a bottle of wine."

"I did," Helen admitted.

"We eat there, too, but out of the dumpster in the back. Occasionally even get a little wine left over in a bottle."

"Show me the wine in your bag," said Bobby, shifting from cordial to commanding.

Before she could pull it out, Bobby grabbed it.

"Fume Blanc, very nice," he said, then turned up the bottled and finished it in two gulps.

The man's aggression alarmed Helen.

"Tell you what," Bobby offered, "You give us $20 and we'll share some beer with you."

Panicked, Helen pulled two twenties out of her wallet and handed them to Bobby.

"Very generous," he said, turning friendly again. He pulled a PBR Tall Boy from a 12-pack, opened it, and handed it to her. "These will buy a few more beers. Take a sip."

The thin, tasteless brew left a mouthful of gassy fizz, which she swallowed, then burped. "Sorry," she said.

"I should go," Helen said, feeling a rising sense of hostility from the group. Still, Bobby introduced everyone. "This is Hoffman, Big Betty, the Irishman, and

I'm Little Bobby. You can guess how I got my nickname." Helen offered a thin smile but said nothing.

For the next few minutes, their attention turned back to a discussion about the best places for food scraps, as if they were restaurant critics.

Helen finished the first beer, and Hoffman handed her a second. Over the next hour, she would recall days later, she must have had at least two more beers. Before she finished the fourth one, her world went fuzzy, then dark.

***

Her head was pounding when she woke up. The sun was coming through a crack in the door next to her face. She reached up and pushed open the door and crawled out onto the dirt. The lower half of her body was in pain; she felt like a horse had kicked her. Worse than that, it felt like she had been twisted and then ripped apart.

When she reached down, she felt naked flesh instead of clothing. Her panties were gone. Probing with her fingers, she felt a sliminess between her legs. When she looked at her hand, it was smeared with blood and something else. Pushing her hand between her cheeks where her thong would be, she also found blood.

What had happened? Why was she half-naked and bloody, lying in the dirt? Where was everyone? Then a vision of drinking beer with a bunch of homeless people flooded her memory.

"Oh my God, what did they do to me?" Helen choked and started crying.

With tears flooding her face, Helen pushed herself into a sitting position and looked down, wiping her eyes and nose on her torn dress and taking inventory. They had ripped her dress. Mud covered one leg. Her shoulders ached as if someone had pulled them back. Her mouth and throat were raw.

When she finished checking herself out, she screamed, "I'm such a fucking loser. What an idiot. How did a sunny day turn into a nightmare?"

CHAPTER ELEVEN

May 8, 2019

Jim Briggs opened the door to his condo, commanded Siri to adjust lighting and music, and headed for the refrigerator. He grabbed an ice-cold pint glass from the freezer, then reached into the refrigerator and pulled down the handle of his copper growler. Sixteen ounces of Fort George Vortex, his favorite IPA, poured out.

He grabbed a bag of salt and pepper potato chips, walked upstairs to his media room, and plopped down on the couch. Kennel cough shots, canine teeth cleaning, bandaging an injured paw, and soothing worried clients who were hand-wringing over sick dogs filled a 12-hour day.

He turned the TV to KOIN news, the local CBS affiliate, and listened to a string of weather and crime reports. Crime news included a video of police rousting the homeless from a cave-dwelling they had dug into the hillside next to a freeway. Fearing the hill might collapse on the cars below, emergency road crews filled the hole and repaired nearby fencing.

The news of problems related to homelessness was never-ending. DIME's suggestions about helping homeless human strays, like Maxine, get to a better place, were taking root. Again, he pushed the thought away and looked out the window and across the city.

What Briggs wanted was a carefree happy hour and a burger with friends. He refilled his beer from his refrigerator and moved to his home office, where he reviewed his business finances and paid bills. He also signed paperwork completing the deal to buy Heavenly Considerations. It was a promising business, but also a paperwork monster with what seemed like a gazillion regulations. To help him get through the stack of paper on his desk, Briggs ordered pizza delivery. Two hours later he had finished the paperwork, along with all but one slice of pepperoni.

Next, he began reviewing resumes from 46 people who had applied to manage his new pet crematory. Their primary job would be to process requests for cremations and manage government paperwork. They would pick up the canine bodies from local veterinary offices, transport them to Heavenly Considerations and handle the cremations, including pulverizing the remains into a fine ash. They would also place the remains into decorative urns and deliver them to local veterinarians for return to bereaved clients.

Most job respondents came from an ad in Craig's List, among them a 60-year-old unemployed marketing executive, a department store shoe sales associate, and a real estate broker, all who claimed to be "great with people." Did they envision themselves as happy pet funeral directors?

Briggs sat back in his chair and rubbed his eyes. He did not need a people-person. He needed someone organized, who understood the animal care industry. The perfect candidate would be an individual who could communicate with clients and veterinary hospitals and clinics and manage business licensing requirements. Yes, good people skills would help, but that was less important than other experience.

He was down to the last application. Why bother reading it? Could the last one be a perfect fit? Based on what he had already read, he had doubts. Briggs put the last application on top, grabbed the two-inch stack of paper with both hands, slapped the ends on the desktop. He took 10 sheets from the top of the pile and was about to feed them into his shredder when he spotted the designation DVM, Doctor of Veterinary Medicine, on the top sheet of the last application.

The resume, from a veterinary researcher, Helen Williams, stood out. He read over her credentials and found that, like him, she had earned a veterinary medicine degree from Oregon State University.

The name Helen tickled his memory—his college girlfriend was Helen—but that memory slipped away as he read her last name, Williams. His Helen had married and was living back East. He did not remember her married last name. But Williams did not sound familiar. The background of this Helen was a perfect match for the job, so he sent her a text message inviting her for an interview the next day.

The woman who appeared for the job left him speechless.

***

As Helen stood in front of the corrugated metal door, a cool breeze made her shiver. It was Spring but on most days too cool to wear the thin dress and light summer sweater she had selected for her interview. The sun felt warm when you were not in the shade. But here she was in North Portland's industrial area, in the shadow of a rusty WWII Quonset hut with small *Heavenly Considerations* and *No Solicitors* signs on the door.

Why was she here?

She did not need a job. Her boss, Susan, had told her to clean up her act and she could come back anytime. Were pride and embarrassment closing that door? What was she getting herself into? Emotionally and physically, she was still raw from the incident in the park. Her memories of what happened—she had drifted in and out of consciousness from alcohol—returned in mental video snippets. The violence to her body was its own blow-by-blow record of the assault.

Helen refused to go to the police. She was too ashamed, and besides, only recalled two names of her attackers, a Bobby and a Hoffman. What would she tell the interviewing officer? "I woke up naked and bloody in a community garden under the freeway, but don't recall who I was with or what I was doing. And, yes, officer, I had four beers, three glasses of wine, and some Scotch before going out for the evening."

"Slut," she could imagine the officer thinking.

Instead, Helen went to the pharmacy, bought Plan B and a Healthy Woman kit that included tests for HIV, chlamydia, gonorrhea, syphilis, and trichomoniasis. She took the morning-after pill but waited 48 hours to take the others. So far, results were negative. She also had scrubbed her skin in the shower with a brush and douched, washing away the evidence.

Now, here she was, in a remote location, by herself, responding to an advertisement to manage a pet crematory where they burned bodies. Flashing red in her mind were scenes from Devil in the White City, Erik Larson's grisly tale of a doctor who lured young woman eager for a job to his office a mile from the 1896 World Fair in Chicago, then killed them and burned up their bodies in the basement.

Was Helen walking into another dangerous situation? Was the owner some creep who put out ads to lure in unsuspecting victims for his sick games, with all evidence of her existence soon after a pile of ashes in a bucket? The ad could be a ruse: you could pull down a magnetic sign in two seconds to erase any attention to the location.

Helen rang the bell and waited for what seemed like forever. When the door opened, the man in front of her sent shock waves through her entire body. He was big. With her sunglasses on in the shade, all she could see was a person's outline filling the space.

"I'm Helen Williams, I'm here for a job… ah, ah… Maybe I made a mistake. I came for an interview for a job." She was on the edge of panic. A bright light coming from inside the building prevented her from seeing the face of the person at the door.

Before she could get out the words, Jim Briggs yelled, "Helen O'Donnell? Is that you?"

She pulled off her sunglasses and peered at the figure.

"I'm Helen Williams now," she said, squinting at the man in front of her. But she recognized the voice.

"Oh my God, Jim? It is. I didn't know this was your business, or that you had moved back to Portland."

"I can't believe it," said Briggs. "Come in. Come in."

"Give me a hug," he said and wrapped his arms around her. Suddenly, she felt safe, warm, and wanted.

Helen let out a sigh of relief. She would not die, at least today.

She followed Briggs into a hangar-like space divided up for offices, a cremation processing room, and a parking area for the Have Paws—Will Travel van. Contrary to the building exterior, the inside was spacious, clean, and light.

"Coffee?" Briggs asked.

"Sure."

"I know just how you like it. A splash of cream and one sugar. The same?"

"That would be perfect."

***

Jim and Helen had been friends and lovers in college, meeting by accident.

Helen remembered the fateful day they met at Oregon State University, where they both had enrolled in veterinary school. It was early summer, 75 degrees, with a light breeze. She sprawled under a leafy alder, her long legs in front of her—a tripping hazard. He tripped over her legs, skinning up both of them.

Embarrassed and horrified at the damage he'd done, Helen recalled Briggs' awkward attempt to apologize, stuttering, "Let… Let me help. I'm an EMT. Well, I mean, I work as an EMT while I'm getting my degree." He had pulled out a small first aid kit and began dabbing at her skinned knees.

Helen also remembered her response: "Keep your hands to yourself. This is the second time you've assaulted me. You fell on me, then started grabbing me."

Despite her warning, Briggs had plopped down next to her with a book on dog anatomy and asked if he could share the shade.

She had nodded, grimacing as she assessed her wounds, then noticed him dabbing at his bloody knee.

Within a month, they were lovers—inseparable for the next three years. They were more like a married couple than two love-struck college students. They became study partners, and both had an insatiable appetite for sex whenever and wherever the opportunity presented itself.

"How long has it been," Briggs asked.

"Five or six years," Helen said.

Helen noticed Briggs' eyes scanning her body.

"Like what you see?" she said, catching him despite his efforts to maintain eye contact. If Briggs could see her cuts and bruises, and feel the pain she was in, he would not be thinking about jumping into bed with her.

Briggs' face turned red. A sheepish grin crossed his face.

"Let me guess," said Helen, never one to be subtle or let an opportunity to embarrass Briggs slip by: "You're thinking I'm older and thinner. You still like my short hair and green eyes. The dress I'm wearing is too sexy for a job interview."

"Got me," Briggs said.

"You're so transparent, Briggs."

"My brain went somewhere a potential employer should not go."

"Like all the times under the goalposts of the deserted football stadium and the stacks at the far end of the campus library," she snapped. Briggs smiled at her and flushed red again. She had him on the run now. He was always so serious, an easy mark for humor. He did not seem to have a funny bone in his body.

"Knowing our history, I guess you'll want me to undress and perform oral sex to secure this job."

Briggs's mouth dropped open. "Damn you, O'Donnell, I mean Williams, you're incorrigible." She raised her eyebrows and flashed a mischievous grin.

"Got me," he said with a goofy smile. "No sexual favors necessary. You're hired."

"That was easy," she said. "You always were a pushover."

"Only for you, Helen. How is marriage? How is Rod?" She frowned, lines appearing on his face as she squeezed her eyes shut and pressed her lips together.

She opened them and stuttered, "He's dead." Again, Briggs' mouth dropped open.

"You got me again," he said.

"No, it's true," said Helen and explained. Briggs slumped in his chair after she told him the story.

"God, I don't know what to say."

"Tell me you want me to start today. I need to get my mind off Rod and start crawling out of the sinkhole that has been my life the past month." Not included in Helen's gruesome tale of Rod's death was the event signaling she had hit rock bottom. Pieces of the nightmare in the park flashed into her mind. She remembered waking up under the freeway, naked from the waist down, pain in every part of her body, with a dim memory of being passed around—gang-raped—by three homeless men, while a female companion watched, and did nothing to help.

When Briggs asked Helen if she had a problem with the homeless—since a piece of the job was to fill in at Have Paws—Will Travel and provide care for the dogs of the homeless, her stomach clenched. A wave of nausea hit.

"Are you okay?" asked Briggs when he saw her grab her stomach.

"Yes, just a burning sensation. Too much coffee," she lied.

"Doing volunteer work will be therapy. It will give me something besides myself to think about."

"Great," said Briggs. "But how are you going to deal with being close to homeless people? A lot of them are rough, dirty, and crude with little hygiene. If they are high on drugs, they will threaten you with verbal outbursts and clenched fists, and glare at you with anger-red faces." Helen held her breath to choke her rage, then said in a soft voice," You can't blame all of them for a few bad actors."

"Fucking homeless," she thought. "Animals. All of them. Killing them, rather than offering kindness, would better describe my feelings." She shared none of her thoughts with Briggs.

"I'm euthanizing a family dog tomorrow morning," Briggs said, breaking the tension. "You can join me."

"You're such a romantic," she said, her face brightening.

Briggs ended the interview, noting it was time to leave for a client appointment. He walked Helen out to her car, gave her another hug, and said he would see her in the morning. Helen climbed in her car, waved as she pulled onto the highway, and headed home. She would need to give Susan the news. Helen would not be returning to Canine Therapeutics. Now, she needed to stay sober so she could show up for her first day on the new job.

"A wee dram of scotch might be nice," she thought as she headed home.

CHAPTER TWELVE

May 10, 2019

The next morning, the chime on Briggs' iPhone alerted him to an incoming client call. The Teller Family's beloved pet Ginger was in crisis, and Ginny Teller was calling to confirm his 10 a.m. appointment at the Teller's Victorian home in Portland's Nob Hill District.

Briggs returned the call and mentioned another veterinarian would accompany him.

Thirty minutes later, Briggs pulled up to the Teller's home and found Helen passed out in her car.

***

Helen had parked her car in front of the Teller home, turned off the motor, opened the glove compartment, and pulled out a bottle of aspirin. After wrestling off the child-proof cap, she washed down four tablets with coffee she had picked up at a donut shop. A maple bar was poking out of a paper bag on the seat next to her. She picked up the bag, looked at the donut, and pushed it back in. The thought of food turned her stomach into a merry-go-round. The pain behind her eyes was pulsing. So much so, she had to close them to block out the light, while squeezing the sides of her head to prevent it from exploding. Despite her best effort to drink up her late husband Rod's fine Scotch, there were still three cases of it left. Here she was, on her first day of work, still drunk. A minute later, she passed out.

A knock on the car window jolted her back to consciousness. Jim Briggs was outside peering in with a quizzical look on his face.

She rolled down the window and greeted him. "Hey."

"You look like Hell, Helen, what happened?"

"I went home from our interview, had dinner, and opened a bottle of Scotch to celebrate the new job. Guess I had a few too many." She tried to make light of her condition. Briggs was not having any of it.

"You can't go into the Tellers like this, reeking of alcohol. Go home, sober up, and plan to start work tomorrow."

Helen offered a weak smile.

***

Briggs had nothing to smile at. He knew Helen liked to drink but could not remember when she had ever been this bad. When she had to study, take a test, or go to a meeting, she had either abstained or kept her intake to a single glass of wine. She had always been moderate.

"Are you all right to drive?"

"I'm fine. I just need some rest and I'll be right as rain."

"Okay," said Briggs. "Drive carefully. I will talk to you later in the day."

Helen buckled her seatbelt, pretended to adjust her mirror, then gave Briggs a wave goodbye as she pulled away from the curb.

"Shit. Shit. Shit. I've got to straighten myself out or I'll end up in the gutter, another homeless person," she said to the woman in the mirror who had tears coming down her face. In the next moment, she pulled the car hard to the curb, leaned her head out the driver's side, barely clearing the door before she vomited.

***

Jim Briggs knocked on the Teller's door, then stood back. He could hear footsteps tapping on a hardwood floor.

When George Teller opened the door, his eight-year-old twins, Geoff and Gina, flanked him.

"Dr. Briggs, hurry, Ginger is sick," said Gina. "She needs your help."

Briggs had been to the Teller home many times over the past few months, trying to nurture Ginger back to health. It had not worked. But the twins were familiar with his effort, which made it easier as he prepared to break the bad news to them. Gina and Geoff each grabbed one of Briggs' hands and led him down the hall to a utility room where Ginger, a 14-year-old border collie, lay on her side, eyes closed, panting. She had survived a severe bout of pancreatitis, but was now incontinent, and the drugs used to treat the disease had damaged her kidneys. Briggs pushed open her eyes and patted her. He went through the motions of doing something for the terminally ill dog for the sake of the children.

"I'll take care of her," Briggs assured them, tears streaming down their faces.

"Kids, go to your room while mommy and daddy talk to the doctor," said George Teller.

"Okay, Daddy," they said in unison.

The children grabbed each other's hands and ran down the hall to their rooms. "The doctor is going to save Ginger," Briggs heard twin Geoff say as the kids disappeared down the hallway. George and Ginny had not shared the plan for their beloved pet.

Turning to Briggs, George Teller said, "Ginny will make a latte for you." He led Briggs to their kitchen. The tall doors and 14-foot ceilings allowed Briggs to navigate his way without ducking to avoid hitting his head—a constant hazard for someone six-feet-six inches.

"Jim, so nice to see you," Ginny said, using her skills as a former barista to pour steamed milk into a white heart shape.

"How do we know if the time is right?" Ginny asked, looking directly at Briggs, ready to verify his answer by the look on his face. Briggs could not believe that Ginny, who had been the founder and manager of a dog daycare center for the past 10 years, could be so ignorant about canine euthanasia. Still, he tried to be calm.

"You can see the suffering. You can feel Ginger's pain, can't you?"

"We do," George and Ginny, like their twins, said in unison as if rehearsed for this moment.

"It's been miserable to see Ginger's decline," said Ginny. "Ginger was like our kid before we had children."

"Do you want the children to witness it?" Briggs asked.

"What's the alternative?" said George. "We don't want to traumatize them."

"I suggest we bring the children in to say goodbye to Ginger," said Briggs. "Then you can take them into the next room while I administer the shots. The kids can come back into the room to say a last goodbye. Ginger will still be warm, so it won't feel odd to touch her. How does that sound?" The Tellers glanced at each other and nodded.

The Tellers said their goodbyes. Like most people about to have a pet put down, it was hard to let go.

Ginger, who just a moment before could barely hold her eyes open as she lay on her side, suddenly sat up in response to all the family's attention. Startled by the sudden movement, the family simultaneously jumped back, and Gina said, "Maybe she's okay, maybe she is feeling better."

Stunned, neither parent could think of anything to say, so Briggs jumped in.

"It's okay, Gina," Briggs said. "Ginger wants to say goodbye and thank you for a good life."

Briggs' little white lie paid off when Ginger settled down, rolled over on her side, and closed her eyes. The children rubbed her fur and gave hugs and pats before George moved the children out of the room. Ginny remained. She had volunteered to be at Ginger's side during her last moments.

In less than a minute, Ginger had received her lethal two-shot cocktail and took her last breath. A moment later, Ginger's slack bladder muscles sent a gush of urine onto the sunroom's red linoleum floor.

After cleaning up, Briggs put a water-absorbent diaper under the dog's body and wrapped her in a blanket. He left Ginger's head exposed so the children could kiss her goodbye and brought the family back in.

"Can we give her one more hug?" asked Ginny.

"Sure, everyone can touch or kiss her," Briggs said.

Helen would cremate Ginger's remains at Heavenly Considerations—if she were sober—and, in a few days, deliver the remains to the Tellers in a brightly colored jar.

They had prepaid the bill, a good business practice because families often delayed payments for months after euthanasia, as if completing the deal was also the last goodbye to their beloved companion animal.

Briggs gave each of the Tellers a hug and said goodbye, carrying Ginger to his van in one of the dog's favorite blankets. He transferred the body to the van's refrigerated unit and headed to the office.

Looking out at the bright day, Briggs thought about how humane euthanasia is for animals.

Jimbo, euthanasia is humane for dogs, why not humans?

"Maybe DIME's right," Briggs thought.

CHAPTER THIRTEEN

May 23, 2019

Briggs's iPhone came to life with a text message alert from the Portland 9-1-1 communications center. He launched his police and fire radio app and listened to the chatter.

"Fire under control. Occupant of a burned shelter suffered minor injuries. Paramedic on scene. We have a 10-11."

Briggs perked up at the 10-11, the code for a dog-involved incident. To find out if he knew the victim and dog, he launched his PupFinder tracking app. His screen lit up with three dozen points of light: white dog symbols, each the location of a homeless client's dog. The GPS chips on their collars helped him keep track since most roamed around the city like nomads.

He tapped on a white dog symbol near the reported area of the fire victim and confirmed it was Pirate Pete, the one-eyed beagle that trailed Jerry Hoffman.

Briggs called 9-1-1, identified himself, and confirmed he would respond and check out the dog.

"This is Mary Philips, Jim. Thanks for responding. You are saving us all a lot of paperwork. What's your ETA?"

"Fifteen minutes max," said Briggs.

"I'll relay the information to the on-scene commander," said Phillips "Hang on a sec."

When she came back on the line, she told Briggs that she had alerted police and fire to his arrival.

"All well with you?" she asked.

"Yeah, Mary, just trying to stay out of trouble. Let's get a beer soon."

"Maybe something a little extra," she teased.

"Been too long," said Briggs. He did not mention he had a girlfriend.

"Great. I'll text you," said Phillips. "Got a crazy schedule right now. Another call coming in. Gotta go."

"Ciao," said Briggs.

Phillips was a former girlfriend lured into engagement by an old boyfriend after Briggs made it clear he was not ready for a lifelong commitment. Phillips and her boyfriend broke off the engagement after six months, but Briggs had moved on by then. Still, he loved Mary's company, her energy, her smile—and her red hair and blue eyes. And they both liked no-holds-barred, no-commitment sex on friend date nights. That was all past with Kim Jansen in his life.

"Sounds like a booty call to me," said Helen. Briggs' fair skin flushed red at the "booty call" comment. Since the Teller euthanasia when Briggs sent her home hungover, Helen had become a constant, reliable companion. She was quickly learning the city layout, the client flow, and the local cops they assisted. She also was taking on more swing shifts to give Briggs nights off.

"Was your relationship with Mary serious?" Helen asked.

"She wanted something long term," said Briggs. "Too much was going on in my life to commit. Now, we are just friends."

When Briggs and Helen arrived on the scene of the tent fire, an emaciated man was sitting on the back of an ambulance being treated for scalp burns. Helen recognized him. Her stomach leaped. It was Jerry Hoffman.

A piece of flaming tent blackened a portion of Hoffman's once gray hair. No doubt the grease in Hoffman's hair fueled the fire. Briggs could not help smiling at the story he recalled from a visit to Amelia Island, off the Florida coast. A hang out for pirates, Blackbird was notorious for twirling his beard into wick-like strands, then oiling and lighting them to scare the hell out of the local population as he walked down the street.

A cop on the scene told Briggs that Hoffman and Pete dove out of the tent a moment before it collapsed in a ball of fire.

While the paramedic bandaged Hoffman, Briggs examined Pete and found the hair on his back had been thick enough to keep most of the fire away from his skin. Briggs trimmed away burned hair, cleaned a small, injured area, then applied burn ointment and a bandage before pronouncing Pete otherwise okay. A leg bandage—from a broken leg Briggs had treated—was dirty and partially shredded, no doubt from Pete trying to pull it off.

"Jerry, by the look of that tent, you're damn lucky to be alive," Briggs said. "What happened?"

Hoffman ignored the question.

"Jerry, I fixed up Pete. He has minor burns from the fire, but the bandage on his leg needs changing. I'll try to find you tomorrow and apply a new bandage. Are you okay?"

Hoffman did not answer, but the fire-paramedic said the burns were superficial, first-degree, like a bad sunburn. In a week, Hoffman would heal up. His hair would take longer to recover.

Briggs knew Hoffman might heal up physically, but mentally, he was gone. Another human stray whose life would end sooner than later. His enormous belly, skinny arms, and buttless body were a tribute to Jerry's daily arm exercises: drinking as much alcohol as he could lift to his face.

Helen stood statue-still during Briggs' conversation with Hoffman. She appeared frozen, her eyes wide as if she had seen a ghost—more like a face-to-face encounter with a wolf in the wilderness. Her fingers went numb, her legs stiff, unable to move.

She recognized the man by the sound of his cigarette damaged vocal cords. He was one of the attackers who left her bruised and bloody in the community garden next to the freeway in the Pearl District. "Helen, are you okay?"

She shook off the shock of seeing Hoffman and looked at Briggs. "I'm fine. Just lost in thought." More like a nightmare. But she was not ready to tell that part of her story to Briggs. He was her boss now, not a boyfriend or a husband. She no longer had a husband, thanks to a fucking homeless stray who forced him into the street in front of a moving train.

"Helen, would you mind taking over for a few hours before going back to Paws? I have a project I'm working on at the library."

"No problem," she said, trying to recover from the shock of hearing the same voice that whispered in her ear, "You're going to love this baby. Big daddy got something sweet for you." She would never forget the words as she felt something jammed into her mouth and down her throat. She stifled a gag.

Helen clasped her hands together tightly behind her back to keep Briggs from seeing that she was shaking. He did not seem to notice.

After Briggs and Helen finished patching up Pirate Pete, she guided the big van down Morrison Street to 10th Avenue to drop Briggs at the Portland Central Library. Briggs was researching the genealogies of homeless clients to find families willing to take them in, maybe save them from dying on Portland streets.

"You got plans for tonight?" Helen asked when she pulled to the curb.

"No," said Briggs, "Just covering the phones, picking up some animals for cremation—the usual. Why?"

"Let me cover tonight's shift. I want to get to know the city better, meet some clients and other veterinarians, get out in the fresh air."

"You're not looking for veterinarians to date, are you? They're a boring bunch."

"I guess that's what I liked about you, Briggs: quiet and kind of boring, but cute."

They looked at each other, and Briggs smiled.

***

May 23, 2019

"Good afternoon, Helen," said Briggs as he walked into the offices of Heavenly Considerations.

"Hi, Jimmy, what's happening?"

"Not much, except I need to track down Jerry Hoffman and Pirate Pete and replace the bandage on Pete's broken leg. He's been pulling on the bandage. It's shredded and dirty. You saw it at the tent fire."

"Yes, I remember," said Helen.

"I'm buried with end of month finances and client follow-up calls. Could you use PupFinder and track down Pete? I also promised to give Hoffman a vitamin shot."

"I'll do it, no problem," said Helen. "I have nothing going tonight except a half bottle of chardonnay and re-runs of Momma's Place."

"I liked Momma's Place, too. But not enough to watch endless re-runs." Briggs was about to leave for his home office when he said, "I thought you were off the booze."

"I'm off whiskey and binging," said Helen. "I think I've got a grip on it. A little goes a long way." Briggs did not challenge her.

"Thanks for stepping in for me tonight," said Briggs. "By the way, on Saturday we are having dinner with Mark and Helen. They are looking forward to meeting you."

After Briggs left, Helen opened the company laptop, which contained all the homeless client files, and launched PupFinder. She quickly located Pirate Pete about a mile away at NW Community Park, where the attack took place. The computer file identified Pete's human companion as Jerry Hoffman. With luck, Hoffman would be alone. She had already confirmed in her own mind that Hoffman was one of her assailants. The time for hesitation was past. She would execute her plan. Or rather, she would implement her execution plan.

Helen climbed into the company van and drove to the community garden. She parked a half-block away, then slowly walked through the garden gate and looked down a row of stone-sided garden boxes filled with plants.

Hoffman was drinking something out of a paper sack and talking loudly to himself. He turned his head her way, making her stomach lurch. It was him: one of her rapists. He eyes were glassy and his head moving from side to side, as if he could not hold it up. He was in another world, stoned on drugs and alcohol. When she realized Hoffman had not seen her, Helen stopped holding her breath.

She would never forget that raspy voice; how he yelped, "Ride'em cowboy" as he rammed her with his penis. She had lost consciousness before he finished and was so inebriated, she could not defend herself or scream. After watching Hoffman for another minute with murderous thoughts rising, Helen decided what she had to do and returned to the van. Instead of rage, she felt calm. This time around, she would be in control.

She took a few deep breaths and decided to come for Hoffman after dark. In the meantime, she was hungry. She would have plenty of time for an early dinner before sunset and darkness.

A few minutes later, Helen was sitting at a window table in a nearby sushi restaurant. As she ate, she watched the sun's glow on adjacent buildings. The setting sun reminded her of times she had evening cocktails with her husband, Rod. They called them 'sunset lounges,' enjoying vodka gimlets as they watched the light fade.

Tonight, she would have a sunset lounge with Jerry Hoffman. But there would be no gimlets. Helen would serve up a mule-like cocktail—something with a kick. A big dose of barbiturate would go straight into his veins. She would offer no anesthetic to soften the blow. His burning chest would buck violently as his lungs and brain screamed for oxygen. His eyes would bulge in terror as he realized Death's hand was reaching out, about to grab him by the throat, and carry him down under. When she finished dinner, Helen drove back to the community garden where Hoffman had been. He was gone. Determined to track him down, she pulled out the PupFinder App on Briggs' laptop. There he was—under the freeway. She knew there was an encampment of homeless in the area.

He would be nearby. Helen clipped her iPhone onto the dash of the van and gave a command. "Siri, play the Moody Blues album *Days of Future Past.*"

***

An hour later, Helen was on her way back to Heavenly Considerations with Jerry Hoffman's body stowed in the van refrigeration unit. One down and three to go," Helen said out loud. "Should I be sorry for what I did?" Nothing popped into her mind. But the Siri came to life and asked, "Who are the three to go?"

"Sorry," must have sounded like "Siri," activating the so-called intelligent assistant. "Creepy," Helen thought. "Is she listening and recording what's going on? Will she be a witness to my meeting tonight with Jerry Hoffman? Can a prosecutor summon an artificial intelligence witness in my trial? Will SIRI tell the jury that it was self-defense? That it was justifiable homicide with Helen acquitted unanimously by a jury of her peers? Her thoughts returned to Mark. If he found out, what would he say about her revenge killing of Jerry Hoffman? Would he turn a blind eye or turn her in? She had no plan to find out.

CHAPTER FOURTEEN

June 1, 2019

Chief of Detectives Mike Melrose reached down and pulled a report from the bottom of the pile and looked at the date. A week old. He knew he had screwed up. Unless you could jump on a case and collect witness statements and other evidence, a case could go cold quickly—especially a missing person's case. A week delay could be the fatal blow for a case—life or death for a kidnapped victim who had gone missing. Of course, he had no evidence of any such crime. Still, he had made a rookie error; an error caused because of his miserable life and the snow of paper mounding on his desk.

"Damn," he said to no one, realizing the whole pile was "aging" unassigned cases. Then he noticed the name of the alleged victim and let out a sign of relief. "Thank God for small favors," he whispered to his empty office, after realizing the so-called victim was nothing more than a missing homeless person. He debated with himself whether he should throw it in the round file. He was not cruel. It's just that with the homeless population's continued growth and their lawlessness consuming the Portland Police Bureau, there was little time to investigate actual crimes.

"Gerald 'Jerry' Hoffman," Melrose thought. "I know this sleaze-bag. He and his friends have been preying on locals and other homeless for years. Why would we want to investigate the report of a missing homeless person? Probably not missing. More like a dazed rooster who could not find his way back to the coop."

The park workers had filled the report with the usual details except for one item found at the scene: a pair of woman's panties. No big deal. But the park worker who wrote the report noted that the panties were very expensive, clean and nearly new. Probably stolen, Melrose figured.

He finished looking at the report and thought, "Good riddance, Jerry Hoffman." His hand hovered over his trash can and stopped. He had an idea: give his new detective, Mark Larson, something to chew on.

***

"Larson, get in here. We need to talk. Now."

The booming voice cut through Mike Melrose's paper pile, shot down the short hallway and shook the quiet.

The other four detectives in the room all stared at Larson, then at each other. Some of them were looking down and others looking away. Several shook their heads.

"What?" said Larson. "You think I'm going to get my ass kicked by the Chief? I've done nothing, yet."

"That's the problem, Larson," said Emily Stinson, a 45-year-old detective with 10 years of experience under her belt. You've been here a week and haven't done shit, except gawk at your shiny, new detective shield." Stinson and the other detectives were doing their best to keep Larson off-balance, part of an informal initiation process. Larson got up slowly, trying the ignore the urgency in his boss's voice. He also wanted to avoid looking like a puppy waiting for a treat. "What's up, Chief?" Larson asked as he stood in Melrose's office doorway, leaning on the jam.

"Vacation is over, Larson. You've had enough time following other detectives around like a dog walker, supplying them with coffee and cleaning up their paperwork messes. Initiation is over. It's time for your own case." He said it loud enough for the other detective to hear, no doubt more entertainment for the troops at Larson's expense.

"What have you got, Chief? I'm ready," said Larson.

"Stop leaning in the doorway like a bored teenager," said Melrose, lowering his voice. "Come in and sit down." Melrose pulled the missing person report from a growing shit-pile of paper and handed it to Larson. "This is probably nothing, but we have a report of a missing homeless man. It's suspicious because a park cleanup crew found an empty tent and wallet with ID and $35 cash. What homeless person would leave behind a wallet with cash?

"The money and wallet is a bit odd," Larson agreed.

"The missing person is one Gerald Robert Hoffman, IV," said Melrose. "You know him, right?"

Larson did not answer, quickly scanning the meager details of the one-page report. "Chief, this report is a week old." Melrose ignored the comment.

"Larson, your first task will be to see if Hoffman has turned up. You know Hoffman, right?"

"Oh yeah, Chief. Had many run-ins with him. He is part of Little Bobby McWhorter's gang, a group of homeless predators who have robbed and raped their way through the most vulnerable in the homeless community. A mean bastard who deserves to be in jail, but threatens retribution to anyone who snitches on him."

"I'm impressed, Larson. You seem to know him well."

"I'm surprised he's still alive," said Larson.

"Maybe he isn't," Melrose offered. "No need to get teary-eyed. Lots of people go missing each year but are found because they were never lost in the first place; they were runaways or victims of abuse. Some just disappear and are never found. The missing homeless may have moved away or found a permanent home. Or have moved their camp to under another bridge on the other side of town."

Larson crossed his arms, his teeth clenched so tight the muscles in his jaw were vibrating.

"What's that look for? You got a problem with the assignment?"

"Permission to speak freely, sir?"

"Give it your best shot, Larson."

"I've been a street cop for seven years, so I'm not some fresh-faced kid joining the force."

"Easy, Detective Larson. I'm not challenging your credentials or your smarts. I guarantee you wouldn't be part of my team if I didn't value your experience. Our crew is so small, we can't afford to be running an internship program trying to bring someone up to speed."

"I understand, Chief. But so much attention to a homeless scofflaw?"

Melrose did not snap off one of his usual sarcastic remarks. Instead, he used both hands to pat a head of precisely trimmed black hair combed straight back. His hair was the only thing in his life not in disarray. Content every hair was in place, Melrose put his hands back on the top of his desk, looking past Larson, his shoulders relaxing. He leaned over and whispered, "Do you ever wonder if some of these people don't just crawl into a hole in Forest Park and die, their remains never found, melting into the earth."

Larson was taken aback by Melrose's daydream, contemplating the mysteries of death, but said nothing. A second later, Melrose snapped back to reality.

"Okay, let's focus on the case. Despite your street experience, you're the new guy, and you need experience. I'm assigning you to Hoffman's case as a start. Go snoop around, check your street sources, talk to folks in the homeless support community. And, yes, buttonhole some homeless. Toss them a few bucks to loosen their tongues. Show them a photo of Hoffman. See what you can come up with. One more thing. You'll find an oddball item in the evidence box: panties with a fancy brand name."

"Thanks, Chief. I'll get on it."

Larson had been one of the most decorated officers on the force. He would know where to look, thought Melrose, and who to ask.

Larson returned to his desk and opened the file. The details included several pages of photos taken at the scene, including some of Hoffman's I.D., and other personal items now locked away in the evidence room. Larson would plan a trip there later to look over everything.

In the meantime, he knew someone who could help his investigation: his friend, Jim Briggs, who operated Have Paws—Will Travel, a mobile canine care service in Northwest Portland. He donated dozens of hours each week to providing free care to the dogs of homeless people. Larson figured Briggs could quickly find Hoffman, putting an end to the case. He looked at the time and realized he was late for a happy hour with Briggs, former patrol partner Kim Jansen, and Helen Williams, the woman Briggs hired to manage Heavenly Considerations.

***

For Detective Mark Larson, it was love at first sight.

Helen Williams was just as Briggs had described her: unimaginably long legs, 5-feet-10, short brown hair, green eyes, and perfect proportions for her height. She was attractive, but Helen's blazing smile riveted him.

"Earth-to-Mark," Briggs said.

"Sorry," he said. "I didn't mean to be rude by staring, it's just that you have a brilliant smile." The comment aroused Helen—the bold, brazen Helen.

"It seems Detective Larson has undressed me with his eyes," Helen turned and said to Jansen and Briggs. Turning back to Larson, she cocked her head slightly, waiting for a response.

He felt like someone shot him with a TASER. Briggs and Kim laughed.

"Meet the real Helen Williams," said Briggs. "I said she was cute. I just left out the snarky part. Figured you needed to experience it firsthand."

Helen continued: "I do like the 'nice smile' line. That's a novel approach. You sound like an old-fashioned guy, a man before his time. I can see you as a clean-cut teen in the 1950s having a Coke and fries at the local burger joint, looking into the 16-year-old girl's eyes and saying, 'what a pretty smile.' Very quaint, don't you think, guys." All eyes were on Larson, whose Nordic face was crimson.

"He is such a sweet guy," said Briggs mockingly.

"Come on, give me a break. I meant it."

"Well, thank you," said Helen, offering a wide grin.

"Let's be on our best behavior," said Kim, winking a Helen. "We are meeting Helen for the first time. We want her to have a good impression since she is Jim's friend."

Briggs smiled at Kim and kissed her, a public affirmation that Kim, not Helen, was his love interest, to avoid any feelings of jealousy. Just in case there were doubts.

"Guys, as you know, Helen had taken over the operation of Heavenly Considerations. Since she is a veterinarian, she will help me with canine care clients. Helen and I were in vet school together.

"That's right," said Jansen. "Briggs told me you met at OSU in the veterinary program."

"We ran into each other one day on campus," Helen said, recounting the meeting. "Or should I say that Briggs tripped over me and fell flat on his face? I yelled, 'Nice move, jerk. Watch where you're going.' He dabbed at my legs and I told him to keep his hands to himself. Afraid to touch me, he bandaged his legs and asked me for a date even though he was hurting." Mark and Kim had already heard the story from Briggs but wanted to hear Helen's side.

To get the focus off Helen, Briggs asked Mark and Kim what had been happening in the police bureau.

"The usual stuff, except a run-in with a little homeless guy—he's tiny, about five feet tall," said Mark. "Robert McWhorter, better known on the streets as

Little Bobby. He had been harassing a Thai restaurant owner who asked him not to camp in his doorway," Kim explained. "The restaurant owner called and said some 'midget' was harassing him and his lunch customers."

"Last year, we confronted Little Bobby," Mark added, "and he took a swing at Kim. She had him locked down in two seconds. He gave up. The last thing he wanted was to go to jail."

"He's got a gang," Kim said. "Every summer, they come together to maximize their wages by panhandling in the best spots—forcing everyone else out—and preying on other homeless, especially those alone or passed out. They swarm homeless loners like a pack of wolves, consuming everything in sight. At night, they hang out in a park next to the freeway, drinking beer and raising hell. The sound of the freeway drowns out their party sounds. Eventually, we pieced together the group's M.O. but never had the resources to pursue an investigation or form a task force to halt it."

"They are bad dudes," said Larson. "Unfortunately, it is rare when someone calls to report an assault or theft. Most of their victims are also homeless and are so dazed and confused, they don't know who attacked them, or won't talk to avoid retribution."

"Bobby and company rape, rob, and beat anyone who gets in their way," Kim said. "Little Bobby's gang members include Jerry Hoffman, Patrick O'Flaherty and a woman, 'Big Betty' Bingham. Big Betty is well over 200 pounds. I recall hearing that Little Bobby and Betty were a couple."

"Oh, come on, give me a break, Jansen," said Larson. "Can you imagine those two holding hands or doing anything else?"

"It is a scary thought," said Kim.

"Well, you might find my day interesting, speaking of homeless gang members," Larson said. "I got my first case as a new detective today. It is an investigation into the disappearance of our very own Jerry Hoffman."

"You are the low man on the totem pole," Jansen said, poking him in the arm. "But giving a homicide detective a missing person investigation is pretty low, don't you think? Those people go missing all the time. And besides, who cares?"

"Exactly what I told Chief Melrose," said Larson. "He told me to get off my rookie butt and get to work." Jansen offered a knowing smile and said, "Sorry."

"Wish I could say my day was interesting," Briggs said. "I picked up a dead dog and took him to Heavenly Considerations, then had a client with a sick Pomeranian."

Helen tried to keep smiling, but her mind crept back to the night of her attack. The description of the gang of homeless was too similar to those who assaulted her to be a coincidence, even though her memory of the night was still hazy, no doubt permanently damaged from the massive dose of alcohol she had consumed.

As she fought off the anger and memory of violence, her smile disappeared.

"You okay, Helen?" asked Larson.

"I'm fine," she said, forcing a smile.

"Honestly? Maybe not. I'm still getting over my husband's death, caused by a homeless man. All this talk about homeless predators pushed a button."

"I'm so sorry," said Mark, reaching across the table and placing his hand on hers. "None of us at this table has a soft spot for the homeless either," said Larson. "Sure, you hate to see families forced to live on the street because they have no money for rent, or a veteran suffering from PTSD slumped lifelessly in a doorway. But I've got no love for the homeless predators, like Little Bobby. They have their territory, and they enforce it. We spend more time responding to crimes by homeless than anything else."

Hey Jimbo, you've got a nice little cabal of homeless haters here. It makes our job easier, don't you think? Maybe you could create your own death squad.

"In your dreams," Briggs' Happy Half countered, just as an alarm vibrated on his phone: a reminder he had a full calendar the next day of client calls. "Siri just reminded me it is bedtime," said Briggs. The three smiled and Kim gibed, "What do you and SIRI have going, Briggs?" She frowned and squinted at him as if waiting for an answer.

"Okay, I get it," he said and smiled.

"If we're lucky, maybe we can get Helen to come out with us again," said Kim.

Helen seemed to shake off the shock of the Little Bobby's story, her smile returning. She had already taken care of Jerry Hoffman. Now that she had learned more about the rest of her attackers, she knew who to go after.

"Text me the time and place and I'll be there," she said, "No arm-twisting or chokeholds required."

This time, Larson did not miss the joke.

"I'll be there, too," he said, perhaps a little too quickly, like an excited puppy. The group broke up with Briggs and Jansen heading out, leaving Larson and Williams alone.

***

June 15, 2019

It had been two weeks since Mark and Helen met for the first time, and she had agreed to a dinner date with him at her townhouse. She was not sure why. She liked Mark, but the thought of cheating on Rod, in the home they had bought together, caused her chest to tighten. Yes, Rod was dead, but she felt him everywhere. Maybe this date was a bad idea. Helen picked up her phone to cancel, tell Mark she was sick. Instead, she took a shot of Scotch, which helped shake off her jitters. She looked around the room to make sure everything was in place: music, place settings, and wine cooling in an ice bucket. A corny scene. "What the hell am I doing," she said, slapping the side of her head like a soda machine that took your money, but delivered nothing. Her thoughts were scrambled; she was having a hard time focusing.

When the doorbell rang, she jumped. Ever since her assault, she had attacks of nerves, jumped at noises outside, and shadows in the hallway to her bedroom. She took several deep breaths and opened the front door. Like their first beers with Briggs and Kim, her eyes locked with Larson's. Helen felt like they remained that way for minutes when it was only seconds. Her eyes scanned Larson: close-cropped blond hair, 200 well-sculpted pounds, and just five-inches taller than her 5-foot-10 inches. He was wearing jeans, sandals, and a long-sleeve shirt with the tails hanging outside his jeans: the perfect Portland look. Her outfit was nearly the same except for her top, which she had tucked in.

Although Larson had grown up in the U.S., he seemed more European: he spoke softly and stood closer than was comfortable for most Americans.

When she talked, he leaned in, as if searching for some hidden meaning in her words. She felt no discomfort or any urge to look away as they gazed into each other's eyes for what seemed like forever.

He walked inside the front door, closed it, and locked on Helen's eyes. He mesmerized her the way you mesmerize dogs with tummy rubs. Mark used the moment to pull Helen in for a kiss. She could not resist. When they parted, Helen said, "Are you hungry?"

"Starving."

"I've heated the barbecue for thick-cut pork chops. Asparagus rubbed with garlic and olive oil is about to go in the oven. A Caesar salad in the refrigerator is ready to serve. For dessert, we'll have chocolate lava cake and espresso."

Helen walked over to a side table, pulled out a bottle of Rombauer chardonnay—$40 bucks a bottle—from the ice bucket, and filled two glasses. She handed a glass to Mark and raised hers in salute: "To new friends and new beginnings."

"I'll drink to that," said Larson.

They both took a sip.

"Mark, you mentioned a case you're working on. Tell me about it."

"You don't want to hear about work crap. We're not even sure it's a case at all."

"Still, I want to hear about it. Your job is a big part of your life, like mine is. It's part of the mating dance, right?"

"Are you preparing to mate?" Larson said, raising his eyebrows. Helen smiled, but was noncommittal.

Helen led him to a sofa where Mark began offering details of the case.

"You no doubt remember the discussion with Jim and Kim about Little Bobby's gang."

"I do," she said. "Go on."

"One of his gang, Gerald Hoffman IV, is the missing person in my case. I didn't want to say anything. It was early days in the investigation. I figured he would turn up. In his abandoned camp, we found his identification and a pair of nearly new, expensive panties with an Agent Provocateur label." Her stomach leaped. Had Hoffman stolen her panties after they pulled them off at the park? She had not found them, she remembered. Helen leaned away from Larson, her mind jumping back to her goodbye party for Jerry Hoffman. Larson noticed the move but said nothing.

"Anyway," Larson continued, "we have no evidence of a crime, nobody, no sign of a crime. Nothing but an I.D. and underwear."

"Hold that thought," said Helen, "I need to use the bathroom. Don't go away. I'll be right back," feigning a smile.

Helen went to the far end of her condo to a second bathroom, bent over the toilet, and vomited. When she returned a few minutes later, she tried to appear calm and said casually. "I'm starved. Let's eat."

After dinner and dessert, Larson excused himself and went to the bathroom. When he walked in and closed the door, his eyes jumped to a bit of white material sticking out of a drawer. Larson walked over, opened the drawer, saw that it was a pair of thong panties. Curious, he looked at the brand. Agent Provocateur. Very nice, he thought, then carefully pushed them back into the drawer and closed it.

'Just as he walked back in the dining room, his phone lit up. "It's the watch commander," he mouthed to Helen. She cocked her head and shook it slightly. She didn't understand the words.

"Who is the watch commander," Helen asked.

"He or she is in charge of managing patrol resources, making the decisions who and how many officers respond to each incident." Helen nodded her understanding.

"I know I shouldn't leave," said Larson. "But patrol needs a detective on the scene of a shooting."

"I need to wind up my day, too," said Helen. "Briggs and I have to put down a dog, the second one this week. The first was a long-time family pet. Today, it's a pound puppy that has a fatal heart condition."

"Never had a dog, so I have experienced nothing like that," said Mark. "I assume it is painful for the family and the vet."

"It is painful to all, no matter how many times you perform the procedure. Most vets can deal with the straightforward application of drugs to euthanize the dogs, but not so much the emotional meltdown of their human companions."

"I'm glad I never had to experience it," said Larson. Helen smiled. For the moment, her clouds of gloom and doom had blown over.

Mark stood up to go. Helen stood as well and closed the space to a few inches. They looked into each other's eyes for a moment, then moved in for a kiss and then a long hug.

"Wow, that was nice," said Helen.

"Until we meet again," said Mark as he turned and walked out the door.

Helen was alone. And a sense of gloom came over her. She knew that If Mark ever learned about what happened to her, she would feel disgraced and used up. Her confession would devastate him. Would he look the other way? "Probably not," she said out loud.

Helen was not sure where her relationship with Mark was going. But she had sealed the fate of Jerry Hoffman and had her sights on Patrick O'Flaherty and Robert "Little Bobby" McWhorter.

CHAPTER FIFTEEN

June 20, 2019

As Jim Briggs approached the *Right To Dream, Too*, the homeless camp better known as R2D2, a line of homeless women and men with their dogs greeted him and Helen. The line stretched more than a block along Burnside Street, Portland's dividing line between north and south. R2D2, which hugged the entrance to Chinatown, was a monument to the city's failed policies to solve homelessness. Across the street was Big Pink, the corporate headquarters of U.S. Bankcorp, known locally for the Italian marble skin that glowed pink at dusk and dawn. Even the rosy glow of the 536-foot-tall tower, where hundreds of people with jobs and homes, could do nothing to brighten the fate of Portland's strays—its human strays. They were 4,000 strong, with 80-100 found dead on the streets each year. Their life was no better than a stray dog.

While Briggs maneuvered the Have Paws—Will Travel mobile canine care van into position to doctor the dogs, Helen spotted a very short man bullying his way to the front of the line. He slapped one man on the back of the head for no apparent reason, kicked another, and aimed his ultimate insult at a woman at the head of the line. He could not have been much over five-feet-tall and 110 pounds, but carried himself with the confidence and power of a much bigger man.

"Briggs, did you see that? That little guy just shoved a woman to the ground and kicked her dog aside to be first in line. What a bastard."

Briggs glanced over for a second, then turned to his backup camera to make sure he not run over anyone.

"That's Little Bobby. He thinks he is the mayor of R2D2. Welcome to Portland and our contribution to community service. He also is, as Kim and Mark described the other night, the head of a violent gang of homeless men. And he's one of our new clients."

"He's a client?" Helen shook her head, her face a twisted mask of pain and disbelief. "You're telling me we are going to provide services to this guy who Mark and Kim warned us about—who just knocked down a lady?"

"No, we are caring for his dog, Juan. Juan is a chihuahua, but not too yappy. He's not a problem."

Helen crossed her arms. "No doubt Little Bobby beats the little guy." Briggs shrugged.

As she focused on Little Bobby, now yelling at someone behind him, a wave of nausea passed over her. A memory snippet of her assault suddenly filled her mind—the name Bobby bouncing around her head. She had been so drunk, drifting in and out of consciousness during the rape, that the details of the nightmare were just beginning to fill in.

"Are you prepared for today given what happened to Rod?" Briggs asked, searching Helen's face for an explanation for why she had become unusually quiet since spotting Little Bobby.

"Just enjoying the clear skies and sunshine," she lied, ignoring his question. Briggs knew she was not one to let a grievance slide. Something was not right, but he could not pinpoint it.

"I'm fine," she finally said.

Briggs let it go.

Hey, Jimbo, get ready for another day of Hell on Earth.

"Worse," Briggs added to DIME's assessment. "More like the City of Joy."

DIME was right. R2D2 was a vision of Hell. Briggs considered R2D2 a lefty liberal's perverted idea of dignity for the desperate and dying, a homeless encampment of tents, tarps, and tiny cubicles that some 100 lost souls called home. For him, it was uncomfortably similar to Calcutta's slum, an area he quickly edged past on a summer trip to India during a college summer break. It was sad, scary, and sickening.

Sure, thought Briggs, these folks have a Right to Dream, too. But other than a fast and permanent way to escape their miserable lives, what could they possibly be dreaming about. DIME, his negative, evil half, clarified it for him.

Jimbo, Don't forget that The Right to Dream comes with other rights—a Homeless Bill of Rights—as city officials and their bleeding heart advocates see it.

Right to panhandle

Right to piss and shit on public streets

Right to harass tourists and locals

Right to sleep in business doorways and frighten patrons

Right to break shop windows

Right to pull people off their bicycles and attack pedestrians

Right to dump trash on sidewalks and start fires

"Harsh, hateful words" Briggs' Happy Half silently protested. But he knew they were true. He was glad Helen could not hear the voice.

They are harsh words, Jimbo. But really, adding this message of hope—RIGHT TO DREAM—to a sign is putting lipstick on a pig; no offense to pigs who live better lives.

"It is nothing more than an advertising slogan," Briggs thought.

Jimbo, welcome to Portland, and the huddled, sick, tired, unsheltered stray mass, longing for death.

Briggs took in DIME's drivel and focused on the task ahead.

When he and Helen climbed out of the van, "Mayor" McWhorter approached. Little Bobby had earned his nickname because of his height. However, anyone who had equated his diminutive size to his ego or his mental capacity was in for a surprise.

His riveting blue eyes and hyper personality, with an intensity to match, could overwhelm you. And he had more than enough intellect needed to outsmart and outmaneuver the other down-and-outers. He was a 100 percent pit bull. He was wheezy from a lifetime smoking habit, and no doubt suffered from COPD. Once a car painter in an auto manufacturing plant, his breathing problems started when he was putting the finishing touches on Mustangs as they rolled off the Ford assembly line.

Away from the safety of the van's steel cab, Helen suddenly felt naked. She stood frozen—the proverbial deer in the headlights—as Briggs approached Little Bobby. After a minute of conversation, Briggs called Helen over. "Come meet Bobby," he urged. He left out the "Little."

Her stomach leaped as another violent piece of her alcohol-infused nightmare flooded her mind. She could hear Little Bobby say, "Take these boner pills, boys. In the meantime, let's enjoy the view of that fine naked ass." They must have stripped off her panties when she was unconscious and had thrown them in the dirt before Jerry Hoffman claimed them as a trophy.

When she realized that Little Bobby did not recognize her, she walked slowly toward him with a medical kit in hand. She would cut the introduction short and begin examining dogs. Little Bobby extended his tiny, dirt-encrusted hand, then pulled it back when he saw Helen looking at it as if it were a snake. "Nice to meet you, Helen," he said. She nodded but said nothing; her face pulled back in a grimace rather than a smile.

She was not sure, but he appeared to inspect her as if she were a side of beef waiting to be butchered, sending another chill down her spine.

"Have we met?" he asked. "Never mind, you're new in town, so it must be my imagination. More likely, my addled brain from all the fumes I breathed at the car factory."

"Excuse me, I need to tend to that lady you knocked down. She appears to be skinned up."

"The bitch should not have tried to keep me from taking my rightful place at the head of the line," Little Bobby fired back, puffing out his chest like the rooster he was.

Little Bobby turned away from Helen and moved next to Briggs. "What's with her?" he asked Briggs, who did not answer.

"Hey, Doc," Little Bobby whispered. Briggs folded his 6-foot-6-inch frame in half to get low enough to hear. "I'm feeling kind of crappy. Was thinking one of your special shots might help." Briggs often gave the homeless shots—mostly essential vitamins—to boost their depleted immune systems.

"First, a little advice about Helen. Like you, she doesn't take any shit. And she is assisting me full-time. That means she may give you your shots, sewing you up, and fix up your dog."

"I get it," said Little Bobby, who offered no apology for knocking down the woman or his comments about Helen.

"Where will you be this afternoon after lunch?" Briggs asked. He could just fire up PupFinder to find the little man later but figured he should not tell him about the tracking device he had surreptitiously attached to Bobby's dog, Juan. He did not want to stir up concern about the invasion of privacy by secretly tracking the homeless.

"After lunch? You're joking," said Little Bobby. "I'll be lucky to get lunch. Come by Pizzicato in the Pearl District around two. Occasionally, I get lunch handouts there. And the pizza is damn good, even scraps on outdoor tables. Better yet, if someone leaves behind a half pint of beer."

"I'll swing by on my way to an appointment or I'll send Helen, so you need to be ready to pop into the van. One of us will give you the shot, and you can be on your way. We probably won't make the Pizzicato meeting. More than likely, it will be late this evening."

"Thanks. I'll be down in my usual haunt, the community garden on 16th and Johnson."

Helen, who had been standing a few feet behind Briggs, listened to the conversation.

"Helen, Bobby is a mean SOB, if you believe Mark and Kim. I told him to be more respectful since you would give him vitamin shots in the future. I would like you to give him a shot tonight."

"I promise to be careful," she said. What she was thinking: "I am going to love to shoot up this bastard with a vitamin shot that will send him to the moon."

"Is the lady Bobby pushed okay?" Briggs asked.

"A nasty case of road rash," said Helen. I cleaned it, applied an antiseptic cream and a bandage. And I advised her to keep it clean."

"Good luck with the clean part," Briggs said. "We better get started on the rest or we'll be her until midnight." Looking at those in line, Helen said, the dogs are nearly as old, ragged, and beat up as their homeless human companions. Among the regulars were Mary with Monte, the Chihuahua (wearing a cloth coat the colors of the Mexican flag), and Kell with Little Debbie, the three-legged Doberman-Basset mix. All were stray dogs no one else wanted. They provided companionship for the homeless—one of their few possessions—and someone to love them unconditionally.

"Briggs, you know you can't save all these people, don't you?" said Helen, this time seriously.

"We can only do what we can do, Helen. As beaten up and scruffy as their animals are, providing a support network for the homeless—with vaccines, first aid, and treatment for urgent care problems—can keep them going for years."

Helen moved next to Briggs and put her mouth next to his ear. "Since when did you become a free clinic and urgent care center for these people," said Helen, hissing the words.

"No big deal," Briggs said. "Regular vitamin shots, some lab testing for chronic problems like diabetes, and some basic first aid go a long way toward boosting what little quality of life they might have. At least, that's how I think about their situation."

When they had finished and were back in his van, Briggs asked for her thoughts about the day. "They are like their human companions: beat up, undernourished, with dirty hair and lice, along with cuts and bruises," she said. "And those like Bobby are monsters."

Helen's description of the homeless as "monsters" jolted him.

"Monsters?"

"Like Little Bobby," said Helen, looking at Briggs to see if he would disagree.

Briggs nodded.

"Did you notice that Little Debbie's three legs hardly slow her down," said Briggs, changing the subject.

Jimbo, Kell's cardboard plea for help would have you believe Little Debbie was literally on her last leg. In reality, Monte and Little Debbie are cash cows, netting an extra $25 a day, their owners freely admit—the donation jar is next to their sad little doggie noses magnets for cash. Drop a dollar, pat Little D, and get a "God Bless" from Kell, who got 30% less per day before he adopted Little Debbie.

Briggs could not disagree with DIME's black-tinted assessment. He could not solve the homeless human problem, he thought, but he could help their pets, which would help their owners collect a few more dollars.

At the same time, he was grappling with how to manage all the requests from the homeless for free dog care, while people living in Portland's northwest neighborhoods, each willing to pay $500 a month for concierge care, were on a waiting list. That's for being available 24/7, quarterly wellness checks, and vaccinations. Everything else was extra. Pet owners never flinched at the cost, sometimes double the monthly retainer.

After Briggs and Helen were back in the van, heading away from Little Bobby and R2D2, Helen considered telling Briggs about Little Bobby and the rape. She decided she did not need to share it with Briggs or anyone else.

***

Treating dozens of dogs and human strays on Saturdays at R2D2 was exhausting. It was an endless stream of mental illness and misery, with no solutions and no end in sight. Who's to blame? His theory: Oregon's progressives, who control the tillers of state and local government with near supermajorities, and the funds necessary to tackle the problem, are ideological captives of the so-called homeless advocates. As proud progressives, the politicos patronize the advocates, who say we should leave the homeless alone; they have a right to roam wherever they like, do whatever they want.

Their advocates also say they are not homeless, they are "unsheltered" as if that were their only problem: shelter them, and all is good. The word homeless had become a dirty word in Portland, no longer politically correct. Even the local newspapers had bought into the word game, calling them *individuals experiencing homelessness*. If you're living on the street without a permanent shelter, aren't you homeless? Can you be experiencing homelessness and not be homeless? Briggs wondered. "Pinning labels on people is negative for them and society," Briggs remembered a college psychology professor explaining. "Alternative narratives can make all the difference in how people with disabilities perceive themselves and how we perceive them." Those called *retards* are now *mentally disabled*; cripples are *physically challenged*; the deaf are *hearing-impaired*, and midgets are called *dwarfs*, *little people*, or *LP's*.

A hearing aid is an *assistive listening device*. Drug abusers are individuals with a *drug use disorder*, and finally, those with autism and similar conditions are *neurally diverse*. Microsoft has created a hiring program for neurally diverse engineers who may have a genius for technology but few social skills.

Terms like crazy no longer applied to people talking to themselves, digging for an unseen thing in a downtown storm drain, eating garbage from trash cans, or yelling at some invisible person. Their diagnoses—divided into many subcategories—could include depression, stress, schizophrenia, obsessive-compulsive, post-traumatic, eating, bipolar, mood, psychosis, anxiety, attention deficit, and emotional-behavioral. That covered just about everyone, Briggs thought. He figured he was somewhere on the list.

Jimbo, crazy is probably a flattering description for a lot of Portland's homeless.

The voice flickered in Briggs 'mind. We don't lock up people in padded cells in insane asylums where one size fits all. We medicate them. No sitting on couches at $250 an hour talking to a psychiatrist, analyzing id and ego—spewing flawed Freudian logic—when a quick consultation and an expensive drug can cure their perceived insanity.

"*Well, Jimbo, maybe some brain shocking, like Jack Nicholson in One Flew Over the Cuckoo's Nest, would be just what the doctor ordered for homeless strays who refuse to take their meds.*"

Briggs tried to shake off the intrusion. But DIME had a point. Unfortunately, many people with access to wonder drugs needed to control their dark impulses, but don't take the pills, cannot be bothered, don't like feeling droopy, or say they forgot. Lots of reasons. Portland's streets are full of them. Those reasons don't apply to alcohol, heroin, meth, uppers, downers, and weed.

Many of the so-called "unsheltered" fall into one of the disorder categories, but without regular healthcare—and no interest or will on their part to comply with a daily regimen—get no treatment. Besides, who cares? As long as they are not hurting anyone. That's one argument.

But saying homeless humans are merely "unsheltered" misses the point, leaving out the important part: why they are without shelter. The *unsheltered* label does not tell the story of the moms and kids living in cars, veterans with PTSD, drug addicts, street bums, panhandlers, and transient hoboes. You can't throw them all in a basket—or insane asylum—and say sheltering them would make their problems disappear. Hell, being unsheltered for some—living in a tent or a cardboard box under a freeway—is freedom, a basic lesson Briggs learned quickly when working with them. He had also come to the opinion—an uneasy feeling, really—that some drug-addicted, mentally ill, and long-time denizens of the streets were terminal, destined to die from the global scourge known as homelessness, like someone with stage four liver cancer. Many homeless wandering Portland's streets might as well be on death row because their fate will be the same. In some ways, death row inmates have an advantage: three square meals every day, a toilet, and a roof over their heads.

For the terminally homeless, Briggs thought, it's as if they have entered one of life's side streets where the signs warn, "Dead End" or "No Outlet." He saw them on the roads every day, their lives seeping away. He wondered if there was a better way to help the homeless. Could he be the angel that helped people like Maxine find rest? He could still hear her haunting plea: "God, please take me."

Maybe not God, Jimbo. But there is a simple solution, one you veterinarians are well trained for.

Briggs' mind tried to turn away from this troubling thought. Then again, it was making more sense.

CHAPTER SIXTEEN

June 22, 2019

A chime brought Helen's phone to life, alerting her to an incoming call from Jim Briggs. "What's up, Jimmy? Let me guess. You and Kim are naked and too tangled in the sheets to make it back in time for your night shift."

"Helen, you're clairvoyant." She could hear the smile in his voice.

"Take the entire weekend. I know that's what you want, right?"

"Well, yes, but I didn't want to ask. You have already filled in the past three days." Jansen and Briggs were at an AirBnB in Rockaway Beach, overlooking the Oregon Coast.

"Doesn't matter. The only thing waiting for me at home is my vibrator and a bottle of scotch. Better that I stay in the van and cover the weekend client calls. The homeless freebies are one thing. But we need to care for paying clients."

"You are as incorrigible as ever," Briggs said.

"Okay, back to business. Did you give Little Bobby his shot?"

"He's scheduled for this week."

"Good luck. Be careful, he's got a temper as you've seen, and can be violent. But mostly he won't hassle you if you're giving him something for free."

"You owe me, Jimmy, bye," she said and hung up.

***

To find Little Bobby, Helen launched the PupFinder app. She quickly picked out Juan, Bobby's Chihuahua, as a point of light on Briggs' laptop screen. She knew Bobby would be nearby. Before driving over to Little Bobby's park hangout, Helen needed to check the location of his other gang members, absent Jerry Hoffman. She knew where he was: in a big black box on the shelf at Heavenly Considerations, labeled 101-JH — a billing code, if anyone asked.

This time she was in luck. Bobby was alone under the 405 freeway that slices through Downtown Portland. While her memories of the rape were still fuzzy, the banner hanging from the fence, declaring the tiny park as "a peaceful urban space" stood out in her mind. It was peaceful unless you were semiconscious, like Helen had been, and were being shaken like a dog with a rag doll, your body being ripped and torn. Worse, after they had finished with her, they pushed her inert body into a shed filled with gardening tools. She had awakened in the dark, a stream of light coming through a crack in the door. Helen had managed to kick the door open and crawl out. Thankfully, no one else was around. Her attackers apparently had their fun, then moved on. She drove a few blocks to the garden and pulled the van to the curb, turned off the engine, got out, and looked around. She quickly spotted Bobby with a 12-pack of Pabst Blue Ribbon Tall Boys, and his dog, Juan. Little Bobby had tipped over three empty 16-ounce beer cans. Juan was lying passively next to a plastic soup container Bobby had repurposed as a water bowl.

Helen walked back to the van, moved it closer to the park so Little Bobby could see it, then got out and approached him.

"Hey Bobby, it's Doctor Helen from Have Paws—Will Travel. Jim Briggs asked me to come by and give you a vitamin shot."

"I remember you."

Did he? Was he thinking about the meeting at R2D2? Or had his memory returned, rape scenes fueling a hard-on? Juan trotted over and jumped up on Helen. "Hey, little guy, how are you doing?"

"He's doing, I'm the one who is dragging," said Bobby. "Actually, I'm a little shit-faced, so it ain't all bad. I thought you were coming last week to give me the shot."

"Sorry about that," she said, "I got tied up with a bunch of client emergencies while Dr. Briggs was away for a few days."

"Hey, I'm a client, too, right? That's what Doc Briggs always says." Containing her anger and keeping her voice steady, she said, "I'm here now. Come over, get in the van, and I'll take care of you." The ungrateful little son-of-a-bitch, she thought.

"Cool. Love ya, Doc." Bobby, unsteady from the beer, stood up, and stumbled toward the van, limping.

"What did you do to your foot?" Helen asked.

"I was just trying to be friendly with some gal—you know, just little pat on the bottom—and the cunt stomped my foot with her boot. Bled like a bitch."

"Maybe I can help with that, too," Helen said, working to keep him relaxed and comfortable while trying to swallow her rage.

Bobby, with Helen's help, stepped into the Paws van. Letting him touch her was painful, but necessary to execute her plan. "Please sit on the table," she said. She pulled out a pillow and urged Little Bobby to relax while she prepared a shot. "Just lean back, take a break." Looking around as if he was in someone's home for the first time, Little Bobby said, "Nice little setup you have here, Doc. A regular fuck pad." Helen stiffened at the remark but stayed calm. Bobby did not tamp down his disdain for women or try to be politically correct. She picked up Juan, placed him on the van floor, and closed the door. When Little Bobby leaned back on a big pillow, Helen opened the medication refrigerator and pulled out Propofol, an anesthesia drug used in human outpatient surgeries. It also was one of the drugs veterinarians used to prevent a dog from suffering when putting it down. It essentially put them in a deep sleep to prevent them from feeling the awful pain produced when a veterinarian injected the kill shot—a fatal dose of barbiturate.

"You ready? You'll only feel a pinch."

"Been ready, shoot me up, doc," he answered as if she were a drug dealer satisfying a user. She inserted the needle, pushed down the plunger, and watched him slip into unconsciousness. He would only be out for about 10 minutes. With Bobby out cold, she pulled out several straps used to secure dogs for neutering and other surgical procedures. The supply company advertised the four straps as "soft and washable." Little Bobby would not need to worry about any of those sales pitches. She locked down Bobby's short, chubby arms and legs and pressed a strip of duct tape over his mouth. Helen unzipped his pants, took hold of his penis—for a little guy it was big, she thought—let go of it, then picked up a scalpel, cut open his scrotum, and removed his testicles. Just your typical neutering procedure for a dog.

Williams completed the minor surgery just as Bobby was waking up. She did not bother to stitch up the wound, adding a clamp instead to prevent excessive blood loss and a bloody mess in the van. As if it mattered. She wanted him conscious for what was coming next.

Although still slightly sedated, Little Bobby felt a surge of pain between his legs as consciousness returned. He tried to reach for his crotch, but the fuzziness created by the anesthetic delayed his awareness of being tied down. Still, he forced his head forward just enough to look down at his exposed crotch. He opened and closed his eyes, trying to squeeze them into focus. Where his balls had been was an empty sack of skin.

"You looking for these?" Helen asked, holding up a pair of bloody testicles. "Looks like you won't have to worry about getting any more bitches pregnant. I've neutered you, just like a stray dog at a shelter." While Little Bobby shook his head trying to clear the cobwebs from the anesthetic, he started yelling through the duct tape she had placed over his mouth, "You fucking bitch, I'm going to kill you." Helen ignored the verbal assault.

"I guess you don't remember me, do you, Bobby? I'm that woman you referred to as a dirty little bitch that you and your gang members raped a few weeks back in this park. What kind of worthless piece of shit attacks a helpless woman drunk out of her mind and defenseless? I guess you didn't care about that. I was just a piece of ass to you. How does it feel to be the helpless victim?" His eyes bulged in terror, and then tears poured down his face as the memory flooded back. Helen took hold of the end of his penis, stretching it out. "Big for a little guy. Fortunately for you, where you're going, you won't need this anymore." Little Bobby screamed a muffled "no, no, no. Stop."

"You want me to stop? Is that what you are saying?"

"Yes, please," came his response as tears left white lines on his dirty face."

"Remember how I begged for you to stop? You answered by jamming your cock in my mouth to stifle my screams."

"Guess what? Shortly, your cock is going to be in your mouth." He looked at her, uncomprehending. She stretched out his penis, gave him a demonic smile, and, with a swift motion, sliced off the tip with four more inches attached. "No, no, no," he tried to scream.

"You just got a little smaller, Little Bobby," she said, admiring her work. He struggled to get the object in focus, blinking away the tears as Helen dropped it into a specimen pan. An instant later, his eyes went wide, and he began screaming and convulsing. The tape on this mouth allowed only a muffled rumble of grunts to escape. Although Helen had clamped off the blood flow from what remained of his penis, a small amount of blood had spread across Bobby's lap.

Responding to Little Bobby's distress, Juan jumped up on the table, walked across his lap and licked at the tape across his mouth. Helen patted him on the head. "It's okay, Juan. Get off Bobby." He jumped off the table, leaving bloody paw prints on the indoor-outdoor carpet.

Helen administered another shot to calm Little Bobby, paralyzing his movement. "Guess what, Robert Brian 'Little Bobby 'McWhorter, this is your lucky day," said Helen. "It's a lucky day for the world, and a good day for payback."

She slipped the tip of the barbiturate-filled syringe into his arm and said, "See this little vitamin shot? In about five more seconds, you're going to be suffering the worst possible pain, and then a few seconds later, you are going to be dead." She smiled and pushed down the plunger. Bobby fought against the drug as his heart stopped and starved his lungs of air. His body fought the restraints. Helen had left out a second dose of Propofol, a courtesy afforded death row inmates as part of the lethal injection procedure.

Little Bobby jerked, bucked, and let out a muffled animal cry for help—his body shutting down, his heart and brain screaming for oxygen. "If there's a hell, you're heading there, Bobby."

In less than a minute, life had ebbed from the man's body. He gradually stopped squirming. Then he stopped moving altogether. His bulging eyes remained open like he saw the Devil waiting for him. She turned her attention to Juan, removed his collar with its GPS tracking device, then opened the van door and gave him a gentle push. The Chihuahua sat on the sidewalk for a minute, then took off, his paws leaving a faint trail of bloody paw prints. After placing Juan outside, she closed the door, reached over and ripped off the duct tape covering Little Bobby's mouth. Pulling the severed penis from the metal tray, she stuffed it in Bobby's mouth, then replaced the tape. "How does it feel Bobby, having someone jam a cock in your mouth?"

Helen was still so angry she grabbed a towel, put it over her mouth to dampen the sound and screamed, then slammed her fists into Little Bobby's face and body. Calming down, she carefully folded the towel and returned it to a supply cabinet, took a deep breath, and rolled the body into the van's refrigerated corpse storage box. After depositing the needle, straps and other used surgical supplies, she headed to Heavenly Considerations to process the body. Her own body was vibrating from the shot of adrenaline she felt when she gave Little Bobby his lethal injection.

After a few minutes, her rage turned to relief. Then, just as quickly, a curtain of dread fell on her as she realized killing Little Bobby only halfway through her quest for payback. Little Bobby and Hoffman were history. Now, she had to deal with O'Flaherty. Helen had not decided on the fate of Big Betty. Betty had witnessed the attack or its beginning before walking away, but did nothing to stop it. How long she remained at the scene, Helen had no way to determine. However, she knew in her heart that if Big Betty had wanted to put an end to it before it got started, she could have.

"Did Betty deserve the death penalty?" Helen wondered. "Wasn't Betty an accessory after the fact? Wasn't she just as guilty because Hoffman, Little Bobby, and O'Flaherty were still planning their attack while they waited for the Viagra to kick in and did nothing to stop it?" Helen cleaned up the blood, locked down the exam table that had held Little Bobby in place, and climbed into the driver's seat. Now, she had to get rid of the evidence. Little Bobby would soon join Jerry Hoffman, their remains in identical boxes, side-by-side in a holding area for cremated dog remains.

***

The furnace was roaring, each moment turning a little more of Little Bobby into ash. Helen stood gazing into the fire like she has done so many times on camping trips. Her mind was blank, caught in a primitive ritual that had survived thousands of years since humans discovered fire.

She stripped off her jacket and sweater, comfortable in her t-shirt. The heat that escaped the BAL1000, 1200-degree furnace's thick walls and glass door melted away the chill left by Little Bobby's death throes.

Mesmerized by the flames, she screamed when a hand came down on her shoulder. When she turned her head, a big man was smiling at her. "Sorry, Helen, I didn't mean to scare you," said Jim Briggs, dropping his hand.

"Shit, I thought you were staying on the coast."

"I did, too. Kim's boss called and said some planned police action required a massive response. She said she could not discuss it. Of course, I said it was no problem. We would pick another time. I was pissed off and disappointed. I can't believe they are so short-handed that they needed her to drive in from the Coast."

Helen took a deep breath. "It's okay. I was just surprised. I was just daydreaming, I guess."

"Who's that?" asked Briggs, nodding toward the object in the furnace.

"Uh… Uh... I don't remember the name," Helen stuttered, searching for an answer, then recovered, "I'm processing a dog for an animal hospital," she said.

"Are you okay?" said Briggs. "You seem distracted. Something bothering you?"

"No, everything is fine. You just surprised me."

"I'll leave you to it. Are you done with the van?"

"Almost. Let me do some cleanup. While you were away with Kim, I stopped by the park and gave Little Bobby his vitamin shot."

"Thanks. He's a piece of work, isn't he?" said Briggs. "He has made so many enemies among the homeless and the police. I'm surprised he's still alive."

Helen smiled. "He isn't," Helen thought.

"Let me finish the cleanup and you can take off."

"Great, but no rush. My first appointment, about 15 minutes from here, isn't for an hour." Briggs turned and left the room.

Once she had finished the cleanup, including running a rag over bloody paws on the van carpet Juan had left after he had jumped into Little Bobby's bloody lap, she brought Briggs the keys. After Briggs left, Helen turned off the furnace.

When it cooled down, she swept Little Bobby's remains, including the DNA-rich teeth and bone fragments, into the cremulator, a high-speed blender that within 20 seconds had pulverized Little Bobby's remains into a fine ash. A DNA lab could not tell if the remains were human or canine. Nothing identifiable remained of the human being formerly known as Little Bobby. Helen secured the bag of ash and put it on a shelf in the back room. Bobby's remains would not go to a loving family or into a memorial wall to celebrate his life. Flushed down the toilet, maybe. Helen hadn't yet decided.

Relieved Bobby was gone forever, she went back to her desk to catch up on paperwork.

CHAPTER SEVENTEEN

June 24, 2019

After vaccinating a client's new puppy for kennel cough, Briggs drove along 16th Avenue below the 405 Freeway through Portland's northwest neighborhood, looking for new homeless clients. He was still short of his goal of caring for 50 dogs. However, given their poor condition and the time to patch them up, he needed a better estimate of how many more animals his practice could accommodate.

As he pulled his van to the curb near a row of tents—which resembled a group camp in a state park—he looked across the street and saw a tent pitched away from the others. It looked familiar. He thought it belonged to Maxine Reid. Before getting out of the van, he launched his PupFinder App to see if he could positively identify her. Sure enough, the dog showing on the screen was Buster. The occupant of the tent would be Maxine, the little lady who had melted down during a drug high a few weeks before.

Briggs closed his laptop, placed it under the front seat so it was out of view of passersby. He got out of his van, locked the door, and walked toward Maxine's shanty camp. As he got closer, he confirmed it was her. She was tying a tarp over her tent against the forecasted rain. She had not seen him yet, so he yelled louder to counter the noise from the freeway above. "Hey Maxine, it's Jim Briggs. I'm the veterinarian who gave Buster a collar last week. Remember, I offered to register him with the Human Society and identify you, Maxine Dorothy Reid, as his owner."

"I remember you. How the hell are you?" she asked, smiling as if they were friends. A contrast to her verbal assault during their first meeting.

"I'm fine," said Briggs, who confided to Maxine that it was his mother's idea to doctor the dogs of the homeless. "She was a big advocate for social justice."

"Good for her," said Maxine. With some rapport established, Briggs felt it was safe to venture into personal territory while bracing for another verbal attack.

"How about you, Maxine, how are you? How did you come to live on the street?" He attempted to make it as non-threatening and conversational as possible.

"You want to know?"

"Sure. I'm the genealogist in my family and I'm always interested in how others ended up where they are. I spent years doing research. . Two years ago, I published a book about the Briggs's line."

Maxine smiled, nodded her approval, then launched into her family history. "The Reids are all dead. My sister was on this genealogy jag and found a long line of our people from Canada, Scotland, and Ireland. It doesn't matter because my sister is dead, too. The Sugar got her." Briggs assumed she meant diabetes. Maxine frowned, apparently saddened by the memory. "She was all I had left. Now she is just dry bones, like all the rest of the Reids."

"What did you do before you were living here?" Briggs asked.

The words tumbled out of Maxine—without hesitation—in a stream of consciousness. Hardly the stuff of dreams. "In high school, I worked summers as a soda jerk in a drugstore for my best girlfriend's mom. I didn't finish high school after I met this older guy who came in every day for lunch. I fell in love, got pregnant. He took off. I got an abortion, found jobs as a server, first in restaurants, then in a titty bar. I had nice ones, tits that is—small, but nice. Want to see?"

Briggs had already seen her tits—now wrinkled flaps of skin falling across her chest. Maxine saw Briggs' jaw tighten and said, "Maybe not," then continued with her story. "I even did a little dancing on stage; made some good tips. I got hooked on cheap champagne the customers bought me for sitting on their laps. I had to sit on a lot of boners grinding into my ass." She stopped and looked at Briggs, who had turned a little red, the color flooding his pale, freckled skin. "Half the time the guys were so drunk, they couldn't get it up. Thank God they didn't have Viagra back them. Once the bar closed permanently, I found jobs in diners and bartending in smoky cocktail lounges filled with drunks. I could still get extra money with lap dances, even though it was illegal. Instead of champagne, I was getting chardonnay—more like Two Buck Chuck—then whiskey shots, and a string of sex partners with no names."

"Do you know what I'm talking about, Doc? At closing time, you look around and find someone as drunk as you are, then go spend the night with them?" Again, she looked at Briggs for recognition.

"I get it," Briggs offered. He had done that more than a few times. It gave him the chills to think Maxine might have been sitting in the same bar, a few seats away. She halted her story long enough to see if Briggs would nod in recognition, then said derisively, "Right, you have never done that." Briggs smiled but said nothing. Maxine continued talking a mile a minute.

"You wake up the next morning hungover, naked, dried cum in your pubes and do not know who is in the bed next to you or how they got there. I tried to get away from all that. First, I went to Georgia to live with my cousins. They were welcoming at first. But it did not take long for their Bible-quoting, trailer-trash husbands to hit on me after they got me hooked on Meth. I escaped that hell hole, got on a bus, headed west as far as I could get on $250, and ended up here. That was nearly 20 years ago. Johnson Street has been my home ever since. Although most people leave Buster and me alone, you could say this place is a hellhole, too. But it's my piece of Hell."

Stunned by Maxine's sour milk of a story, Briggs tried to sweeten it up a bit; put a cherry on top. "Did you stay in touch with your girlfriend from high school, the one you worked with at the soda fountain?"

"Melanoma, dead at 37," Maxine answered, no sorrow in her words. Cool as ice. "She was the only friend I had left."

Later he would jot down as many details of her life as he could remember. Her full name and family origin would give him what he needed to search the genealogy websites. She said she had no close living relatives. But Briggs would not give up hope he could find a distant cousin willing to take her in. Sure, a $1.50 syringe filled with a hefty dose of barbiturate would solve Maxine's housing problem permanently and grant her wish for death. But Briggs was not planning to play God soon.

Next stop: the public library to verify Maxine's story and search for relatives. Maybe even find her a permanent home.

Just as he was planning his escape to the library, a client 9-1-1 call lit up his phone. Husbands Mat and Murphy Black were in distress.

***

When Jim Briggs pulled into the driveway of a cottage style house on NW 26th Avenue, Mat Black raced out the front door and pressed his face against the van's tinted window. He started yelling frantically, "Come now. Mike is dying. Oh, God, you need to hurry."

Briggs opened the door, careful not to knock down the distraught man.

"It's okay, I'm here. I'll just get my medical bag and come right in."

While Briggs gathered medical supplies, Mat was grabbing at his arm. "You've got to hurry." Life Partners Mat and Murphy Black, married now two years, were the parents of Mike, a 12-year-old white Bichon Frise, fuzzy-faced breed, cotton balls for a face. Mat's companion since he was in fifth grade, Mike had picked up a case of roundworm at the local dog park. The cause, Jim Briggs explained, was no doubt the result of munching on a dead rodent. The guys didn't believe him. They said they would never let such a thing happen.

Briggs lifted Mike onto the dining room table and pulled out his stethoscope to listen to Mike's lungs and heart After the roundworm clawed its way into his lungs, Mike began coughing. He had eaten little in a week, was underweight, his head almost too heavy to lift in his weakened condition. Briggs placed Mike back in his pink furry bed and turned his attention to Mat and Murphy, who were holding hands. Mat was crying as Murphy hugged him and made assurances that Mike would be okay.

Briggs knew better. He had warned them of the consequences of not treating Mike more aggressively on a previous visit when their dog's condition might have been reversed. But vet visits aren't cheap, and the guys worried about their financial well-being ever since Intel laid off Mat. Murphy had been the stay-at-home partner. Now it was too late. Speaking in a quiet, soothing tone, Briggs said, "I know this is painful for you. I've been there." He then shared the story of his own dog's death when he was a kid. He retold the story to clients often to show his empathy. Murphy got up from the couch and pulled Briggs aside, while Mat dropped to the floor and began kissing Mike. "My poor baby," he cried.

"I can't do it," Murphy said, half pleading for Briggs not to tell him the only option was to put Mike down.

"Ok, let's give him the de-worming treatment and some fluids and see what happens," Briggs said. Murphy nodded. He turned to the two men who had moved Mike's bed to the sofa where they were sitting and whispered, "We've done everything we can for Mike. I've given him some medicine that might help.

The best thing we can do is monitor him and let him rest. Time will tell if he will get better. Let's be optimistic."

Wiping his eyes, Mat said, "Okay. I know there is only so much you can do." Briggs patted the dog, promised to call early the next day for a follow-up, and headed out.

***

As Briggs climbed back into the van, a text came in from Detective Larson, who had become a workout buddy shortly after they met at Maxine's meltdown. "Let's have a beer and get caught up," said Larson. Briggs texted a thumb up to meet Mark on the rooftop at 10 Barrel Brewing. "C U in 45." What Briggs wanted to do was crash after his meeting with Mat and Murphy. Briggs knew he could have done more to keep Mike alive a bit longer, but the cost would further drain the men's bank account. With expensive medications and lots of fluids, they might be able to keep Mike alive for a week or two more. Briggs would donate the roundworm medication. He drove home, parked his van on the street, and walked eight blocks to his meeting with Mark.

***

Jim Briggs's height always created a stir when he walked into a restaurant or pub. If someone caught his eye as he walked by a table, he would offer, unsolicited, "I'm six-feet-six" and "enjoy your beer." To avoid height questions and eye contact, he would look straight ahead over the heads of potential inquisitors. When he reached the rooftop bar, he ducked under the headrail and emerged in the open space. Mark was sitting at a table in a corner with good privacy. Briggs fist-bumped Mark and sat down, a beer already at his place.

"Apocalypse IPA. Nice choice, Mark. Thanks." Briggs lifted the 16-ounce glass and drained a fourth in three gulps.

"Stressful day, Briggs?"

He explained his last call. "It was a killer day. Nonstop. I've put down plenty of dogs but dealing with clients distraught because they know they will have to decide to euthanize their pet is the toughest part of my job."

Changing the subject, Briggs said, "How is your case going?"

"The case is expanding," said Larson. "It started with Jerry Hoffman missing. Now Little Bobby McWhorter has disappeared.

"Hoffman and Little Bobby are clients," said Briggs. "I've been caring for their dogs. I've also stitched up Jerry a few times and dressed open sores on his feet. He must have been a big, rough guy at one point. Now, he's a broken-down alcoholic just hanging onto life. He seems miserable. And, he is miserable to be around. Of course, Little Bobby is in his own special category of miserable people you wish would go away."

"Like Kim and I were telling Helen the first night we met at the pub, Little Bobby's gang is bad news. Or was bad news, depending on what has happened to the little man. When was the last time you saw Hoffman or Little Bobby?"

"Last I saw Hoffman, he had nearly died in a tent fire. Don't remember the date. Just saw Little Bobby in the last week at R2D2 pushing his way to the head of the line of homeless needing care for their dogs."

"I can look it up the Hoffman fire incident," said Larson, pulling his phone out of his pocket and scribbling a note.

"I know all of Little's Bobby's gang and take care of their dogs," said Briggs, who began calling out the names and their dogs. "Betty Ann Bingham has Sepp, a Schnauzer; Little Bobby's companion, Juan, is a Chihuahua; James Patrick "Big Red" O'Flaherty takes lousy care of his lame Scottie mix he named Laddie, and Gerald "Jerry" Robert Hoffman is with Pirate, his one eyed Beagle." Briggs said he had given Hoffman 25 stitches once after four homeless men attacked him. Hoffman claimed he did not provoke the attack. More likely, he was the attacker who got on the wrong end of a blade. Larson didn't ask for details. Instead, he gulped his beer. "This is better than mother's milk," he said, savoring the hoppy bitterness.

"Why continue to focus on a missing persons case when the homeless come and go? Briggs asked.

"Melrose says he considers it a legitimate case, but I have my doubts," said Larson. "The homeless disappear all the time, and no one gets excited. It's just one less person to hassle us. Besides, it's not like we don't have a load of actual cases to work. Why the hell should I get saddled with a missing person case?" Just then a server brought two fresh glasses of beer. Briggs and Larson clicked classes, and each took a long drink. "I wanted us to get together for a beer today to BS and catch up, but I also wanted to see if you could help me find Jerry Hoffman and Little Bobby." said Larson.

"I'll check my database," said Briggs. "I know where most of my strays—humans and dogs—hangout." He wasn't sure why he decided not to tell Larson that his database system included PupFinder and GPS devices attached to the dogs.

"Did you just refer to the homeless as strays, like dogs?" Larson asked.

"Why is that so strange?" Briggs countered. "Think about it: they live on the street or under bridges or abandoned buildings and eat out of trashcans and dumpsters. Like stray dogs."

"I see the logic," said Larson. "Just had not heard anyone describe them like that. It's not very politically correct. I guess it's a veterinarian thing. No doubt you like sex doggie style, right Briggs?"

Briggs looked up, taking a moment to get the joke. "Hilarious Larson," he said, giving his friend a playful arm punch.

"Are you required to keep records on these people and their dogs?" Larson asked.

"No, I don't since I am acting as a volunteer. It's all free, a charitable contribution. It was my mother's last wish in her will."

"A real momma's boy, aren't you Briggs?"

"Fuck you, Larson," Briggs growled, a scowl on his face. Again, slow to get it, he admitted he was a bit of a momma's boy; raised without a father, how could he not be? "She left me a pile of money and real estate, so I can't complain," Briggs said.

"Veterinarians legally can't give shots or apply basic first aid to humans," Briggs continued. "But I was a certified EMT in college to help pay tuition, so I have the experience, if not an up-to-date license."

"How many dogs of the homeless do you care for, Briggs?"

"Forty-five, I guess. My goal is 50, but I'm not sure I have the time or energy to take care of that many."

"Mark, I'll check out the last place I saw Jerry Hoffman and call you if I find him."

"That will work, thanks."

"If I help you find Hoffman, you'll make points with your boss."

"That's the idea."

"One odd find in Jerry's stuff was a sexy pair of high-priced women's thong underwear," Larson said, as if it was an important piece of evidence that needed following up. "They were new and clean. A very bizarre item for a homeless guy to have, don't you think?"

"Who knows," Briggs said. "This Marie Kondo downsizing craze has people donating everything in sight. So, maybe some rich babe discovered the next big thing in panties and donated last year's model, which ended up at the door of the Goodwill store where Hoffman found them."

"Maybe."

For the next half hour, Briggs and Larson drank beer and talked about nothing too serious before Briggs' phone vibrated. He pulled it out, read the caller I.D., and sent the call to voicemail. Two minutes later, he checked voicemail and determined a client wanted a wellness check on her poodle.

"Client call, Mark. Gotta go."

"You shouldn't be driving," Larson warned.

"I walked here. Since the call is not urgent, I will go home, give myself a couple of hours to sober up, then grab my medical kit and ride my bike over. The ride is all of ten minutes."

"Hey, Briggs."

"Yeah?"

"Didn't you forget something?"

Briggs gave Larson a devilish smile.

"No, buddy, I didn't forget. You get to pay today for all the valuable information I provided," Briggs countered. "Ciao."

Larson would have protested, but figured Briggs' help with his case was well worth a burger and two beers.

The pantie mystery, however, left Larson with an uneasy feeling.

CHAPTER EIGHTEEN

July 1, 2019

Maxine Reid had pleaded for death when she was under the influence of a near overdose of methamphetamine. DIME had suggested granting her wish. Briggs argued with his internal opposite that he was not the *Make-A-Wish Foundation* and had no intention of putting Maxine down like a dog—as painless as the process was. He wanted to find her a home and had come to the Portland Public Library to scour ancestor databases to determine if she had any living relatives. If he could locate someone who knew Maxine, he would try to convince them to take her in. Maxine was among the 1.5 million unsheltered citizens in the U.S—about the same number as stray dogs euthanized each year. "But I'm not going there," Briggs thought. The ethics of killing—when it was okay and when it was not—troubled him.

Jimbo, it must have been a sadist who thought it a good idea to give a Death Row inmate a ceremonial last happy meal. After a big steak and baked potato, the guards walk them down the green mile to a surgical steel cold room where they are strapped down with arms out—like Jesus on the cross. Tubes are then shoved in theirs arm while an audience sits fidgeting behind one-way glass, waiting for the lethal injection.

"Rather than a filet mignon, how about a sleeping pill to knock them out, followed by an overdose of barbiturate? Discretely," Briggs responded to DIME, his nemesis. "Assisted suicide in Oregon, which is killing, is okay."

"*Jimbo, turning off life support for a terminally ill patient is also killing. Putting them out of their misery, like a dying dog, is an act of humanity. Remember, the syringes are cheap.*"

"We can debate the ethics of killing all day, but I'm not killing anyone," said Briggs.

Jimbo, not yet. But you will come around.

Briggs turned away from the hateful thought, found an open library computer, and logged onto Ancestry.com. It was accessible from home, but he loved the comfort of the high ceilings and stunning open spaces created in the

1913 Georgian Style building. The grand space dwarfed him, and he liked it. He didn't look so big and drew fewer stares.

Briggs's mind returned to the light airiness of the library just as Lily Goodrich appeared. "Hi Doc," said Lily, an energetic middle-aged woman who spoke in bursts, the go-to librarian for genealogical research. Briggs snapped out of his daydream.

"Hey, Lily, what fun project are you into today?"

"Just got back from a Genealogical Society of Oregon seminar on the home building techniques of early Portland settlers."

"Wow, sounds stimulating," Briggs said, feigning excitement. She smiled. She knew he liked genealogy, but not so much local history.

"How about you? What's up with you, Doc?" Lily always said something that lifted your spirits, if not an eyebrow, like this corny joke.

"I was looking into claims that one of my homeless clients, Maxine Reid, had an extensive family history, that her sister is dead, and she has no children, parents or anyone to look after Maxine. I keep hoping I can find families willing to take care of some street people whose dogs I doctor."

"That's a very compassionate goal, Dr. Briggs."

"Thanks. Call me, Jim."

"Any luck, Jim?"

"I found an Aunt Daisy Reid. She is the twin sister of Maxine's mother. I found her pretty quickly. I think Maxine can't hold out too much longer; she's frail, got COPD, and is nearly a skeleton."

"I read recently," Lily said, "a lot of the unsheltered disappear, or die on the street. We see the homeless in here all the time, searching the web and charging their $10 flip phones. You recognize the regulars. One day they're here, then gone the next. If you ask another homeless person about a missing individual, they usually give you a blank stare or say something about barely being able to care for themselves, let alone worry about another homeless person."

"I've read the same statistics on missing homeless people," said Briggs. "Shameful, don't you think, that we let our fellow citizens wallow in the gutter. Isn't that what death penalty opponents call cruel and inhuman treatment?"

In a whisper, Lily said, "I agree wholeheartedly. I have to be careful about making judgments about people. It's a library policy. I am as outraged as you are." She smiled and offered, "Give me a holler if you need help."

"You want me to holler—in the library?" Lily stopped for a second, then they both chuckled.

What Briggs didn't explain to Lily was his mission to find homes for his homeless clients rather than euthanize them to put them out of their misery. So far, he had not crossed the red line between murder and helping. He had grown to like Maxine and was in no hurry to put her down, terminal stray or not.

Beautiful sentiment Jimbo, but consider: under our plan, the forever-homeless won't suffer forever.

As Briggs continued his research into Maxine's family, a skinny man with shaggy gray hair appeared in his peripheral vision. It was Chuck Grayson, former newsman and editor of the blog, UrbanStreetPDX.

***

"Doc Briggs, we have to quit meeting like this," said Chuck Grayson with a devilish grin.

Briggs' head swung around, then back at the screen.

"Hey, Chuck, what's up with you?"

Briggs tried to be polite to Grayson, a retired newsman who had been his dad's best friend. Chuck had been in the newsroom when Jim Briggs Sr. keeled from a massive heart attack. Briggs, only 12 when his dad died, remembered that Grayson and his dad spent a lot of time after work at the Press Club, a local bar for reporters. They smoked camels and drank gallons of Pabst Blue Ribbon, also known as PBR, $1 for a 16-ounce can.

"I'm working on an offshoot of the Grayson family," he said. "It has been a lifelong hobby. At least once a month, I make some small breakthrough. How about you, Doc?" Briggs turned away from the screen and toward Chuck. He could see it was useless to ignore the man.

"I met a homeless woman who claims to be from a proud clan of Scots," Briggs explained. "Says she has no one left in Denver where the family had settled in the early 1900s. How she got to Portland is a long story. For the past decade, she has lived on methamphetamine, while creating chaos for police and her social workers."

"I know who you're talking about. Maxine. I remember I've seen her name in police reports so often. And I just wrote about her meltdown during rush-hour traffic. I covered that."

"Yes, I remember. "I was there and you quoted me.

"So you're looking up relatives for Maxine Reid. Why do you care about that homeless bag of bones?"

"Chuck, I'm trying to be civil, here. I know you were a friend of my dad. But I also know you're looking for news. I've read your blog. I am not newsworthy. I'm just an ordinary citizen who thinks he can help save a stray or two."

"Calling them strays is an odd way of describing our unsheltered citizens," said Grayson.

"Your words, not mine," said Briggs. He never even looked up to see if Grayson reacted. Grayson said nothing, no doubt contemplating if there was a better solution to solve homelessness. "With so many homeless dying on the streets each year—of natural causes or by violence—it is hard not to imagine a better way," Briggs added. "Veterinarians put down nearly a million and a half stray dogs each year."

Grayson was taken aback, intrigued by the thought, but also disturbed that anyone would consider—even for a millisecond—euthanasia as an antidote to homelessness in Portland. He would leave that out of his next blog post.

Briggs gambled that if he made a ridiculous statement, Grayson would see right through it, and avoid creating a firestorm by publishing it in his blog.

Briggs looked at Grayson, who was staring off in space. He knew the broken-down old newsman's brain was already spinning a tale about Brigg's efforts to find permanent shelter for the homeless.

"I was just kidding," said Briggs. "I would never advocate killing homeless people to save them from the vagaries of street life."

Jimbo, yes you would. Of course, Chuck can't see that dead spot in your heart like I can.

"Chuck, I understand that although you're retired, you're still a journalist at heart, and when you latch onto what you think is a good story, you are like a dog with a bone. But I would appreciate it if you didn't report my every move regarding the homeless, including my research."

"I'll think about it," said Grayson. "But you know that's like putting a red flag in front of a bull—telling a reporter not to print something."

"I'm well aware," said Briggs. "Heard it from Dad many times."

"As long as you understand the rules: everything is fair game. But since your dad was a friend of mine, I'll consider easing up. But no promises."

Briggs could not wait to read Grayson's column later that day. In the meantime, he logged out of the library's Ancestry account and stood up. "Chuck, I've got to go. I have an appointment to check on a sick dog I will need to put down."

"Is this a stray person or dog?" Grayson said sarcastically. Briggs looked at him like he wanted to choke Grayson but shook his head and walked away.

The next day, Briggs checked UrbanStreetPDX to see if he had escaped the spotlight, read the headline and first paragraph, then yelled, "That fucking Grayson. Why can't he leave it alone?"

***

A Viking of a Man With Big Ideas for Solving Homelessness

By Chuck Grayson, Editor, UrbanStreetPDX

JULY 2—I met a man yesterday, hiding out in the reference department of the Multnomah County Library. He wasn't plundering cities. He was performing humanitarian service to the community.

I know. That hardly sounds like news. But this individual has a big idea—an idea as big as he is. He stands 6-feet-6 inches tall with a bright red beard and massive hands to match his height. We met at the public library, where he was digging into the family history of a homeless woman who has been living on the street for nearly two decades.

His name is Jim Briggs, a local veterinarian who provides free care to the dogs of homeless people.

Yesterday I looked over his giant shoulder as he searched on Ancestry.com for relatives of Maxine Dorothy Reid.

Briggs is a rather quiet man, not the type to crow about his charitable work. It seems he has become friends with the meth-addicted skeleton of a homeless woman who just a few weeks ago police tackled to save her from getting hit by a car in the morning rush-hour traffic. As is policy, the cops took her to a nearby emergency room for a 24-hour hold. Reid has a lengthy arrest record. Dr. Briggs is the same person you see around town in the green van with the business name, *Have Paws—Will Travel, and a line of white paws* on the side. Words below describe him as a purveyor of loving canine care.

Turns out, Dr. Briggs not only operates a concierge on-call pet service for the privileged but cares for dogs of the homeless at no cost. And he assists the Portland Police Bureau when dogs run amok at emergency scenes like fires and major traffic accidents.

Why was he researching Maxine Dorothy Reid at the Multnomah County Library?

It seems Briggs has some notion that verifying homeless claims of once being part of a proper family adds dignity to humans who have nothing more to lose. Many are literally at the end of their family lines. Miss Reid told Briggs she is the descendant of a proud Scottish Clan. Her story checks out.

Said Briggs: "These poor souls are just like you and me. They have a heritage, a history, and once had families. Maxine must have someone who cares about her and would take her in. The research into her past hopefully will bring me closer to finding a permanent home."

I was best friends with Briggs' father. When Briggs was growing up, I recognized his love for animals and am pleased to see he has made helping dogs a passionate pursuit for the good of Portland. We need more Vikings like Jim Briggs, people willing to pillage and plunder our petty prejudices and misconceptions about Portland's citizens experiencing homelessness.

Please leave comments below:

"*A beautiful story, but I'm not buying it. Briggs can do all the research he wants, and it will make no difference; nary a dent in the problem.*"—Skeptical in Portland

"*The Vikings were short, Mr. Grayson.*"—History Nerd.

"*Hooray for Dr. Briggs. But if the city and county with millions of dollars can't figure out how to solve the problem—or make a dent—how can he expect to make a difference. Can't condemn him for trying.*"—Hopeful in Downtown Portland.

CHAPTER NINETEEN

July 5, 2019

When Helen pulled the van to the curb, James Patrick "Big Red" O'Flaherty—one of Little Bobby's rape gang—was walking in circles in the warm summer rain, criss-crossing the street near 12th Avenue and Morrison Street. He had draped a faded purple sleeping bag over his head, its sides flowing like a king's robe. The sleeping bag, his shoes, and his pants were soaked from a passing squall. O'Flaherty's dog, Laddie, walked behind him, a plastic bag with holes cut for his head and tail. O'Flaherty had the presence to look out for his dog's welfare, if not his own.

Helen figured the best way to get O'Flaherty's attention was to call his dog. "Laddie, come boy," she said, kneeling on the wet sidewalk to greet the little mutt, his soggy tail wagging. The aging dog walked toward her slowly. His arthritic hip appeared painful.

"Mr. O'Flaherty, I would like to feed Laddie and give him a shot to ease the pain in his hip. And a vitamin shot to you. Dr. Briggs said it will boost your immune system and energy."

"Whatever," the man mumbled but seemed to snap out of his daze. He watched Helen take Laddie inside the van while leaving the door open.

"How about a sandwich?" she offered. "Come on inside and get warm."

"Okay," O'Flaherty said, realizing he had not eaten all day, and noticing—apparently for the first time—he was drenched. Helen closed the van door, handed O'Flaherty a towel to dry off and set down a bag next to the big man with a ham sandwich, some chips, a small tub of potato salad, and watermelon slices. The van smelled like wet fur, the humidity spiking with the body heat and wetness in the closed van. Helen reached over and turned on the air conditioner button to dehumidify the space

When she turned back and realized O'Flaherty's face was only inches from hers, her stomach clenched, and her chest tightened. Her hands started shaking as a rush of fear and claustrophobia closed in. She looked away and pulled back from the man, taking deep breaths to calm down and re-center herself as she prepared a syringe for O'Flaherty.

Helen tried to remain calm and be friendly. If O'Flaherty thought he had been identified as a rapist, he would have become spooked. He could easily go wild and kill her in the compact space. However, she knew that when the needle was slipped into his arm, there would be the tiniest pinch, nothing alarming. She would be home free.

"Ham or turkey?" asked Helen, her voice slightly shaky.

"Ham," said O'Flaherty. "Turkey is tasteless."

"Enjoy," Helen thought. "It's your last."

As O'Flaherty focused on his sandwich, something loud slammed on the side of the van, and a voice yelled, "Police officer, open up."

Helen jumped, her heart racing. This can't be happening, she thought. Not now. What was she going to do? She was on the edge of panic. Then she realized she recognized the voice.

As her heartbeat slowed slightly, Helen slid open the big side door, revealing the scruffy man sitting on the van worktable with a dog at his feet.

Looking at the syringe in Helen's hand, Detective Larson said, "What are you up to, young lady? Looks like no good."

Helen forced a smile and said, "Just helping Jimmy out. He's back at the office doing paperwork. Asked me to cover."

"Please step outside and close the door," Larson said in his best police officer commanding voice. "We need to talk."

Helen closed the door.

"Seeing you in the middle of the day is such a sweet surprise," Larson said, pulling her in for a hug. "The dog has a problem?"

Helen let out a big breath. "Larson, you scared the shit out of me. But I am glad to see you. I was just thinking about ways to surprise you on our next date." The rain had stopped and both looked up as the clouds made way for blue sky.

"I can't wait for our date," he said, the thought turning him on. "Detective Larson, do I see something coming up?" Larson blushed and buttoned his coat. She gave him a sly smile and acted as though she was going to reach down and touch him. Larson moved back a few inches. "No more," he begged. "I'm on duty, for god's sake."

"If you need to know what I'm up to besides evil ways to torture you, I'm giving OFlaherty's dog, Laddie, a pain shot for his hip and a vitamin B1 shot to our dear friend in there. It helps with digestion and a few other ailments, like alcoholism.

"Since you aren't an M.D. Helen, I am going to assume that giving shots to humans isn't exactly legal," Larson whispered.

"I didn't know officer, please give me a break," she cooed in his ear.

She then stepped away from the van so she could talk with Larson privately.

"All right, Dr. Williams, I'll let you off this time for good behavior. Or should I say, your bad behavior in the bedroom?"

"As payback, meet me at 10 Barrel Brewing at 18:30 hours for a beer and a burger. And dessert afterward."

She smiled and said, "I assume giving a cop a pay-off isn't exactly legal, either."

"Got me," Mark said, smiling. Just then, a call came in on Larson's radio. He listened and said, "Been summoned back to the office. See you soon."

"Looking forward to it," she thought. "Lucky your suit coat is covering the damage."

"Gotta go," Larson said.

Helen waited until she saw Larson roar off to an urgent call. A woman waiting for a bus got soaked when Larson's car zipped through a deep puddle and accidently sprayed her with water. As Larson pulled away, Helen remembered she already had plans to meet Briggs. Normally, Larson would have been welcomed. Not tonight. Tonight would be a come-to-Jesus conversation—one Mark couldn't know about. "Sorry, Mark, Briggs and I have business stuff to take care of," Helen texted. "I forgot. Will call tomorrow and make it up to you."

Helen locked the van door, then finished preparing the syringes and put one containing Propofol back in the refrigerator. "Ready to feel better?" Helen asked O'Flaherty.

"Yeah, give me the shot, Doc," he said, without hesitation.

O'Flaherty swallowed the last bite of sandwich and washed it down with a swig of Gatorade, while Helen pulled out a fresh syringe, opened the refrigerator, and removed a single vial. She filled a syringe, put the bottle back into the refrigerated drug cabinet and said, "Relax."

The needle didn't alarm O'Flaherty because Briggs had given him several vitamin shots to counter the ravages of alcohol and meager diet of leftover trash scraps.

She was about to insert the needle and push down the plunger. The short-acting anesthetic filling the syringe would give her a chance to tie down O'Flaherty. But first, she wanted to get to a less public space. O'Flaherty's usual hangout under the freeway would muffle the sound. She started the engine and drove a mile to the park where her assault had taken place. O'Flaherty continued eating. He said nothing on the drive over.

After she parked, Helen gave O'Flaherty a shot of Propofol to knock him out. Like Little Bobby, she tied down O'Flaherty's arms and legs, put tape over his mouth, then prepared a syringe for Laddie. Laddie was chewing on a bone, a rare treat for him, giving Helen little notice. She inserted the needle and was about to knock him out, then decided she could not do it, despite his physical problems that would continue to plague him. She had taken an oath as a veterinarian to do no unnecessary harm—comfort and quality of life as the key factors to consider before euthanizing a dog. Instead of killing Laddie, she removed his tracking collar with the PupFinder GPS tracker and put it aside, then opened the van door and encouraged Laddie to jump out. Laddie looked back when O'Flaherty didn't follow.

"Go find a new home," she commanded. Laddie looked at her for a moment, then ran off. He wasn't as attached to O'Flaherty as she had thought.

Helen closed the van door and refocused on O'Flaherty, who was waking up. She pulled a vial from the refrigerator and prepared a second shot, this one filled with a deadly dose of barbiturate.

O'Flaherty felt his limbs come to life. He could not open his mouth, not understanding or able to see the tape. Gripped by panic, O'Flaherty struggled against the restraints, freeing an arm. He started swinging wildly, hitting Helen in the head. Stunned, she fell on her back, unable to move.; the needle was rolled free toward the back of the van, out of reach. As her vision cleared, she turned her head and saw that the single dose of killing barbiturate was still intact.

Helen slowly rolled over onto her stomach and got to her knees. She had only been out for maybe 20 seconds. O'Flaherty was trying to yell through the tape, grabbing at it with his free hand, desperate to free himself. Fortunately, he had chewed off his fingernails and had nothing to pry up the end of the straps.

Helen knew she had to act fast, or she'd become the man's victim again. This time she would not escape with her life. Frantic, she spotted the van fire extinguisher by the door, unlocked it, and swung it at O'Flaherty's head. The glancing blow stunned him. When he dropped back onto the table, fear and a surge of adrenaline allowed her to grab the end of the strap on O'Flaherty's free hand and wrap it around a hook on the table, immobilizing him. It took all her strength to lock down the arm. Once he stopped moving, she secured the tie and moved above him. He looked at her; his eyes wide, trying to understand what was happening. He was shaking, but it was hard to tell if it was from sheer terror or hypothermia from being soaked in the 48-degree rain.

"Look at me, Patrick. Do you know who I am?"

Trying to clear his eyes and shake off the blow to the head, out came a response that sounded like "Oc-or ill-ums."

"Yes, I'm Doctor Helen. But I'm also Helen Williams, the woman you, Jerry Hoffman, and Little Bobby raped in the park. And guess what," she continued, "Now, I'm going to fuck you up." She leaned over and got the poison-loaded syringe off the floor. "Only you will not recover."

Recognition filled his eyes and tears started flowing down O'Flaherty's face as he shook his head back and forth.

"You're sorry, aren't you, Patrick?" He cried and nodded. A minute later, he stopped struggling altogether as if he were a Death Row inmate who had come to terms with his crime and punishment.

"I would like to say you are only going to feel a pinch, but that would be a fat lie. You're not getting the anesthetic that would have allowed a pain-free death. In just a moment, your brain will scream, and your heart will buck from lack of oxygen. You'll think you're about to see the Angel of Death coming for you, and you won't be wrong."

She inserted the needle into his vein and stopped.

"Take a second and think back to that little Viagra party in the park."

"Fuck you," he responded as if false bravado would make what was coming less painful.

"Yes, you already fucked me, Patrick. How's that working for you? Enjoy your memory. It will be your last. A minute from now you won't remember anything because the pain will erase every other thought."

A second before Helen pushed down the syringe plunger, she whispered: "I'm going to cut off your dick and stuff it in your mouth. Thought you might enjoy the experience."

She pushed in the plunger and an instant later, every nerve in O'Flaherty went on red alert. His heart felt like it was going to explode, while his brain screamed like it was sliced into pieces.

When O'Flaherty stopped moving, Helen said, "Say hello to Satan."

She rolled him off the procedure table into the van's refrigeration unit.

A moment later she was sitting in the driver's seat, listening to Verve, one of her favorite chill music groups. Helen had selected their Urban Hymns album. She turned up the music and closed her eyes. When the first song ended, she opened her eyes and looked out. A man with an REI bag was passing by. He did not look up. As her heart rate was returning to normal, her phone rang.

"Hey, Jimmy. What's up?"

"What have you been up to?" Briggs countered.

"Just doing God's Work, helping more homeless and their dogs."

"O'Flaherty?"

"How did you guess?"

***

Helen had arrived at 10 Barrel Brewing first and ordered beers and wings from the happy hour menu. Briggs arrived a few minutes later. As always, he had to duck under the doorway to avoid bashing his head. He spotted Helen and took ten long strides across the room, slid into a booth, and moved toward her. She reached out, grabbed him, and gave him a hug and a kiss on the cheek. The intimacy of her action sent a flush of warmth through his body. They pulled apart and took long drinks of beer, looking around to make sure no one could hear their conversation. Even when it was not very crowded, the cacophony of conversation made it nearly impossible to discern what one person was saying to another.

Still, they moved in closer, a few inches apart.

"Helen, this will sound weird," said Briggs.

He wanted to tell her about DIME and the pull to kill homeless people—with canine euthanasia drugs rather than with kindness. She would think he was demented. Instead, he said, "I have begun thinking my mission to find homes for the homeless is hopeless. I'm not giving up yet but haven't found any relatives willing to take in Maxine. And she is just one of thousands who need help." He stopped speaking, took a sip of beer, and looked at Helen for a reaction.

"What do you mean hopeless?" Helen asked.

"The more I work with our homeless clients, the more I believe most will die on the streets, featured in the annual coroner's report. Putting down someone like Maxine would be a relief to her—palliative care for a miserable life that will no doubt end badly from a meth overdose, hypothermia, or street violence."

Helen also took a long drink of beer. When she put her half-empty glass down, she nodded and said, "Go on."

"I rejected the idea at first, wondering if there was a better way. I thought if I scoured genealogy databases to find their families and contact family members, I could facilitate a reconciliation. It seemed like a logical plan. The more I know about my homeless clients and why they are living on the street, the more I realize how naïve I am; no amount of family therapy or effort can help people like Maxine."

"It isn't a bad plan at all, but not realistic," said Helen. "No one will stand up to the social justice zealots who go nuts when you suggest city officials should force homeless into shelters where they can get food, medicine, toilet facilities, and counseling. The laws of common decency, if not civic ordinances, should prevent human beings from sleeping on the streets, harassing people, tossing trash everywhere, and using business storefronts as bathrooms."

Briggs said nothing but nodded in agreement.

Even though Helen had left clues for Briggs to figure out what she was up to, she decided it was time to confess. Her revenge campaign could jeopardize his business and reputation if anyone found out what she had done. She would make it sound clinical, matter-of-fact, leaving out the bloody details. She knew Briggs well enough to know he would be sympathetic. He would understand. He wouldn't push her away. Or would he? Helen hesitated, then said,

"I also have a confession to make." Briggs pulled away from her, put his beer glass down, and gripped the sides of the table.

I didn't tell you everything that happened to me before I applied for this job. Rod's death and losing our baby are all true. But there is one more thing."

Should she tell him? Wouldn't he be obligated to fire her and call the police? Mark would be his first call. Mark would come down to Heavenly Considerations, handcuff her, and tell accompanying patrol officers to lock her up on suspicion of murder in the first degree.

"Two months ago, I had dinner and a half bottle of wine at LeJoyeux, then walked home. On the way, I stopped at that urban garden on 16th Avenue under the freeway when I heard a bunch of people partying. I followed the noise and soon found myself in the circle of homeless people and started drinking beer with them. It seemed harmless—a bunch of drunks laughing and talking—until I passed out."

Helen recalled as many of the gory details as possible and finished her story with a list of participants. She also described how she woke up, half-naked, bloody, and alone in a dark maintenance shed where the group had tossed her.

"Oh my god, Helen, I'm so sorry. I didn't know."

"I wasn't going to tell you or Mark. I washed away any evidence and my physical injuries have healed. Why put myself through the judicial ringer?"

Briggs looked down at the table and into his glass. He appeared to be looking at the contents as if it were a witch's caldron about to reveal the answer to how this could have happened. But from Mark and Kim's description of Little Bobby and his gang, he now understood. "I regret taking them on as clients, even if we were helping their dogs. If only I could wave a magic wand and make them disappear. I would do anything to prevent them from attacking another woman. Or anyone. I don't know what else to say." Briggs reached and grabbed her hands, tears streaming down his face.

Helen didn't want to tangle Briggs in her mess or make him an accomplice by confessing what she had done. But she felt she was bursting; she could not keep everything bottled up inside. She needed someone to tell her it was okay, that she was doing the right thing.

"It's okay, Jimmy. If it makes you feel any better, no one needs to be frightened of Little Bobby, Jerry Hoffman, or Patrick O'Flaherty any longer. All three are sitting side-by-side, lined up with other cremated remains at Heavenly Considerations, waiting for disposition."

Briggs pushed back and slid down in his chair. He took a deep breath, then two gulps of beer. He opened his mouth, but nothing came out.

"I labeled each with a number and letter—like we do with other clients. I haven't decided what to do with the remains. Are you shocked?"

"You euthanized the dogs as well?"

"I could not do it. Could not violate our oath as vets. I let all of them go and removed their tracking collars.

Briggs didn't want to know any more details.

Now he understood what was going on: Helen had been on a murder spree. What else could it be, Briggs thought. He had considered killing the homeless to put them out of their misery, humanely. Helen was in a rage, out for revenge.

Could Briggs do anything about it? Did he want to? Didn't Little Bobby and his gang get what they deserved? Maybe the death penalty was too good for them. As his mind ping-ponged over the morality of killing Helen's rapists, he also knew there was nothing to do at this point. It was premeditated. But only he and Helen knew why the Bobby's gang members were disappearing.

Helen is doing wonderful work, right Jimbo? A woman after our own heart. Got to love her.

"I'll be on Death Row with her," he fired back at DIME. "How great is that?"

Helen didn't let the subject drop. Part of her self-appointed therapy was the verbalization of the crime and the punishment.

"Trust me, they're in the place they deserve. As for getting off easy, after I drugged and then tied them down and taped their mouths, I made them understand who I was and why they were about to die. They got their so-called vitamin shots, each filled with an extra big dose of barbiturate. I left out the Propofol."

Briggs cringed, his mouth pulling back in a grimace, exposing his teeth. He had witnessed the death of a dog in veterinary school that didn't get an anesthetic before the kill shot. You never forgot the sound of a dogs' yelping in pain or the twisting and jumping of their bodies as the pure barbiturate exploded like acid in their bodies. The thought raced through his mind, but he said nothing.

Helen left out the bloody details. Telling Briggs she had cut off their penises and stuffed them in their mouths was more than even she wanted to share. It would sound like sick, ritualistic murders.

"So, here we are," Briggs said.

Helen had crossed the line Briggs had been toeing for some time as he grappled with the fate of Maxine Reid.

"Here we are," Helen repeated, who offered no apology for her feelings, words—or deeds.

"We need to get the cremated remains out of Heavenly Considerations. I'm no legal expert, but I'll bet having the ashes of dogs associated with three missing persons is enough circumstantial evidence to send both of us to jail, if not Death Row. We will toss the human ashes from the cliff of the Chamberlain Rest Area into the Columbia, where they will wash out to sea."

"And the dog collars?" Helen asked.

Briggs looked across the room over the rim of his beer mug into the distance as if daydreaming, then said, "I have a perfect spot in some trees behind my place in White Salmon. I'll create a pet cemetery."

"I like the idea," said Helen, who could not help thinking about Stephen King's novel, Pet Cemetery, a creepy, scary story, one of her favorites. "Maybe we should take a trip out there this afternoon."

"Listen to me. No, listen to us," said Briggs. "We sound like cold-blooded killers."

He thought he said it too loudly, swiveling around to see if heads turned their way. None had.

"Three down and one to go," she said.

Briggs just nodded, paralyzed by the thought. He understood her "one to go" reference: Betty would be next.

And Maxine will make five, Jimbo.

He ignored the interruption and repeated, "There is no usable DNA—nothing that could confirm we burned up their bodies." After he said it—a little louder than intended—he looked around and saw a lone woman looking at him. "Talking about a TV script," Briggs offered. The woman smiled.

Helen agreed, "Jimmy, the cremulator has eliminated that problem."

They finished their beers and headed over to pick up the remains of Little Bobby and Company.

They would put the dog collars in Briggs' cemetery, which would include the still-active PupFinder GPS tags. He figured he could log on to PupFinder.com and see tiny points of light concentrated in one spot: his pet cemetery. As long as the lights remained lit, the dogs would remain alive in his mind. Their power sources would stay charged for up to a year.

Nice touch, Jimbo. Anytime you get lonely for your doggie pals, day or night, you'll be able to log onto your computer screen and see their points of light on the screen. They'll be a reminder of all your charitable work.

CHAPTER TWENTY

July 10, 2019

When Larson walked into Chief Detective Mike Melrose's office, he thought he was in the wrong place. Sitting behind the desk, with only five or six files on top, was a man whose hair was neatly trimmed, tie cinched, sitting up straight. The man appeared to be Chief Melrose. For a moment, Larson was not sure. He had rarely seen his boss out from underneath the paper mountain that filled his office. You could not sugarcoat it: Melrose was a hoarder.

"Chief, is that you? What happened to this place?"

"Don't be a wiseass, Larson."

Miserable and lonely because of his broken marriage and in trouble with the brass over the condition of his office, Melrose had relented and called Marty Simpson, the consultant the Portland Police Bureau had hired to streamline operations. When Melrose dialed the contact number, he figured he would get an answering machine, a callback a week later, and an appointment in a month or two. Instead, a man answered the phone. He said Marty, the organizational consultant, had been helping another department head one floor down and would drop by in a few minutes.

The person who showed up left Melrose's mouth agape: she was wearing a crisp state police uniform with a lieutenant rank on the shoulders.

"I think there's been a mistake," said Melrose. "I'm expecting a civilian, a guy named Marty, to come up and help me out with my apparent hoarding addiction."

"That's me," said Simpson, a fresh-faced woman, about 40, with stylish, short brown hair, brown eyes, and a smile that lit up the room. "Would you have preferred Marie Kondo, Captain?"

Melrose got up from behind his desk, shook hands with Lt. Simpson, who explained, "The bureau figured hiring an outside consultant with no understanding of how police operations function wouldn't work. Instead, they found me. I have had special training in time management and several other specialties, such as hostage negotiations. I'm also good at cleaning up messes."

Suddenly self-consciously about his lapses in hygiene and appearance—at home and in the office—Melrose straightened his jacket and tie and patted his perfectly cut hair to make sure everything was in place, and said, "The only hostage here is the crap on my desk. I need help to free it."

For the next several hours, Melrose and Simpson reviewed the piles, decided what was essential to keep, and what they could toss. They tossed nearly everything into boxes destined for shredding. Melrose felt like a new man when he went home that night.

Instead of plowing through a six-pack of beer while plopped in front of the television, he took his dog for a long walk and picked up Japanese takeout on the way home. He had one beer with dinner, washed a week's worth of dishes, and put his socks, underwear, and gamey pajamas in the wash. And he thought about how he could spend more time with Marty Simpson.

Although Melrose found extra energy in a clean office and thoughts of a girlfriend, he maintained his tough exterior. He figured he needed to put a boot in Larson's ass and push him forward, help him get moving on the case.

"Two more homeless people have disappeared," said Melrose. "The case now stands at three missing persons. Besides Jerry Hoffman and Little Bobby, Patrick O'Flaherty has joined the rolls of the missing. Bill Blaise, who works security for crews cleaning up homeless camps, says he hasn't seen any of them lately. He was unable to pin down the last encounter he had with any of them, except Jerry. He was there the day park workers found Jerry's abandoned camp. However, Blaise recalls seeing Pirate Pete, Jerry's one-eyed Beagle, wandering around without Jerry the other day. Again, he wasn't able to pinpoint a time or a date."

"Do you think somebody has taken them out in retaliation for all the nasty shit they've done?" Larson asked.

"That's a question for you to answer, Larson. Go find out."

"Got it, Chief."

Turning back to the condition of his office, Melrose answered Larson's question. "What happened here is that I got rid of the useless crap on my desk."

Larson asked no more questions. He had seen Melrose's so-called clean up consultant, Lt. Simpson, hanging around. No one in the detective bureau missed the change in Melrose's appearance or his demeanor since she arrived. Or the closed doors which stayed that way during the hour-long Lt. Simpson consults with the detective chief.

"Okay, Chief," said Larson. "I'll get on it."

As he sat down as his desk, a wave of anxiety struck Larson as the image of Helen in the Have Paws—Will Travel van with O'Flaherty two days earlier appeared in his mind. He felt like a sneaker wave has struck him, tumbling him uncontrollably in the surf. His breath came in gasps as he tried to push away the thought Helen might be involved.

Melrose's addition of a potential victim not only ramped up Larson's investigation, but for the first time gave him the feeling something wasn't right. The homeless come and go, and they die on the streets each year in increasing numbers. But they rarely disappeared without a trace, as if an alien spaceship had sucked them up, never to return. He had discovered no bodies, nor any evidence of a crime. Still, Larson knew he would need to dig deep to find the truth. Even if it led to Helen. "No way," Larson said out loud, his colleagues looking askance.

While waiting to get the DNA analysis of the panties and a possible suspect, Larson would rely on old-fashioned shoe leather in his search for information. As he had as a patrol officer, he would go back on the street and talk to the people who lived and suffered with the missing. He knew where to start: SugarBurst, a donut shop on 23rd to talk to Kenny, a savvy homeless man who was a keen observer of life around him. Kenny had been one of Larson's best informants.

Larson found a rare parking space a half block from Kenny's hangout, put his city parking permit in the window, and walked toward SugarBurst. If Kenny wasn't around, Larson could at least enjoy a donut or two and a cup of coffee.

When Larson came around the corner onto 23rd Avenue, Kenny was in his regular spot, sitting on a bright green plastic tote box. But today, he was holding a red umbrella over his head to shield himself from the afternoon sun. The temperature was in the low 80s. The ubiquitous cardboard sign the homeless display to plead for cash contributions declared Kenny a veteran working his way out of homelessness. Kenny displayed four signs telling his life's loves and losses. What was new on his sign was the fact that a local community college had accepted him into a training program and that he had found temporary housing.

Despite his good fortune, it was difficult breaking the habit of hanging out in front of the gourmet donut shop where tourists and locals paid $4 for a donut and were generous with donations. How could they not be? They sat gorging themselves on gourmet donuts, looking through a large picture window at Kenny, who sat half slumped on the sidewalk a few feet away.

"Hello," he called out to Kenny.

Kenny got up and stood at attention. Suspicious of Larson's intentions, he asked, "Did I do something wrong, detective? I'm a U.S. Navy Veteran. I've had some hard times. Just trying to get by."

"Come on, give me a break, Kenny. You know me. Officer Larson. We've talked many times. I just got a promotion to detective. Maybe my suit and tie disguise has confused you."

Kenny looked closer, searching Larson's face. "Now, I recognize you," said Kenny, whose shoulders relaxed in a less defensive posture.

"You're not in any trouble," said Larson, trying to ease the man's anxiety. "Remember, like you, I'm a Navy Veteran. I served as a weapons control officer on the U.S.S. John McCain.

Kenny stood erect and patted his hair to make sure everything was in place the way a soldier might check his things before an inspection. "At ease, sailor," said Larson. "This isn't about you.

Kenny's shoulders and hands appeared to loosen, his posture relaxed. "Have a seat," Kenny said, as he dropped back onto his plastic crate and cleaned off a second one for Larson.

Larson sat down and said, "Kenny, I have a case with three homeless people missing. I think you know them: Little Bobby, Jerry Hoffman, and Patrick O'Flaherty."

"Yeah, I know those assholes, they attacked me one night and took a day's wages, nearly $150. I was going to fight them, but realized it would he hopeless. They are a mean bunch."

"So, you haven't seen them here?"

"No, the only other homeless person I've met at SugarBurst is Big Betty."

What is Big Betty's last name?"

"Bingham, I believe," said Kenny. "I remember the name because of the three B's in her name. And I remember Miss Triple B because she is about three times the size of the average person."

"The woman is at least 50 pounds overweight," Kenny continued. "I'm not sure how someone living out here could be so fat. I wasn't too happy when she first appeared with her dog and started cutting into my donations."

"Donations?"

"Yes, donations, the money I get from generous people to help me get off the street and into permanent housing. I got off the streets for a while after a school accepted me for a technical training program. The training didn't take. Guess I'm an old dog who could not learn new tricks." Larson listened without comment.

"Betty, I remember her," Kenny continued. "Like I said, a big lady. She came every day for a month, then just stopped."

"Do you know why she stopped coming?" She was not part of Larson's case, but that fact that she had been part of Little Bobby's gang and his former girlfriend set off an alert in Larson's head.

"Given her daily take of cash—$150 a day in the summer—I'm not sure. Add it up. It's $3,000 a month and all tax-free."

Larson frowned. He did not like the idea Kenny was proud of cheating the government out of thousands in income tax payments, part of which would have been used to pay for Kenny's healthcare, veteran benefits, social workers, and city bureaucracy that cost millions of dollars a year to maintain.

"Where did she go?" Larson asked. "Was she ever threatened? Was there anyone who approached her, maybe scared her away?"

"Whoa," said Kenny, holding up his hands like he was waiting for someone to rain down blows on his head. "That's too many questions. You're going to make my head explode."

"No, I never threatened her," Kenny said. "I admit it pissed me off the first time she showed up, but she rarely came when I was here. When we shared the sidewalk, Betty was a wonderful conversationalist, and our dogs got along, which was a plus. Donations from passersby this summer have been generous, plenty for both of us." Larson noted that Kenny's repeated use of the word "donations." Did these people keep track, file 1040 tax forms, and claim thousands of dollars in charitable giving? Larson did not share the thought with Kenny.

"Hey, wait a minute, are you accusing me of hurting Betty?"

This was the first time Larson has heard that Big Betty Bingham had joined the list of missing homeless. All were part of Little Bobby's gang. Was someone out for revenge—payback for the violence the group heaped on others? Larson wondered.

"I'm not accusing you. Just asking. Betty and some other people have disappeared. I'm checking into it."

Larson moved closer to Kenny. In Sweden, where Larson's parents were born, a person's personal space was smaller than in the U.S. They felt comfortable standing closer to strangers. Larson had learned that closing up the space between him and someone he was interviewing made them squirm. And made them more likely to tell the truth, just to get away. Up close, Larson could see their eye movements better to determine if there were signs of lying. While the rancid breath of the homeless would offend most people, Larson felt it gave him a better sense of a person, and what they ate or drank—his breathalyzer for pot and alcohol.

"The disappearance of other homeless people isn't unusual," said Kenny. "I find stuff abandoned all the time. Get some of my best things from piles of belongings left behind. Most show up later. They replace their lost things in a day or two of salvaging. It would amaze you how much stuff people dump on the street." Larson knew the figures. The amount of trash park maintenance people picked up every day and took to the dump was staggering.

As Larson moved closer, Kenny got jumpy.

"Come to think about it, there was one guy who approached Betty. He was a big guy—a giant with long red hair. A veterinarian, I think. Yeah, Briggs, Dr. Briggs. He helped my dog and me, and Betty's dog, who had a bad leg." There it was again: Jim Briggs name associated with the missing.

But as Briggs has said, that's not unusual given his volunteer work with the homeless. Still, it made Larson uncomfortable that the only connection to the missing homeless was his friend, Jim Briggs. Could Briggs have something to do with the missing men?

Larson pushed the thought away. "Kenny, thanks for your help."

"No problem," he said, as Larson walked away.

Kenny raised his umbrella, then thanked a woman and her little girl who had dropped $5 into Kenny's U.S. Navy-issue cloth cap, known as a "dixie cup." The cap was round and very white, a prized possession of Kenny's Navy service days. It was a memory of better times when he could count on three squares, a bed, and a roof over his head, and a family waiting for him back home.

Larson found it hard to feel sorry for Kenny, whose panhandled earnings—if you could believe the amount—totaled $3,000 a month tax-free. And all for sitting on his ass, begging.

"I could get a dog, buy some clothes from Goodwill, share Kenny's space, and retire," Larson thought. "I could use the donations and unemployment benefits to pay for an apartment. I could pretend to be homeless."

Back in his car, Larson's uncharitable thoughts turned to happy thoughts of Helen. They had a date the next night. He wondered what surprise she would spring on him. He had mentioned one of his fantasies to her during their last date. The possibility made him smile.

***

Helen suggested their second date with Mark Larson be at his place. She felt seeing how he lived would give her a better sense of the man. Was he a neat freak? A slob? Were there pictures on the walls and modern furniture? Was his home just a place to crash at night?

Although she hadn't asked Mark, she planned to spend the night and brought a change of clothes and personal items she would need in a large soft shoulder bag.

She arrived right on time for their 7 pm date, knocked on his door, put her bag down, unbuttoned her coat, and waited for him to open it.

When the door swung open, Mark barely got "Hi" out of his mouth before Helen pulled her coat open and said, "Ta-Da."

Larson's mouth dropped open. No words came out. She was naked and smiling.

"Don't you like my body? I can leave?"

Larson decided a sassy comeback was his best weapon.

"Go into the bedroom, take off the coat, climb into bed, and I'll be right there."

"Now, we're talking," said Helen, her smile electric.

When she got to the bedroom, Helen removed her coat but left the boots on—a Larson fantasy. While he removed his clothes, careful to fold them on a chair, she set the bag on top of the bed.

"What's that?" Larson asked.

"Sex toys."

An hour later, they were both in robes in the kitchen cooking and drinking wine.

"You're spoiling me, Williams."

Larson, like most cops, called people by their last names. Suspects—even those given traffic tickets—were *perps*, also known as perpetrators. It was a habit, and he was no different with Helen.

He walked outside to the Weber and put on the skewers of shrimp.

Helen's mouth dropped open at the sight of Larson's apartment, stunned by its beauty. A Scandinavian flair with sleek, clean Swedish furniture and modern lighting gave the room an airy feeling. Minimalist. She loved it.

He had covered the walls with huge photos on canvas from vacations Larson had taken around the world, from the Great Wall to Barcelona's Basilica de la Sagrada Familia to St. Michael Church in Bratislava. They were a riot of bright colors, all with a focus on ancient architecture.

"Your home is beautiful," said Helen.

"My mother's influence," said Larson. "She helped me decorate. We did it last year when my folks came for a month-long visit from Sweden."

Once the shrimp was grilled, they sat down for dinner and talked about the day.

Larson poured each of them a glass of wine and toasted, "To Helen, the light of my life."

Normally, Helen would fire back to keep him off guard. Instead, tears started flowing. "This is the first time in months I've felt good. I don't mean just from the sex. That was great."

Larson raised his eyebrows, waiting for more praise.

"I feel connected. I don't mean to frighten you because our relationship is just starting. But today I feel like I'm a member of a family. Today, you're my family."

She could tell him that she had temporarily disabled the shield she had erected which allowed her to accomplish her mission of revenge. Larson teared up. He raised his glass again in a silent cheer. Then they began eating dinner. They said little while eating, glancing at each other, neither feeling embarrassed nor uncomfortable. They only rarely broke eye contact to spear another bite of food.

"Helen, I have a very unsexy question for you I hope won't dim the glow we are both feeling. When I came to your house, you explained how upsetting euthanasia is for the dog owners—and for you. We didn't discuss the actual process. I understand it is similar to the lethal injections process on death row. Could you explain the nuts and bolts?"

The request alarmed Helen. "Is this work-related?" she asked.

"No, not at all," he lied, forcing himself not to blink or break eye contact.

She explained it was rather simple.

"Dogs have always been part of human packs. But now, more than ever, people think of their canines not as pets, but companion animals. Have Paws—Will Travel provides basic veterinary services much the same way your primary care physician takes care of you. Jim and I provide a soup-to-nuts pantry of care options: vaccinations, exams, lab tests, and urgent care and emergency care. And, when all else fails, because of age or illness, we euthanize client dogs. The conversations are emotional. We answer their questions and try to reduce their anxiety. They treat their dogs like their children and spend nearly as much on them. No matter how many times you've put down an animal, it's difficult. You hate to take a life, as diminished as it might be. And you have to absorb the blast of client emotional upset that comes with euthanasia. Otherwise, it is all very mechanical: give an anesthetic to put the animal into a deep sleep so they feel no pain, then give them the killing shot to stop their heart. It's quick and easy."

Larson nodded. "Sounds tough."

"To put it in perspective, Jim said it was easier to decide to turn off his mother's life support than watch his beagle put down when he was a kid. He knew his mother was near death. Dogs are harder. Not only is the family stressed, but they put extra stress on us with their questions, hoping we will come up with a cure and offer a reprieve. As a result, I always wonder if I could have done something different to save them or extend their life."

"What happens when a family wants a cremation?"

"Again," Helen explained, "there is an emotional element and a physical process. The process is straight-forward. You put the dog in a furnace cranked up to 1200 degrees and at the end of a cycle that lasts one to two hours depending on the size of the animal, you get a pile of ash and bone. Those bits go into a commercial grade, high-speed blender, pulverizing everything. The end product is fine dust, leaving no evidence of life or DNA; you can't tell the difference between a human and a dog."

"Very interesting," said Larson, twisting his face into a frown with his lips pressed together like he was about to ask her to confess to killing and burning up his four missing homeless. He had just heard an explanation about how his so-called victims could have been killed, and all traces of their existence wiped away.

"When I saw you with Patrick O'Flaherty, didn't you promise me dessert tonight?"

Helen burst into a smile. "Well, Detective Larson, I was just going to suggest we move to the last course of the night. But you already got dessert. Are you sure your diet can handle a second?"

"I'm full but not that full," he said, grinning.

"In that case, let's go," she said, heading to the bedroom.

CHAPTER TWENTY-ONE

July 12, 2019

Near the end of his morning walk before making Have Paws—Will Travel client calls, Jim Briggs' sweet tooth alert sounded. A half-block away was his favorite donut shop, SugarBurst. Not only was he craving a treat, but his body was shutting down.

"It's like a car running out of gas," Briggs described the feeling to his doctor. The doctor could not explain why Briggs had sudden drops in blood sugar since he had no signs of diabetes or other ailments. The tests were all normal. Even though the incidents were rare, Briggs found them disturbing, especially for someone like him in his mid-thirties, who could ride a bike 30 miles and have energy left to spare.

He would order a latte and three donuts: a crème brulée, a maple-bacon with chunks of real bacon—none of those fake bacon bits—and a fat powdered donut with a Meyer lemon-key lime curd filling. When he walked inside, a group of women ogled the donuts, trying decide which ones to buy.

A few minutes later, he was sitting on a stool looking through a picture window at a massive woman with a tangle of dyed red hair in her early sixties.

The homeless are like ants in the house looking for water on a hot day, right Jimbo. You don't know where they come from and can't seem to get rid of them.

For once, he agreed with his dark inner voice.

He recognized the chubby-faced woman from his recent visit to R2D2. She was "Big Betty" Bingham, with her schnauzer, Sepp. Betty was a battleship of a woman, six-feet-two inches tall, 250 pounds. This was the woman Helen said left her to the mercy of Little Bobby and friends.

The last time he stopped at SugarBurst, a homeless military veteran, Kenny, was sitting on the same green plastic box Betty now occupied. Briggs didn't know if they shared the space, or if it was first-come, first-served.

Her cardboard sign pleaded, "Need $35 by 4 pm for cancer treatment co-pay and $18 cash for a room for the night." Briggs knew the room she was talking about had nothing to do with the hospital. For $18, you'd be lucky to find a room in a hospital broom closet with a dried up mop for a pillow.

The week before, about six blocks down the street, he had met another homeless woman with a dog who claimed the same sad story of cancer and chemotherapy. Were they a mother-daughter tag-team—two people with no cancer—who knew their story would spark the sympathy of passersby and generate bigger donations?

After finishing his donuts, Briggs went outside and introduced himself to Betty. Before their conversation was over, he had tagged her Schnauzer Sepp with a PupFinder GPS chip. He kept a supply of the chips and some basic first aid in a messenger bag he carried with him everywhere.

Helen's story of Betty leaving her vulnerable to assault by Little Bobby's gang slashed at Briggs' heart. He could not imagine how one person could be so cruel to another, let alone the woman not coming to her rescue.

"Your sign says you have cancer and need money for chemotherapy," said Briggs. "Oregon provides free healthcare to the homeless last time I checked."

"The bastards say I don't qualify," said Betty, whose massive body did not appear to be wasting away from disease. "Now, I fight every day to stay alive. It's a day-by-day battle. No co-pay, no chemo."

Briggs shook his head when she finished talking. He did not believe her.

Betty searched Briggs's face for recognition and sympathy, but found neither in his neutral expression.

"Here's my pathology report," she said, pulling a crumpled piece of paper from a pocket.

Briggs took it, recognized the pathologist as one of Providence Health Care's best, and read the diagnosis: Stage 4 metastatic breast cancer. Prognosis with expensive life-extending drugs, two months.

Carefully folding the report, Briggs handed it back to Betty. "Sorry," he said, then pulled out his wallet and handed the woman three twenties to cover her room and co-pay. Betty grabbed the man and hugged him. She reeked of garlic, overripe cheese, and body odor.

Betty looked up at Briggs like a lover, gazing into his eyes, before he pushed her gently away. He had tears in his eyes. "It's okay, big guy. Wherever I'm going next can't be much worse than trying to survive on Portland streets."

Briggs had just met this woman and was feeling sorry for her, despite what Helen had told him. Just when he thought he might escape, Betty said, "Grant me one dying wish."

The wish Briggs had for the woman was a premature death. And death was coming at Betty like a freight train. He wanted nothing to do with last wishes.

Betty called Sepp and scooped him in her arms. She kissed him and then pushed him toward Briggs.

"Doc, please take care of Sepp when I'm gone," Betty pleaded.

Briggs hesitated and then reached for Sepp. His veterinarian training wouldn't let him say no.

"Okay," said Briggs. "I'll take care of Sepp. Don't worry. For now, he needs to be with you." Briggs handed him back.

"Now, I'm ready to die," said Betty, her body suddenly drooping as if she were a balloon deflating. Briggs passed Sepp back to her.

Jimbo, luck is with us. We just got permission to kill Betty. She's begging for it. Put her in the van and get on with it.

A client 9-1-1 call rescued Briggs from DIME and Big Betty. He listened to the message and told Betty he had to go.

"Where will you be this evening, Betty?"

"I can give you a shot to help with the chemotherapy effects," he lied. The shot he was talking about, to boost her immune system, post-chemo, cost $10,000 a dose, one small syringe.

"Sepp and I hang out in the park at 16th and Johnson, under the freeway. I used to go there with friends, but they've disappeared. I guess it's just me left. And I will not be here much longer either." He knew she was talking about the members of her homeless crime family but showed no sign of recognition.

"Who are the friends missing and for how long?"

"They disappeared over the past week or two. I'm not sure. I think they have abandoned me when I need them most." Tears started down her cheeks. "How could Little Bobby do that to me? We've been a couple. Never married. But I've been a wife to him in so many ways." Briggs didn't want to count the ways.

Despite death coming for her soon, Briggs was having a hard time choking up over Little Bobby or the couple's so-called marital problems.

"I'll come by tonight after work, about 8 pm, or my colleague will. Her name is Helen Williams, and she is also a veterinarian. One of us will give you the shot and check Sepp's health and give him whatever he might need."

Briggs' only question: would he apply the death penalty or would Helen? When he got home from his walk and encounter with Big Betty, he texted Helen. "Just met Big Betty and her dog, Sepp. She'll be in the park tonight. She has terminal breast cancer. I told her one of us would show up after 8 to give her a shot to boost her energy after the chemotherapy. Will you do the honors?"

"With pleasure," Helen texted back.

CHAPTER TWENTY-TWO

July 13, 2019

The next day, Briggs tracked Maxine Reid to a corner in Portland's Pearl District where she and Buster were collecting donations. When she saw Briggs, Maxine smiled and said, "Hey Doc, sit down and join us." Buster ran over, wagging his tail, trying to lick Briggs's face.

After settling next to her, Briggs said, "I've got a surprise for you."

"A carton of smokes?"

"No cigarettes, Maxine. I'm not feeding that habit. You know that. I watched my mom die from burned-out smoker's lungs."

"Yeah, yeah, yeah," Maxine shot back. "Save the lecture."

"I've been to the library several times searching your family roots, looking for some of them who might still be alive."

"I already told you they are all dead, or didn't you listen to me?" Maxine said, glaring at Briggs.

Briggs ignored her rant and continued. "This morning I discovered you have an Aunt Daisy. She's very much alive, living in Denver, Colorado, and she would like to talk to you." Maxine's head jerked toward Briggs.

"Who the hell is Aunt Daisy?"

"You don't know?" Briggs pulled back, looked down at Maxine, and waited for her to respond. He did not believe her.

"I have a faint memory of a lady in a photo who looked like my mom, but don't recall my mom ever talking about her. When I asked who was in the photo, Mom closed the album and said, 'no one important. A person I knew at one time.'"

Briggs stopped for a second to consider whether to lay out the story, giving her the ugly reality of the affair that split the family apart. He gave it to her straight. He first sat down in the van doorway so he was at eye level with Maxine, who was standing on the sidewalk. Buster jumped in his lap without being called. He had that effect on animals. Especially cats that never got into anyone's lap.

Despite being a veterinarian, Briggs did not like cats. Too much bite and scratch for his taste. He knew a veterinarian who contracted Cat-scratch fever and needed heart surgery to repair the damage left by the disease.

Speaking slowly so Maxine could take in his words, he said, "Daisy is your mother's identical twin sister. She claims her husband, Jack—your father—had an affair with your 17-year-old mom and got pregnant with you."

Maxine shook her head. "Sounds like Mom. Could not keep her pants on from what I heard. Mom married at least four more times after my dad died, one of them Jack. I barely remember him. I was only five years old. So, Mom cheated on her sister and then blamed Daisy, and cut my aunt—her twin sister—out of her life. And I'm old Jack's bastard child. I can see why she never mentioned Daisy."

"Daisy is alone," Briggs explained. "She has a big house that she will share for a little help with cleaning and grocery shopping. She said you and Buster are welcome to live with her."

Maxine did not respond. Instead, she rattled her cup full of coins and yelled, "A little help needed." The shrill cry turned heads and made people stop and look. A dog bowl with a few dollar bills and change was just inches from Buster's nose, a beacon for donations. Buster was resting, taking in the scene. A woman jolted by the cries for help took off her headphones, stared at Maxine and Buster for a moment, then reached into a fanny pack, pulled out a $5 bill, and dropped it into the bowl. "God bless," Maxine offered. The woman smiled, put on her headphones, and hurried away. Maxine picked up her cash pile, putting most of it in a big pocket on her skirt. She left a dollar and change, just enough to generate pity and draw other contributions from people who might feel sorry for the ragged little woman and her dog.

"Doc, I guess I would talk to Daisy. But as bad as it is out here, I'm not sure it would interest my aunt having a burned-out meth addict and a beat-up dog live with her. I would have to clean up my act. Not sure I'm ready to do that." After a pause, she added, as if thinking out loud, "But what the hell, what have I got to lose?"

That's funny, Jimbo. What's she got to lose? How about her fucking miserable life? Time to put this stray out of her misery.

Briggs countered, "We found a home for Maxine—hope for at least one Portland stray."

Turning to Maxine, Briggs set his plan in motion: "I will call and plan for you to talk with Daisy tomorrow."

"Okay," she said. "I'll be right here, same time, same station."

Briggs' phone lit up with a text from a client who wanted a wellness check for her dog. "Gotta go, Maxine," he said, pushing himself up and heading off to help a paying customer.

***

After tracking Maxine to the rear of a local market the next day where she was preparing lunch for her and Buster from dumpster scraps, Briggs called her over to his van and offered her burgers and fries from MacDonald's—her favorite.

"Ah, big man, you are the best. Eating lettuce and rotten fruit ain't no taste-treat. But Buster and I love Big Macs and fries!" Briggs had seen Maxine collect at least $50 in 15 minutes the day before. Why would she be eating garbage?

Instead of challenging Maxine, Briggs said, "Come on in and eat," while he unfolded his work table and added a small tablecloth as if she needed an enticement beyond the fast food.

"Table cloth? You're going to spoil me, Doc."

Briggs joined in the feast. He also liked the burgers. The fries were not as good as those at Tilt, a half dozen blocks away, but they were crispy and salty, two essentials for decent french fries.

Briggs watched Maxine gulp down half the burger, then feed the rest to Buster. She wiped her face with her end of her skirt and let Buster lick the salt from her fingers.

"Ready to talk to Aunt Daisy?"

"As ready as I'll ever be."

"Briggs made the call, then handed over his iPhone to Maxine. He stepped out of the van to give her some privacy. A half-hour later, he heard, "Hey, Doc, let me out." He pulled open the door and saw Maxine dabbing tears.

"Are you okay, Maxine?" Maxine tried to cover up the emotions. "Fine, just got something in my eye."

"Did you and Aunt Daisy hit it off?" Maxine sighed and looked away, her eyes watering. "She sounded like my mother. It was like Mom had come back to life. She even used some same expressions as Mom." Maxine used the end of her dirty purple skirt to wipe her eyes. "Aunt Daisy seems like a gracious lady. Said she loves dogs."

"I did it, I found a home for Maxine," Briggs thought, a broad grin on his face and a mental high five.

Before Briggs could ask, Maxine said, "Life on the street is pretty shitty. I know my time is short. That doesn't worry me. Knowing this could end anytime is comforting in a way. Life might be better with Daisy. But I can't see myself living in a neighborhood with a house, a kitchen, a warm bed, and all that shit. Very tempting. But I'm too old to settle into someone else's life—even someone as nice and welcoming as Daisy. I'm staying here. I just pray that one day I won't wake up. I don't care what they do with this old bag of bones. Buster will find his way with another street person."

Briggs' heart sank.

You tried, Jimbo. Maxine is hopeless. You heard her. She's done with this life. Worn out. If we don't help her, the mean streets will.

"What other choice to do I have," Briggs said, agreeing with his dark impulse.

For the next few minutes, he and Maxine sat in silence. "Doc, I gotta go."

Briggs did not try to stop her. He opened the van door and helped Maxine out. Buster followed.

"I know you are trying to help. So thanks for that," said Maxine, then gathered her panhandling cash and cardboard together, and wandered off. "See you around. Come on, Buster."

Maxine turned around, looked back, and smiled at Briggs. Tears filled her eyes.

Were the tears because she missed her mother? Or a future she knew could not exist? Briggs would never know. He knew what he had to do next.

CHAPTER TWENTY-THREE

July 14, 2019

Kim Jansen texted Jim Briggs, "We need 2 talk."

As usual, Kim liked to keep Briggs in the dark, her way of ramping up the excitement. She knew it also ramped up his anxiety. He always expected the worse. He had explained that his fear was a leftover scar from his mother's approach to raising him with no father. She never praised him. More often than not, she would say, "You screwed up. You can do better."

Kim used her key to unlock Briggs' townhouse. The three-bedroom, three-bath home, covered 3,500 square feet. Often, she had to search to find Briggs. On two levels, you could scream from the lower level and he could not hear in his office, which was in the back of the upper story.

As she stood on the front steps, about to unlock the door, she got the feeling someone was watching her. A voice from behind her called out. "Is there a problem, officer? I live two doors down. We've had no problem before."

Dressed in her full Portland Police Bureau uniform and duty belt loaded with a gun, mace, baton, and taser, Jansen looked out of place among the million-dollar townhouses. An occasional burglary or smashed car window was a "crime wave" in Briggs's neighborhood; an armed police officer knocking at someone's door was a rare bird.

A white-haired woman, holding a chihuahua wrapped in a knitted pink sweater, stood behind Jansen, her lips pressed together in a look of concern. She adjusted her glasses and waited for an answer.

"Hello," said Officer Jansen, in her friendliest voice possible.

"No problem here. I'm coming to visit my brother," Jansen lied.

Jansen hoped by suggesting a sister relationship, rather than a cop girlfriend dropping in for a bootie call, she could prevent any rumors from flying among Briggs' neighbors.

"Your brother is a big man," she said. "You're tall yourself, scanning Jansen's 6-foot height. Looks like you both have good family genes." The woman seemed relieved the visit didn't mean trouble. She was also probably relieved a blue-collar cop was not living on her street. A visit was okay. The woman no doubt knew that a patrol officer in the Portland Police Bureau could not afford to live in Briggs's $1.5 million home. Inherited from his mother, Briggs was in the enviable position of having no mortgage and living in the Pearl, one of the city's trendiest neighborhoods.

"I'm Martha Maywether," the woman said.

"Nice to meet you, Mrs. Maywether. If I'm ever around and can do something for you, please let me know."

"You're very sweet," the elderly lady said. "Please call me Martha."

"Martha, My brother and I are having dinner and I'm helping cook, so I better get inside and change," she said, trying to get away from the woman.

"Always nice to know girls still learn to cook these days," Mrs. Maywether said, as she continued on her walk. As Kim finished unlocking the door, the handle twisted in her hand.

"Hi sweetheart," said Briggs, swinging the door open wide.

Once Jansen had stepped inside, she turned around and waved to Mrs. Maywether, who was watching Briggs' greeting but was too far away to hear what they were saying.

"Briggs, be quiet, don't call me sweetheart." His eyebrows raised in a questioning look.

She explained her white lie to Martha.

"Good thinking, Kimmy."

Once they were inside and the door was closed, Kim grabbed a handful of Briggs' Hawaiian shirt decorated with green pineapples and pulled his head down for a kiss. As he smiled and backed away, she looked closer at the shirt. "The green pineapples are unappetizing," said Jansen. Briggs owned about two dozen in every imaginable color and pattern. She loved most of them. But not the pineapple.

"What have I done officer?"

"You'll find out. Just do what I say and no one will get hurt. Turn around."

A moment later, he heard her handcuffs come out and open with a loud click. "Put your hands behind your back," Jansen commanded. He did not resist.

Once she had his hand locked, she marched him to the bedroom, told her to turn around, and started undoing his belt and then the zipper of the loose shorts he always wore. His shorts dropped to the floor.

"Officer, I don't think you can hold me here. I've done nothing wrong."

"We'll see about that," she responded.

Kim reached down and squeezed him through his briefs, which were already swelling with excitement.

Jansen then put a hand on his chest and pushed him back on the bed. His 6-foot-6 body fell like a redwood tree, shaking the bed and the floor. She then rolled him on his side to unlock the cuffs, and said, "Don't make any funny moves, Dr. Briggs."

Within two minutes, Kim had shed and folded her uniform, climbed up on the bed, and stripped off Briggs' underwear. A half-hour later they both collapsed, exhausted.

"What was that for," Briggs asked, smiling.

"That was the first part of a multiple-part celebration of my promotion to sergeant. I passed the fucking exam, top of my class."

"Give me a high five," said Briggs

"I'm so proud of you," he said.

"Nice sentiment, Briggs, but I want action, not platitudes."

An hour later, Briggs was pleading for mercy. "Kim, honey, I've got nothing left, you've got to release me."

The words came out with little urgency. The warmth of being inside her and watching her find a half dozens of ways to satisfy herself while he lay helpless, lingered.

"I'm not sure I'm done with you," she said, curled up between his legs with her hand a few inches from his now spent manhood. "Look at me," she demanded, her blond hair falling across an ice blue eye. "You have nothing left?" Just as he was becoming aroused, Kim stopped. "We need to talk. First, we need food."

Afterwards, they collapsed in front of the TV, drinking microbrews, watching the six o'clock news, and waiting for pizza delivery.

"Police are cleaning out the homeless camps along the Spring Corridor," the newscaster reported. "The homeless are upset and their advocates are angry over the latest police roundup."

"Officer Jansen, according to the news, you've been harassing poor homeless people, while I'm helping them."

"You're such a saint," she said, punching his shoulder.

"Jimmy, I talked to Mark earlier today, and he said his case now has four missing homeless."

"Four? Last time I talked to him, Little Bobby, Jerry Hoffman, and Patrick O'Flaherty had all disappeared."

"Who else got added to the list?"

"Big Betty Bingham," Kim said. "It's weird that all four members of Little Bobby's gang have disappeared. No one has seen them. And the only evidence of their existence has been Hoffman's welfare identification card and a pair of high-priced panties."

Briggs' white freckled face flushed red.

"Are you okay, Jimmy?"

Tell her you're happy as hell, Jimbo. Four down and one to go.

"DIME, aren't you having a problem with math," Briggs' happy half thought. He refused to add Maxine to the tally.

"I saw Betty two days ago in front of SugarBurst Donuts. She had a sign begging for cash for a chemotherapy co-pay for cancer. I thought it was a con job until she dug a crumpled medical report out of his pocket and gave it to me. It was from a respected Oregon pathologist. She's got stage 4 breast cancer, dead in months, regardless of treatment. I promised to take care of her dog when she died."

"You need to give that information to Mark. What a terrible way to go."

Kim's mother had died of breast cancer when Kim was 14, so she knew the pain and suffering of the disease up close and personal.

Kim shifted her attention back to their celebration.

"You know, Briggs, we ought to do our own film and submit it to the HUMP Festival," Kim said.

"What's the HUMP Festival? Briggs said, although he had attended the last two at a local movie theater.

HUMP, Kim explained, is a film festival featuring short dirty movies—each less than five minutes—all created by people who are not porn stars but want to be for a few hours. That's the pitch, anyway. They screen the movies all over the country, from Portland to Missoula and Minneapolis to Manhattan. Conservatives and liberals alike suck them up.

"Kim, maybe we should observe. Appearing in a porn movie wouldn't be good for either of our careers."

"I'm kidding, Briggs. But hell yes, let's go watch."

“Ready for another round of loving?” she asked, rested, ready for her own HUMPfest with Briggs as her co-star.

“You might persuade me, officer. No need for cuffs or ties. I’ll go willingly.”

Afterward, they each sat up and checked their texts. Briggs had one from Helen: Confirm plan to head out to your place in the Gorge.

Briggs responded: Meet at the office. We’ll leave at nine.

Helen sent a thumbs-up emoji.

CHAPTER TWENTY-FOUR

July 16, 2019

Mark Larson agreed to meet Jansen at Via Romana, a cozy bistro serving Mediterranean and Italian food deep in the Pearl District neighborhood. Just five blocks from Briggs's townhouse, it was a perfect place to escape Briggs' cavernous home that made her feel lonely after he had left for work. Although Jansen still maintained her modest apartment, most nights she stayed with Briggs. She and Briggs were close to making the move permanent.

Her favorite table was a private spot behind a sculpture of a life-size olive tree. Most mornings, she would treat herself to a cappuccino and pastry, while reading the digital edition of the Oregonian, Portland's daily newspaper. She always wore jeans and a hooded sweatshirt, with her hair down. It was a perfect disguise when she was out of uniform.

She had gotten to know most of the Via Romana's staff, who now called her Kim. She had only said hello once to Antonio Sabino, the owner, a distinguished-looking man with thick silver hair and a slight Italian accent. Sometimes at lunch, on her days off, Jansen would come for a pasta lunch, but skip the food and go straight to a pint of the homemade gelato.

Today, when she entered Via Romana in full uniform with her hair pulled back, Antonio was standing behind the cash register with a server next to him waiting for customers.

"Are we in trouble, officer?" asked Antonio. That's what everyone wanted to know: were they in trouble? Didn't matter if they were 80 and walking with a cane, it was always the same. Everyone felt guilty about one thing or another and were just waiting for the law to catch up with them.

Before she could answer, the server recognized her and blurted out, "Kim, how are you? Nice to see you. I did not know you were a police officer." She wanted to say that being a police officer was just a job like everyone else's in the working world. But she knew that wasn't true on many levels. And she also knew the public wouldn't see an accountant and a police officer in the same light.

The young man turned to Antonio and said, "You remember Kim, don't you, Mr. Savino? She comes here all the time."

"Yes, now I remember," he said, but Kim could tell from the glazed look in his eyes he did not know she was a nondescript lady in jeans who came in three times a week. She was anonymous, which she liked.

The young man put his hand over his mouth, horrified for using the familiar 'Kim,' instead of Officer Jansen. "I am very, very sorry. I didn't mean any disrespect."

"You can always call me Kim," she offered. Changing the subject, she alerted the man to Larson's arrival. "I have a friend coming to join me for a quick lunch to celebrate my promotion to sergeant."

The formal introductions over and her identity established, she reached out to the owner, shook his hand, and complimented him on his food and staff service.

"Thank you," he said. "Don't forget to come to dinner sometime. Congratulations on your promotion."

Jansen ordered two cappuccinos and headed for her table, which had views of Tanner Springs Park, a natural spring set among high-rise condominiums. Occasionally, Portland streetcars would block the view for a minute or two before moving on toward downtown. In the back of the restaurant, her uniform would be less visible, with fewer prying eyes.

Larson stepped inside the front door, looked around, and walked toward Jansen, who waved him over. They hugged and sat down. "Perfect timing," she said to the server who delivered their cappuccinos.

"I don't think I've ever been here," Larson said, looking around. "Is the food good?"

"I know the pastries and gelato are good. I'm usually with Jimmy in the evening at his place cooking. This is my morning hang out."

Larson took a sip of his coffee and lifted his cup to Jansen, "Congrats on your promotion. Next stop, the detective bureau."

"Good luck with that. I took the test a year ago and haven't heard a word from anyone. I won't hold my breath."

"Larson, Briggs says you've added Big Betty to your missing list."

"Yeah, Briggs said he saw Betty recently. Oddly, it was right after I spoke to Kenny, a homeless guy who hangs out at SugarBurst Donuts. Briggs said Betty was a regular in front of the donut shop. I don't recall if he mentioned a date.

Briggs said he would check his database to see if he made a note about treating Betty's dog. He might know about other hangouts, in addition to SugarBurst.

"I know what you're thinking, Jansen. You're right. If you include Betty in the tally, all four of the missing were part of Little Bobby's gang. Good riddance. I do not know where they went, nor does anyone I have interviewed. I don't want to care about this case. However, Melrose says I better care or else."

"Larson, how long have you been working on this case?"

"About a month and a half. It started after Jerry Hoffman went missing in May. I got the case on June 1, and over those eight weeks, the bodies have been piling up. You already know that."

"That is the problem, Larson. You've got no bodies and no evidence of any crime. And nothing new to add to the case."

"Brilliant deduction, Jansen. Maybe I should turn my shield over me you and let you run the case."

"Your so-called victims have disappeared off the earth, yet various people you have interviewed claimed to have seen their dogs running around," said Jansen.

"So far, you are 100% right," Larson said, waiting for her next deduction.

"You've got shit, Larson."

"You're right. It's also evidence that the end of my career as a detective can't be far off. Melrose expects results. Or at least progress. I've got neither."

"If I didn't care about you or your career, I would agree with you. I would reinforce how much of a loser you are, especially if it would up free up a detective shield for me."

"Fuck you, Jansen," Larson mouthed, overly sensitive about his progress in the case.

Changing from "Jansen" to friend mode, he said, "Kim, there are two clues that any other detective with a suspicious mind might have concluded were enough to make arrests. One is that Helen and Jim are both connected to all the victims because they care for the victims' dogs. They have access to killing drugs. They euthanize dogs with drugs that work on humans. Briggs burns up dog corpses at Heavenly Considerations, and Helen wears the same brand of panties as those found in Jerry Hoffman's tent."

"Are you sniffing panties Larson," Kim said, working to get a rise from him.

Larson rolled his eyes. "If you must know—and you don't—Helen and I have rounded the bases. Not that it's any of your business. At first, she was very standoffish. Then one evening she called and invited me over and we were in bed minutes after I walked into her place. Later, when she went to the bathroom, I looked over and saw the panties."

Kim shook her head in disbelief. "Come on, Larson. Do you think Jimmy and I are stupid? The way you guys were undressing each other with your eyes the last time we got together, I'm surprised you waited more than a minute."

Larson's fair skin turned red.

"Tell me about the panties."

Larson filled her in on the discovery of the Agent Provocateur brand panties in Jerry Hoffman's abandoned tent.

"Give me your hands," Jansen said, reaching out and taking Larson's hands in hers.

She leaned in closer to Larson, pretending to use his technique for making suspects squirm.

"I don't smell weed or alcohol on your breath, so dementia must be settling in."

Smiling, Larson said, "Got me! Nice one, Jansen."

"I know it makes no sense when you consider that Jim and Helen are all over the homeless caring for their dogs 24/7, no doubt leaving behind bucket loads of their DNA," he said.

"Larson, Agent Provocateur is a popular brand. I even have a pair, despite my pitiful salary."

"Mark, have you asked Jimmy to look at his PupFinder tracking program?"

"What is it?"

"Since the homeless roam like free-range chickens, Jimmy's marketing consultant found PupFinder. Along with the App, she supplied a box of GPS tags which he has attached to the dogs of his homeless clients. When he wants to follow up on a dog with a health problem, he logs onto PupFinder and his screen lights up showing a tiny white dog on the screen and its exact location. He knows whereever the dog is, his homeless owner will be nearby."

"You know it's a Class C felony to track a person or their car with GPS without their permission?"

"Technically, he is tracking the dog. As far as I know, the dog has no legal protections."

Larson sat back in his seat and thought about it for a moment.

Jansen raised her hand to get the server's attention, then called out, "Two pastas with clams, please."

"Coming right up," the young man said.

"Mark, Jimmy hasn't been keeping it a secret. When he told me, it was just matter-of-fact. With 50 homeless client dogs on his roster, it's the only way he can keep track of them. Jimmy will tell you where to find the missing dogs. I'm sure he'll be glad to help. You are friends, after all."

"Helen must know about PupFinder," said Larson.

"Of course, she does. She helps manage his two businesses. She also has been filling in for Jimmy the past couple of weeks to give him and me a chance to get away to the beach."

"I'll give Briggs a call this afternoon and ask him if he can give me the locations of the dogs. I'll go check out the dogs and see if any of my so-called missing homeless are lying low to avoid the law. Little Bobby's gang was always up to no good."

A few minutes later, the pasta arrived.

Larson twirled a string of pasta around his fork and lifted it into the air.

"Salut, Sergeant Jansen."

"Sergeant. What a sweet sound," she said.

CHAPTER TWENTY-FIVE

July 23, 2019

It had been nearly seven weeks since Larson began his investigation into the missing homeless, with little to show for it. The street people he interviewed remembered little about Maxine and the other missing. Most of the homeless he interviewed didn't like Maxine. Several called her a "nasty bitch." If anyone had a clue about the disappearance of Little Bobby McWhorter, gang leader and unelected mayor of R2D2, the homeless camp downtown, they weren't sharing it with Larson.

Given that many of them suffered from a mental illness or were addicts, he wasn't surprised at their hazy recall. The cops were not their friends, so why help him.

Despite his years of daily interaction with the homeless, Larson felt he needed to refresh his memory of statistics related to those killed, found dead, or missing. Statistics, he knew, could show patterns, identify trends, and reveal anomalies.

Larson powered up his computer and Googled Portland, Oregon homeless, and scanned the first of a series of stories in the Oregonian newspaper on the plight of the homeless. One fact caught his attention:

Homeless men and women still die on the streets of Multnomah County at the rate of over one a week, despite renewed focus from city and county leaders. The death rate prompted social justice advocates to renew their call for more solutions and more money.

The story noted the victims were an average of 45 years old. According to the number cited, homeless deaths had taken a big jump. What Larson needed to know was whether the number of missing homeless persons also had spiked. He scanned the database, looked at the totals, and a rush of adrenaline flooded his body. The data showed a spike: a 20 percent jump in missing persons in the past two months. Was it a coincidence? Did it mean anything? He made a note to re-check the evidence box with Jerry Hoffman's personal effects, including the panties—if you could call them his personal effects. A possible clue connecting someone to the case, they were out for analysis. Finally, he listened to a voice in the back of his mind telling him to return to the scene of Hoffman's abandoned camp.

Larson read the original report on Jerry Hoffman's abandoned camp, identified the general location—in a grassy patch under the freeway near 16th Avenue and Overton Street—and drove to the area.

He scanned the report again, noting where Park Maintenance Workers Muncie and Hobson had swept away Hoffman's encampment. When he arrived in the area of Jerry Hoffman's abandoned tent, Larson expected to find nothing more than piles of discarded cans, bottles, and food wrappers, and a "No Camping" sign on a massive freeway support pillar. Instead, he spotted a tent planted right next to the sign, got out of his car, and walked through the weeds and trash toward the illegal camper. Had Jerry Hoffman returned with a new tent and set up camp again? Larson could only hope. When he was standing in front of the tent, he yelled, "Anyone home?"

A moment later the tent opened and out stepped a woman with a greyhound trailing her.

"Can I help you?" she asked, then spotted the detective shield on Larson's belt and backed away. "You're not here to kick me out, are you? I've got no other place to go."

"I'm Portland Police Bureau Detective Mark Larson," he said, handing her his card.

"I'm Alison Meyer," she said, suddenly wrapping her sweater tightly around her body and pulling her dog close to her leg. Then she started running her fingers through her hair like she was combing it. Larson's presence had triggered Alison's anxiety attack.

Larson made a mental note that she was overly thin, 5-feet-six, about 110 pounds, hair flowing to the waist, and a pair of jeans and worn-out work boots with a chunk of leather missing near the big toe.

"Who is this handsome guy?" asked Larson, looking at her dog.

"It's Winnie. A girl. She's a rescue dog. They dumped her after her racing days ended."

Larson petted Winnie and turned back to Alison.

"Alison, I'm looking for a missing person. His name is Jerry Hoffman. He was last seen right where we are standing. The city cleared out his tent after they found it abandoned."

"I saw them," Alison said. "As soon as they left, I moved my stuff and claimed the site for myself."

"Right under the 'No Camping' sign, I see," said Larson.

Alison shrugged.

Before he could get out another question, she said she had seen a dark figure help Jerry into a van the night before crews cleared Jerry's things. She said Jerry was always drunk when she saw him, and he appeared to be struggling to stand up.

"Could you tell if the person helping Jerry a man or a woman?"

"It was too dark. But the person seemed shorter. Which isn't surprising given Hoffman's height. He's at least 6-feet-3. Anyone would look shorter.

"Did you see the make or model of the van?"

"It was really dark. But I do remember the moon was rising and I could light reflecting off the side of the van they got in. There was a line of what looked like white paws across the side. I could not make out the words above the paws."

Larson felt a pulsing pain behind his eyes. Hoffman was big. He wouldn't seem big, however, next to Briggs, 6-feet-6. That left Helen. The thought of Helen, his girlfriend, wearing the same brand of underwear found in Hoffman's and description of the van made his head feel like it might explode. The van could only be Have Paws—Will Travel. And there were only two people who drove the van: Helen and Jim Briggs.

"So, Hoffman didn't get sucked up by an alien," Larson thought.

"Anything else?" Larson asked Alison.

"I went back to bed. Whatever was happening was none of my business."

"Thanks for your time," he said. "Just so you know, the park people patrol this area and every 10 days to clear out campers."

"I'll keep that in mind. Thanks, Detective."

Larson closed his notebook, put it in his coat pocket, and walked back to the car.

Lightning struck as he considered the significance of the sighting.

"It's got to be Jim Briggs' van."

He would check for security cameras in the area and see if he could pin down the time and location the van was in the area.

CHAPTER TWENTY-SIX

July 24, 2019

The next time Briggs saw Maxine, she was slumped against the side of a concrete pillar under the freeway. Her head was poking out of a mountain of blankets. Her eyes were watery, a slight smile on her face. She was in another world. She must have recently had a fix and was still on the high side of feeling good. The sun had just set. The city streets in this mostly residential area were deserted. You could hear a whistle coming from the Portland Train Depot and the rising sound wave of afternoon rush-hour crossing the Fremont Bridge, heading north.

Briggs was not surprised Maxine had been sleeping outside her tent on a night when temperatures were above 70 degrees. Buster, who by now recognized Briggs's voice, appeared out of the pile of cardboard stacked up next to Maxine to see the intruder, then disappeared.

Briggs spoke to Maxine in a stage whisper. "Good evening, Maxine. How are you?"

"Who's there? Get away from me. My dog will rip you a new one." Even though Buster had already acknowledged Briggs, he growled like there was some other unseen invader.

"It's me, Doc Briggs."

"Is that you, Doc? You come to see Buster?"

"I'm here for you today, Maxine. I have something special for you. Something that will make you feel better."

"I'm good right now. Got some magic pipe a few hours ago."

"Let's get you over to the van. You and Buster can come inside, rest a bit out of the weather. I've got some food, too."

Maxine, with considerable effort, given her tiny frame and weak muscles, pushed out of the enormous wad of dirty blankets. Apparently, the warmth of the evening wasn't enough for Maxine, who was skin and bones. Briggs helped her into the van and then lured Buster. He looked around to make sure no one else was watching and closed the door.

"Watch my stuff, Doc. Don't let no one get my stuff."

"Don't worry, I'll watch it," he said. "I'm going to give you two shots now to make you feel better."

"I like shots," she said.

Briggs rolled up her sleeve and wiped off her arm with an alcohol swab. He wasn't sure why he bothered. Where Maxine was going, she wouldn't need to worry about infection.

Briggs stopped for a moment and closed his eyes. Yes, he had tried to find a home for Maxine. He found one, and she rejected it. Yes, she had said during her methamphetamine meltdown that she wanted God to take her. She was used up and no doubt would soon to be a name on the coroner's list of street people who died. But did that justify taking Maxine's life—even if she wanted to die? He wasn't a doctor. He could not prescribe the drugs for assisted suicide. Why kill her now? Or ever? His desire to help Maxine, coupled with the tragedies Helen had experienced at the hands of the homeless, had pushed him over the threshold between helping and killing. He opened his eyes and saw Maxine staring at him.

"Are you okay, big man?" she asked. "I'm fine," said Briggs, who smiled weakly.

"Are you ready, Maxine? You'll just feel a pinch."

"Give it to me," said Maxine. She smiled. Briggs smiled back. "You're an angel, Doc," she said. Briggs paused again for a few seconds before delivering Maxine's shot. He thought back to her family history and what he had learned about her life on the streets: beatings, rapes, thefts, arrests, and drug abuse. Her life story firmed his resolve to do to her what he did so often with dogs: put them out of their misery. Then he delivered the shot.

"Goodbye, sweet little lady. Your suffering is nearly over. No more sleeping outside in the cold and rain, no more dumpster diving for dinner."

"God bless you, Doc Briggs." Did Maxine think she was getting a feel-good vitamin shot? Or had she finally come to terms with her fate. She seemed happy. She was lucid enough to say goodbye and ask him to care for Buster. Filling the first syringe with Propofol, he gently inserted the needle into Maxine's emaciated body, and pushed down the plunger. Maxine slipped into a calm sleep, completely anesthetized. She would feel no pain. Then, with one more push of the second drug, Briggs said goodbye to Maxine Reid.

Buster sniffed Maxine, and he knew something wasn't right.

"Buster, what do you think, little guy? Stay with Maxine or go on your way?"

Buster instinctively knew what Briggs was asking, and he decided he wanted to be with Maxine. He dug into the covers, then curled up between Maxine's still warm body and her thin arm. Briggs offered him a chewy, which he took and began gnawing with no notice of Briggs as he inserted a needle. For Buster, like Maxine, a painless death would offer freedom. The anesthetic would quickly numb and relax the scroungy mutt's 4-pound body, just before the second shot lovingly stopped his heart.

The entire procedure, practiced in veterinary school and the actual world, would take Briggs less than a minute. Nothing cruel and unusual about this needle. Like Helen, he couldn't go through with it. Killing Buster would be violation of the oath all veterinarians take. Similar to medical doctors' claim to do no harm—which isn't in the Hippocratic Oath—veterinarians put the dog's welfare and humane treatment first and foremost.

He removed Buster's collar, opened the door, and gave him push. He placed Maxine into a body bag and placed her in the van's cooler, then headed to Heavenly Considerations to cremate her. Briggs felt calm, the heart rate reading on his fitness watch a healthy 55 beats per minute. The number didn't move either before or after he sent Maxine and Buster on their way. A moment later, though, his heart began racing as a wave of anxiety struck—a reaction to the crime he had just committed and doubt over his future with Kim Jansen. Still, he felt satisfaction knowing he had given Maxine some peace.

"I would like to say that God took her," Briggs thought. But he knew God had nothing to do with it. Briggs was her angel on this day.

***

Briggs opened the big metal double doors of Heavenly Considerations and drove in the van. He hit the close button, shutting off the inner workings of his pet crematory from prying eyes.

Disposing of Maxine's meager remains—all 80 plus pounds (about the size of a large dog)—would take about 120 minutes.

Two small dogs he was processing would take half as long. Still, he was looking at a long night; state and federal rules governing crematory operations were a bureaucratic nightmare, and there were no shortcuts.

It would have been easy to cremate Maxine and the dogs together, but he tried to live by the industry ethics regarding the almost sacred handling of dead animals. That covered stray humans, Briggs thought.

Beer or caffeine? That was his next thought. It was still early in the morning, but Briggs chose both a hefty dose of Stumptown nitrogen-infused cold brew coffee and a beer to follow.

He placed Maxine on the incinerator table, kissed her on the forehead and wished her a pleasant journey in her new life—if there was one. He pushed her in, closed the door, turned up the heat, and went to his desk to fill out the state-mandated paperwork for his canine cremations.

Briggs looked into the cremation chamber and watched Maxine's emaciated body disappear.

See no evil. Hear no evil. Speak no evil, right, Jimbo?

As Briggs peered into the fire, Helen walked back into the crematory and stood next to him. He did not know Helen was working late, catching up on a mountain of paperwork. Briggs jumped, looked at her, and answered—before being asked, "It's Maxine." They looked at each other. He knew then he would eventually join Helen on Death Row.

"Let's be careful we don't spill our guts to Mark," Helen warned. "I can see in a moment of tenderness—in the throes of intense sex and the afterglow—I could see myself bursting out with a confession. You know me, I have a hard time bottling up any thought that comes into my head."

"Join the club," said Briggs. "This will have to be a secret forever."

"Odd, don't you think, Jimmy, that our best friends and lovers are cops. My boyfriend is the chief investigator of the missing homeless. I'm his girlfriend and the missing link in his case."

"Helen, does he have any leads?"

"Not a clue, as far as I can tell. And I want to keep it that way."

***

Determined not to let his first investigation fail, Larson went back out on the street for more interviews and clues. "All of us try to get away from the chaos of the city and make our way to a quieter spot in the suburbs," said one homeless woman he interviewed. "We jump on the Max Train, go as far as we can, get off and find a hidey-hole."

"A hidey-hole?"

"A place you can get away from other people and can hide your stuff so no one steals it," the woman explained.

Larson wondered if his missing were holed up because of a crime they committed and would return to their regular haunts in a few weeks. All the missing had three things in common: they had no permanent shelter, they owned dogs, and they were pro bono clients of James Allen Briggs, DVM. Briggs was many things to many people close to Larson. He was Larson's best male friend and boyfriend to Kim Jansen, Larson's ex-Portland Police Bureau partner. Briggs was the employer of Helen Williams, who was Larson's girlfriend and lover. Jim Briggs, everyone said, was an all-around stand-up guy and noted humanitarian. Larson could not argue with the characterization. A random twisted thought jolted Larson: Briggs regularly puts down and cremates dogs. He gives vitamin shots to the homeless. Briggs and I have talked about euthanasia, the death penalty, and an easier way to eliminate the contentious debate over lethal injection for Death Row inmates.

"No way in hell," Larson barked out loud to no one and pushed away from the thought. "I'm done with this case. I feel like a dog chasing his tail." He wasn't ready to put Briggs in the crosshairs of his investigation. Larson spent the next three days merging notes and writing his "final" case report. After reviewing the draft, he realized there was still one enormous hole: DNA test results. He called the lab and got a vague answer about possibly getting something in a week. He would have to submit his report to Melrose and insert the lab results later. Still, he didn't expect to find anything.

CHAPTER TWENTY-SEVEN

July 27, 2019

Briggs and Larson met for one of their usual beer and bullshit sessions, this time at 10 Barrel Brewing, and sat outside in the rooftop bar to make the most of the summer weather.

After their usual high fives and delivery of beers, Briggs spoke first.

"Mark, you look down, like you've lost your best friend. But, hey, I'm right here, so what gives? Problems with Helen?"

"No, we went from zero to 100 miles per hour soon after we met, and it hasn't slowed down."

"Then all is good," said Briggs.

"No, this is about my case."

"Okay. So, that's not a new topic," said Briggs. "What gives?"

"I've just come out of a meeting with Chief Melrose. He has reviewed the file and believes you're a person of interest. He wants you to come into the station for an interview. He believes you are a suspect.

"A suspect? Suspected of what?"

"You're not making this easy, Briggs," Larson sighed. "Suspected of having something to do with the disappearance of five homeless people and their dogs."

Careful Jimbo. Mark is weaving across the line between being a police detective and best friend. The last thing you want is to get hit by the oncoming car.

DIME was right. This conversation felt different. Melrose wouldn't give Briggs the benefit of the doubt like Mark would. As chief of detectives, Melrose was all about boosting his solve rates, according to Larson.

"Mark, don't worry about it. I've got nothing to hide. I'll do it. Just tell me when."

"Tomorrow at 10?"

"I'll be there."

"Let's order another round, drain a little tension from your shoulders, give that giant detective brain of yours a rest."

"Helen and I are getting serious," Larson offered, changing the subject. He was pushing off his suspicions about Helen. He hoped that neither she nor Briggs were guilty of anything other than helping the dogs of the homeless. But he would not allow himself to believe Helen was involved. As much as it might hurt to consider, he would prefer that Briggs take the fall—if that's where the evidence led.

"Meaning what, exactly, Larson? Come clean."

"I'm going to propose."

"Detective. Husband. Father. All three titles fit those broad shoulders well," Briggs said.

"Easy, Briggs. The Detective title is good. Husband sounds okay. Don't push the father thing."

"I didn't realize Helen was eager to jump into another marriage. Her husband died not that long ago. Did she tell you she wants to get remarried?"

"No, we haven't discussed marriage, children, or buying a home together or even living together,"

"What's the rush to get married?"

Larson took a sip of beer and looked directly at Briggs and mumbled, "She's the one."

"I hope you know what you're doing, Larson? She may be the one, but marriage seems a long way off."

"Has Helen said something to you, Briggs?"

"No, I guess I'm being protective, cautious. You don't want to drive her away."

"I get your point. I'll think about it."

"No secrets between you and Helen then," Briggs blurted.

"What do you mean secrets?"

Oops, Jimbo, you may have just stepped in a pile of shit.

Briggs quickly recovered. "Secrets people share like how many people they've slept with; if they have ever cheated on a spouse or significant other."

Briggs could have revealed Helen's trauma. But it wasn't his truth to tell.

"Another?" Briggs asked, holding up his empty glass.

"Thanks, Jimmy. But I need to get some sleep. Honestly, making you—my best friend—the focus of a murder investigation exhausts me."

"No problem, buddy. And hey," Briggs said, then waiting until Larson brought his head up and their eyes met. "It's not a problem. I've got nothing to hide. I might even help with the solution. Maybe Melrose will squeeze out some information I hadn't thought to share."

Larson seemed to brighten. They fist-bumped, and Briggs offered to pay the bill. "Take off Mark, I'll pay this check."

"Wait a minute, Briggs. You offering to pay? That's suspicious. You're always rushing off to client emergencies, sticking me with the check."

"I confess," Briggs said, stopping for effect. Larson looked confused. "I am going to stay behind, catch up on my email, and have one more brewski. And don't worry, detective, I won't drink and drive. Remember, I live nearby and have no clients tonight. Helen is covering for me."

Larson could not help smiling, then turned and headed out the door. "Later, Jimmy."

When Larson was out the door, Briggs expelled a massive lungful of air. He didn't realize he had been holding his breath as Mark was leaving.

Stay focused, Jimbo. No evidence exists that you are involved.

DIME was right. Police would find no DNA or witnesses. Just some dog collars in Briggs's pet cemetery. By now, the river would have carried the remains of homeless victims to the ocean.

For the first time since Melrose assigned Mark the case, Briggs wasn't so sure. He needed to talk to Helen.

***

It was nearly 7 pm when Briggs arrived back at Heavenly Considerations. He had called Helen and asked her to hang around. He wanted to fill her in on his conversation with Mark.

When he arrived back at the office, Helen handed him a beer. "It's still happy hour," Helen declared. They clinked glasses, and Helen said, "Here's to old-fashioned frontier justice, like Have Gun—Will Travel. Which one of us is Paladin?"

"I think you would get the starring role, don't you?" Briggs said.

Jimbo, I'm proud of you. And Helen, too, even though I can't tell her.

Briggs wasn't proud of himself or Helen. They had killed five human beings: Helen out of revenge and Briggs out of his sense of humanity. However, Briggs understood that in the eyes of the law, it didn't matter that he had euthanized Maxine humanely, granting her wish the day she had her drug meltdown and urged God to take her. He was not licensed to offer her death with dignity under Oregon State Laws governing assisted suicide. Revenge would never hold up as a defense for Helen, no matter what Little Bobby and company had done to her. And Briggs was complicit in Helen's acts.

"Briggs, Mark is all over this case. It's weird sleeping with him and having him offer details of his investigation. Which is going nowhere. He's desperate to find a clue, but there is nothing to find. Imagine if he knew we were involved. Ironic, don't you think?"

"Listen, when Mark and I met earlier, he asked me to come in for an interview with his boss, Chief Melrose. I'm guessing Melrose is doing it as a favor to Mark since Mark and I are friends and doesn't want to be grilling me."

"Are you nervous?"

"Should I be? I think we are both in the clear. There is nothing to find."

"Good luck with your interview," said Helen, who put down her beer and took Briggs' hand in both of hers. "I love you, Jimmy. I know putting down Maxine was difficult. And knowing you, you'll fret about it for a long time. I honestly think you performed an act of kindness. And Maxine was grateful."

Briggs teared up. "Thanks, Helen," he said.

She moved closer, then leaned in to kiss him. Briggs didn't resist. She always made him feel better.

Helen sat back in her chair and said, "If I hear anything from Mark that might help you, I'll text or call you later tonight. Probably late. He and I have our date night. Usually, there is more touching than talking, but I know he feels frustrated by his lack of progress in the case, and no doubt will want to talk afterward."

***

The intercom on Michael Melrose's desk buzzed, and he hit the receive button.

"There's a gentleman at the desk, a Dr. Briggs, who says he has an appointment with you."

"I'll come out and get him," said Melrose, who decided a chat in a conference room would be more productive than putting Briggs in an interview room. "Dr. Briggs," Melrose said, as he reached out to shake hands, looking up at the man who nearly towered over him by a foot. "Nice to meet you. Come on back. I've reserved a conference room."

"Coffee?"

"Sure," Briggs said. "Black is fine."

"That's the way I like it, too."

When they arrived at the conference room, Melrose dropped the shades on the side adjoining the detective work area and slid the "in use" sign in place.

Melrose set down his mug and grabbed another, put a French roast pod in the Keurig, and waited for it to finish, then carried it over to the table.

"I noticed that all your mugs have dog breeds on them," Briggs said.

"That's my doing. I'm a big dog lover. Since I'm the boss, I figured I should make the choice. The staff hasn't complained."

"Dr. Briggs, may I call you Jim?"

"Sure."

"Did Detective Larson tell you why we invited you in this morning?"

"Because I'm a suspect in Mark's missing person case?"

"Partly true," said Melrose. "Think of it this way: we have five homeless people and their dogs missing, and the only obvious connection between their disappearance is you."

"I know you and Mark are friends, which is complicating the case for him. So, he asked me to talk to you. If nothing else, you might have some insights to help us solve the damn thing."

"I am recording this because it's standard procedure," said Melrose. "To be honest, I told Mark that you are a person of interest. Which means, as far as we can tell, you are connected because you provide free care to their dogs. So, think of this as a conversation, rather than inquisition. First, tell me about your business and how you got into it."

Briggs spent the next ten minutes giving Melrose a rundown of his time in Chicago, the death of his mother and return to Portland, and the launch of Have Paws—Will Travel and Heavenly Considerations.

"My mother regularly volunteered at downtown homeless shelters, serving food, and helping clean up. In her will, she asked that I use some of my inheritance to give back to the community, and suggested I help the dogs of the homeless."

Without Melrose asking, Briggs offered, "She left me her mortgage-free townhouse in the Pearl District, which last sold for $1.2 million, and nearly $1.3 million in investments. My business launch was well funded."

Briggs explained that his colleague Helen Williams was also a veterinarian. She was helping him manage his businesses, which included about 100 wealthy paying clients and 50 homeless clients with dogs who got free care.

"That's a lot of people to manage."

Chief Detective Melrose asked the next obvious question, which he had not seen in any of Larson's updates. "How do you keep track of the homeless when they run all over the place? It's a big city."

"PupFinder."

"What's that."

"It's a dot-com based company with hardware and software to track pets," Briggs explained.

"I have added a GPS tag to each of the dog collars I give the homeless. I have registered their tags with PupFinder. Anytime I want to find a dog, I launch the app which shows a tiny white dog symbol over a city map. I can tap on the dog symbol and feed it into my phone and get the exact location, and use navigation to take me right there."

"Do your homeless clients know you are tracking them?"

"Technically, I'm tracking their dogs. They never ask. The free collar is a valuable thing for them. They won't want to risk losing their dog by questioning the ethics."

"Is it ethical?" Melrose asked.

"Tracking an individual with a GPS device without their permission is against the law, as I'm sure you know. I did the research."

"Is it ethical?" Briggs repeated.

Briggs wanted to challenge Melrose. Ask him when he quit being a detective and started being an ethicist.

Briggs thought about it for a minute and said, "I realize it's splitting hairs, but the homeless are so poor and have so many needs, including caring for their beloved canines, I believe practicality trumps everything else."

Melrose could see the pieces coming together: missing homeless, a way to track them, a crematory to burn up their bodies, and dog euthanasia drugs to kill them. Briggs had the means to make them go missing, but no apparent motive.

"Jim, do you like homeless people?"

"Some. They are a mixed bag, like those who aren't homeless: you find the good, bad, and ugly. People like Little Bobby McWhorter, who pretends to be the mayor of R2D2, can be an obnoxious. Others, like Maxine Reid, can be grouchy and angry one minute, then funny and likable the next."

"I would have a hard time thinking anything that meth addict said or did could be likable," said Melrose.

"You'd be surprised," said Briggs. "I've been researching her family and discovered she comes from a Scottish clan, including an aunt who agreed to take her in, get her off the street."

Now you put your foot in your mouth, Jimbo. Maxine's gone for good. Calling attention to her puts one more nail in your coffin.

Briggs ignored his internal warning. "I had hoped I could reunite Maxine with her family. I recently talked to her Aunt Daisy in Denver, who said she would take Maxine in. Maxine talked to Daisy for nearly an hour and said there was no way you could live drug-free with her dog in a nice suburban home."

Melrose's look hardened. He sat up straight, scanning Briggs's face for signs of deception.

"She's one of the missing," he said finally.

Briggs didn't look surprised, but didn't show any signs of deception either, Melrose thought.

Instead, Briggs raised his eyebrows and shrugged his shoulders.

"Chief Melrose, the homeless wander all over the city. They will disappear for a few weeks and then show up again at their old haunts. Who knows where they go."

"Could you try to locate some of those we are talking about with PupFinder?" Melrose asked.

Briggs could have pulled his laptop out of his messenger bag and located any of the missing if they were still alive and their dogs had been wearing their collars. Briggs knew Buster's collar, still active, was at Heavenly Considerations. He would have to get back to the office and destroy the GPS tag so it wouldn't appear in PupFinder.

"I don't have my laptop with me," Larson lied. "When I get back to the office, I'll run a check and call you with a location if I have one."

"That would be great, Jim."

Melrose had heard all he needed. Instead of excusing Briggs, he launched into a discussion about his dog's skin and digestive problems. A half-hour later, Melrose stood up, thanked Briggs for coming, and escorted him to the front door. The two men shook hands.

"I'll call you in the next hour about the location of Maxine's dog."

"Thanks, Jim."

Briggs let out a sigh of relief, then felt a wave of panic wash over him.

He needed to destroy Buster's collar ASAP. He and Helen needed to destroy all five collars, which included the four Helen had removed from her victims' dogs.

Briggs texted a 9-1-1 to Helen and said, "Urgent we meet."

He and Helen figured they were safe from getting caught, with no identifiable DNA from the cremated remains of homeless bodies. However, existence of the collars with the GPS chips, Briggs realized, were enough circumstantial evidence to sentence them to life in prison.

***

Larson saw Briggs leave the bureau's main conference room with Chief Melrose.

Instead of stiff goodbyes, Larson heard them laughing but avoided showing his face. Instead, he waited for Briggs to leave, then walked into Melrose's office.

"So, what did you think, Chief?"

"I think you have more work to do," Melrose concluded.

"Did you find out anything useful, Chief?"

"Probably just the clue you need to put an end to this case," Melrose tossed out.

"What are you talking about?"

"Larson, did you ever think to ask Briggs how he keeps track of his homeless clients' dogs?"

Larson looked puzzled.

"He visits homeless camps, places like R2D2."

"Guess again."

"I give up, Chief."

"He attaches a GPS chip to the dog collars he gives them and uses an App called PupFinder to track them on his laptop. He can log in and see where every dog is, with the likelihood their owner will be right there with them."

"I just found out about that yesterday," Larson confessed. "I called Briggs, and he said he would help."

"If we had known about this at the beginning of your investigation, we could have put this case to bed," said Melrose.

Larson sank in his chair opposite Melrose. He closed his eyes and waited for the inevitable words, "You're an incompetent Larson, you're fired. Turn in your badge and leave the station immediately."

Why the hell hadn't Briggs told him about PupFinder?

"Chief, I want to bounce something off you. Might sound crazy, but I'm already deep in a hole on this case, so things can't get any worse."

Melrose put down the desk cleaner that had turned him from hoarder to clean freak.

"I'm listening, Larson."

Larson shared his theory that Briggs might think he could solve homelessness the way veterinarians eliminate more than a million dogs a year who aren't adopted: they euthanize them and use drugs similar to those used to kill Death Row prisoners. And he noted Briggs' reference to the homeless as 'strays,' like stray dogs that are homeless.

"That is twisted," Melrose agreed.

"Chief, I want to get his drug supply records and see if his barbiturate purchases are in line with industry practice. A friend over at Lynch Martin Animal Hospital will help me out."

"Larson, you're going to have to ask Briggs for his records. We have no evidence of a crime or suspicion that would justify a court order."

"I'll ask him."

"Larson, sit down for a minute. You seem antsy. That's not like you. You usually seem relaxed."

"I'm pissed at myself for not being more thorough, for knowing about the tracking software. I'm also working hard to make sure I don't let my friendship with Briggs impede my police work."

"Dig some more, Detective Larson. Are there other suspects you might have overlooked? Go over the case files again. Talk to Kim Jansen. She may be Briggs' girlfriend, but she's also a good cop, an honest cop. You two can figure it out." Melrose stopped for a minute and looked off into space. The coziness of Briggs to his investigator and Jansen made him feel uncomfortable. Having two reliable cops so close to the only suspect, was reassuring.

Melrose picked up some notes in front of him. They were tips for taking care of Melrose's dog. He and Briggs talked a lot about canine care after the interview. Not very professional, of course. But a welcome break for Melrose who felt Briggs was innocent.

Larson stood at the door, waiting for Melrose to speak.

"You might also check out your girlfriend," Melrose instructed. "She has access to the same drugs, the same crematory, and interacts with the homeless, same as Briggs."

Larson closed his eyes, put his face in his hands, and rubbed his temples. His head was throbbing.

"You okay, Larson?"

"Just peachy," Larson said sarcastically.

"Good. Get out and go detect. We need to finish up this case and move on."

Larson looked up at Melrose, who was back buffing his desktop — already gleaming — to a shine.

"I'm on it," said Larson as he turned and headed out the door.

"Fuck," he said to himself. "My best friend is a suspect, and my boss wants me to check out my girlfriend to see if we might connect her to the missing. It's a real shit-show."

CHAPTER TWENTY-EIGHT

"Jim, it's Mark."

"Hey, pal. What's going on?"

"Chief Melrose said you two had a pleasant talk. However, he has asked me to follow up on a couple of items: the location of Maxine's dog, Buster, and your permission to look at your drug supply records."

"Larson, why would you want to look at my drug supply records?"

Larson looked down into his hands, closed his eyes, and rubbed his face. He was stalling.

"To compare the amount of barbiturate you order to number of dogs you euthanize."

"Mark, this is getting to be ridiculous. You tell me I'm not a suspect but keep coming back to my business looking for answers. I don't get it."

"Blame Melrose," said Larson. "I'm following his orders. He thinks you're a saint but won't let any stone go unturned. He would tell you it's routine."

Briggs let it go, moving to Mark's request for the location of the dogs of the missing.

"Buster has disappeared off the radar, like a plane in the Bermuda Triangle. And no one has seen Maxine. I also ran location checks on dogs of the other people missing in your case. None of the dog collars are active."

"What does that mean?"

"It means the collars have been removed from the dogs and the trackers disabled, or the GPS batteries have gone bad. That's not likely. They are guaranteed for 10 years."

"Can you tell when they went silent?"

"No, I just can tell if they are switched on or off."

"Damn," said Larson, his frustration coming over the phone line.

"Hey Briggs, why didn't you tell me about the PupFinder App sooner?"

"I don't remember you asking how I kept in touch with the homeless. Helen uses it all the time, so she knew. Kim has been with me when I'm using it. No secret."

Larson dropped back into his seat, defeated. "Sorry. Melrose got on my case about it. He said we could have used the knowledge weeks ago to determine if any of the missing homeless had moved."

"Mark, I don't want to be critical of you. But this seems a little desperate. Still, I'll give my supplier the okay."

***

A few hours later, Detective Larson had a complete supply of everything used at Have Paws—Will Travel and had made an appointment with Jennifer Limm, DVM, to look over the records. Dr. Limm, co-owner of Lynch Martin Animal Hospital, had a sterling reputation as a veterinary surgeon. She also was Larson's former girlfriend. When he arrived at Lynch Martin, the receptionist seated him outside Limm's office. He had to wait nearly an hour after arriving for a 3 pm appointment with Dr. Limm while she finished up an emergency surgery.

"Detective Larson, please come with me," Limm said coolly, unconcerned she had forgotten to remove her surgical gown, which was covered with blood. She saw him scanning her from head to foot. "You like this look, Detective Larson?"

"Sorry, there is a lot of blood. I meant to change before I came out."

"Did the dog survive?"

"He did, despite considerable blood loss, multiple fractures, and internal injuries. We've been operating for hours. It involved three surgeons, including a canine ophthalmologist who removed a ruptured eye."

Larson cringed. "Spare me the details," he said.

After stripping off the surgical gown, she hurried across the room, grabbed Larson, and hugged him.

As she wrapped her arms around him, she cooed, "Have you come to arrest me, Detective Larson? You know how much I enjoy wearing your handcuffs." An old joke. Neither of them was into bondage.

Larson shifted gears.

"I need you to look at a few documents and give me a professional opinion. I am working on a case involving several missing homeless, and a local veterinarian who may have something to do with their disappearance."

"Are you talking about stray dogs or human strays?"

"There's that term again: referring to homeless people as strays."

"You shouldn't be so surprised at the comparison since we deal with so many homeless stray dogs. I know it's not politically correct. But they live on the streets. What are you looking for?"

"Drugs used for euthanasia. I can't tell you who these are for," Larson added before she noticed the blacked-out name.

She scanned the sheets, looking mainly at injectables.

"Looks about right for a busy vet practice."

"The person in question has about 100 clients, picks up dead and injured dogs for the city, and cares for the dogs of the homeless at no cost. Euthanasia is a routine part of the job."

"So you're talking about Jim Briggs."

"I guess there's no way to disguise the person of interest in this case."

"Jim Briggs is a person of interest? Give me a break, Mark. Really?" She picked up the sheets and examined them. "Are you suggesting Jim Briggs is using veterinary drugs to kill homeless people?"

"Yes. Maybe. I don't know. He is the only link to all the victims."

"Victims? I thought they were missing persons."

"It's complicated. My boss thinks it's odd that this one group of homeless has gone missing. Four of them were part of a gang of homeless predators. They were feared throughout the homeless community for preying on the weakest among them."

"That could be something to consider, I guess," she said, unconvinced. Jennifer picked up the 10-page list and scanned the columns. "Our industry is highly regulated. The law doesn't allow much room to game the system. Records of euthanized animals have to match up with drug orders. Of course, you can fudge the records the same way you can in any industry. I see nothing out of the ordinary. These drugs have a short shelf life and can become outdated quickly, and we accidentally drop and break the vials routinely. So, while there is close monitoring, state regulators can only do so much. To make a comparison, you need to measure the supply against the number of animals euthanized. I don't see that information here."

"I don't have that," Larson admitted. Another screw up, Larson thought. "Thanks, Jennifer." They hugged.

"I miss you, Larson."

"I miss you, too, Jenny. We seem to be out of sync. I break up and you have a boyfriend. You break up and I'm going with someone." He knew he could not have Helen as his girlfriend with someone on the side, as tempting as Jennifer might be.

He was about to leave the Limm's office when she said, "I believe Helen O'Donnell is working for Briggs. She also is a veterinarian. Did you look at her records?" Larson stopped. He squinted at Limm, trying to focus on her words. "Did you say, O'Donnell?"

"Yes, Helen came here to discuss a position as a veterinarian, then backed out. I'm not sure why. Her application used her maiden name, which is on her veterinary license. It lists her as Helen (Williams) O'Donnell. I recently heard that she had joined Jim Briggs' practice. But she'll have her own supply list of prescriptions as a licensed veterinarian."

Larson suddenly had an uneasy feeling. Why hadn't Helen mentioned her maiden name? But why would she? He knew he hadn't asked her about it. Briggs' purchase records were a dead end. Helen's maiden name is O'Donnell. Was there any reason to believe Helen was a person of interest or that her records would be any different? The evidence was thin.

CHAPTER TWENTY-NINE

July 30, 2019

Mark returned to the police bureau office and began scribbling a summary of case facts:

-Regular contact with homeless and dogs: Williams and Briggs

-The same panties that Williams wears were found at the abandoned campsite.

-Van and dark clothed figure helping a big man into a van (note: witness said she saw what looked like paws on the side of the van, but said it was very dark out; Briggs and Williams regularly give vitamin shots? But in the middle of the night?

-O'Flaherty was in the van with Williams getting a vitamin shot around the time he disappeared.

-Williams and Briggs have access to drugs to kill animals and humans.

-No bodies

-No sign of foul play

-Motive: Little Bobby and Gang were predators. Plenty of reasons and victims.

(How did Maxine fit in?)

Note: what motive could Briggs and Williams have?

-DNA on panties–still waiting

Larson grabbed his list and marched over to Chief Detective Melrose's office. The door opened just as he was reaching for the handle.

"Hi Detective Larson," said Lt. Marty Simpson, department consultant for management improvement, and Melrose's apparent new girlfriend.

"Hi, Lt. Simpson. I just need a few minutes with the Chief."

"We just finished up," she said, straightening her uniform jacket. "Go right in. I've got an appointment up on the fifth floor."

She turned and said goodbye to Chief Melrose, in a sweet, flirty voice. "Michael—I mean Chief Melrose—keep up the outstanding work."

Somehow Larson felt keeping her happy was Melrose's new full-time job. Which was okay, since the chief of detectives had been in a better mood for the past few weeks. Could this help with Larson's request?

"Come in, Mark," Melrose said, obviously still spellbound by his new friend. Melrose never called him by his first name.

"Chief, I want to run something by you. I have reviewed the files, pulled together key discoveries, and re-read my interviews. Williams and Briggs, as we've said, are right in the middle of everything. But everything they are doing is normal operating procedure. Today, I got back the DNA from the panties. It was a very good sample, but the none of our databases could identify the person wearing them."

"Get on with it, Larson, I'm in a good mood, but my patience is thin."

"Do you remember the case of the Golden State Killer, who was tracked down by genetic genealogists?"

"An amazing piece of work," Melrose said.

"It was," said Larson. "The genealogists used public DNA databases to trace the killer to a particular family, including a long list of cousins. The detectives in the case traced it to one individual, who turned out to be the killer."

"I want to submit my DNA sample to Parabon NanoLabs for analysis. They could very well help us solve the case, discover the motive, and make a bunch of links we need to solve this case."

Larson told him the cost, $4,000, and waited for an answer.

"That's a chunk of money. I'm feeling good, and I want you to solve this case. I'll approve the expenditure."

"I'll get on it right now," Larson responded. He was suddenly standing tall, shoulders back, a grin on his face. Damn right, he was going to solve this case.

"But what if Helen's family name, O'Donnell, came back as a match?

Larson slumped in his chair. He leaned forward and put his face flat on the desk, banging his head on the surface again and again. Things could not get any worse, could they?

CHAPTER THIRTY

August 1, 2019

The next afternoon, Briggs and Helen were sitting in Adirondack Chairs at his getaway, watching the windsurfers streaking across the Columbia River.

Both of them sat quietly, watching kite surfers sail over wind-whipped waves.

Helen reached out and put her hand on top of Briggs's hand.

You never forget your first girl, right, Jimbo? Like the slogan on St. Pauli Girl beer bottles.

He would never forget Helen, his first. How could he? Helen, still beautiful, was sitting right next to him. She sent his pulse racing. The warmth of her presence stirred old memories and better times.

Briggs had been a late bloomer. Frustrated by "near misses." He and a high school buddy each promised to get laid by the end of the summer before entering college. Bad enough to suffer the indignities of freshman-hood, but to add the title of "virgin" at 18, going on 19, was humiliation. His friend, who had traveled cross-country to Martha's Vineyard for the summer, had met a girl with the same goal, setting off a summer-long sex fest. No such luck for Briggs. He would be 20 when he met Helen. Then it was "Katy bar the door." But not in a bad way. Helen lost her virginity at 16 and found she had an insatiable appetite to try anything new. Including new guys. Lucky for her, she escaped a reputation because she picked the quiet types, like Briggs, who didn't feel it necessary to boast about notches on their bedroom wall.

Briggs was the beneficiary of Helen's experience and never told a soul. Now they were colleagues, former lovers—and some might say—cold-blooded killers. How else would you describe two people who conspired to kill five people and cover it up?

"How long before Mark figures this out and locks us up?" Briggs said.

"Gee, you're a party-pooper, Briggs. My mind had jumped back to happier times when you and I were together in college and then the early days of my marriage to Rod. After I lost the baby, Rod and I both seemed lost."

The weight of the tragedy appeared to be smothering Helen. She took a deep breath and let it out, then another—working hard to get air into her lungs.

"The end of our marriage was in sight," she said, her eyes filling with tears.

Helen wiped her eyes, then brightened, "On the morning of Rod's death we made love, kissed each other goodbye, realizing we had found our way out of the abyss and back into the light. The future was a blinding light of hope. Then he was gone. And here we are."

"We need to agree on where we are," said Briggs. "Mark could be your future. Kim is definitely in mine. What we tell them or don't tell them will have consequences for the rest of our lives."

Dreams of warm memories turned to the cold reality of life in prison—or worse yet—Death Row for one of them, or both.

"I'm no detective," said Helen, "I feel like these months with Mark, listening to how he analyzes his work, has given me insight into the man."

"Let me summarize," she said. "The DNA is destroyed. Mark has no evidence of a crime. If someone stumbled on your pet cemetery, they would find a single grave marker with name Patches. We could pull the marker off the grave and no one would ever find it. If they do, they will find five dog collars. That could be decades from now when the trees in your backyard are cut and the stumps drug out. The collars alone would mean nothing to anyone.

"Plus, I'm sleeping with Mark, and he tells me everything going on in his head and with the case," Helen added. "Just relax. The human remains are making their way to the ocean in the Columbia River as we speak."

When they dumped the remains of Hoffman, McWhorter, and O'Flaherty into the river from a grassy little pull-out on the Washington side of the Columbia River, Helen silently offered a "Good riddance motherfuckers." Killing them had released her anger.

Maxine Reid's ashes had been lovingly scattered into the Columbia River as Briggs offered some final words. "You finally got your wish for God to take you, Max. Sleep well tonight and for all time."

Betty's remains also got a river sendoff. Briggs said a few words, while Helen remained silent. She had no regrets about killing Betty, and could not stop herself from feeling anger about the woman who left her for Little Bobby and company to savage. Betty, who Helen considered an accomplice, got a gentle death. Riddled with cancer, her death was kinder and gentler than suffering the pain as cancer finally overwhelmed her.

Briggs took a pull on his beer and watched the windsurfers battling the wild waves on the river below him. On most weekends, he would ride with them, skimming across the water.

Today, he imagined Maxine Reid taking her wind-whipped ride—this one for the ages.

"Jimmy, come with me," Helen urged as she grabbed his hand. He knew what she wanted, and he knew they shouldn't, as colleagues and employee-employer. And both in relationships with other people who were lovers and best friends. The pressure and stress of Helen and Briggs dealing with the homeless had fractured the norms. Briggs did not resist.

Their lovemaking was a part celebration and part catharsis. Each had accomplished their goals, as perverse as they were.

They were still lying in bed when Helen's phone came to life.

"Hey, Mark, what's happening?" Barely recovered from their sex, and conflicted by their betrayal, she revealed none of her genuine emotions to Larson.

"Helen, where are you? I'm at Heavenly Considerations, and there is no one here. The door was unlocked and partly open, so I went in thinking I would find you."

"Must be the cleaning crew," said Helen. "This is the third time this month they finished and left the door open. Do me a favor and check it out, then lock it up for us."

"No problem."

"Briggs and I are at his place in the Gorge, drinking beer and watching the windsurfers. Come join us. Stay the night."

"Wish I could, but got to work this weekend. The case of the missing homeless has expanded to five. Capt. Melrose worries something else is going on—like one of those serial killers who victimize prostitutes and never get caught."

"You think your missing persons are victims of a serial killer?" Helen asked.

Briggs rolled over and propped himself up on his elbow. He had a look of concern on his face. A pang of panic gripped his chest.

"No, I think this is a waste of time," said Larson.

"Mark, we've talked about this before, but I'm still mystified why this case is so important that Portland Police Bureau is assigning a homicide detective full-time to investigate," Helen said. "They go missing all the time. No big woop."

"You and I agree," he repeated. "Makes no sense."

What Larson didn't share was the worm of doubt burrowing into his brain: Briggs and Helen cared for the missing men and their dogs. Helen wore Agent Provocateur underwear like they found in Jerry Hoffman's tent. The idea Briggs and Williams might be involved—even though there was no evidence—made him nauseous. He was doubly troubled by contact with Helen the week before in front of Starburst Donuts. She was in the van with O'Flaherty, about to give him a shot. She said it was a vitamin shot—that explanation from a veterinarian skilled in euthanizing animals. What motive would Helen have for killing a bum like O'Flaherty? Yes, he was a member of Little Bobby's gang terrorizing other homeless and evading the law, but what else was new. Helen had nothing to do with any of that. After she hung up, she turned to Briggs. "Ready for a rematch, Jimmy?"

Briggs smiled at her.

"None of this little celebration gets back to Kim or Mark, right Briggs? No getting weak-kneed in a moment of ecstasy with Kim and confessing. The aftermath wouldn't be pretty. You have to take it to your grave."

"Right," he said.

With Larson digging in, Jimbo, that might be sooner than you think.

The thought jolted Briggs. DIME was right. A picture of walking down the green mile filled his mind.

"Let's enjoy the moment," said Helen.

"Helen, I started this journey to help the city eliminate homelessness—put the terminal homeless out of their misery by connecting them to family, not killing them. But after failing to get Maxine and her aunt together, I realized how naïve I have been about improving the lives of Portland's homeless. It's hopeless."

"Think of it this way, Jimmy. We both have achieved our goals. You provided a gentle send off for Maxine. She would have died soon, anyway."

"Besides, dogs are like family to the homeless," she said. "Keeping their dogs halfway healthy is a humanitarian act itself."

If he were honest with himself, he felt nothing but joy for Helen, and for helping Maxine.

You did good, Jimbo. You rescued Maxine and, with Little Bobby's gang gone, the other homeless human strays are safer.

Briggs listened, then dived into another round of love-making with Helen.

***

Larson ended his call with Helen and, as promised, walked around the building to make sure no one was inside and nothing was out of place.

He quickly located the furnace where they cremated dogs and walked through a thick, insulated door. He expected it to be cold, like the rest of the space under the metal roof with no insulation. Instead, a rush of warm air surrounded him. The room was still cooling down from a cremation. The furnace, the room, and floors were immaculate, like the cleanroom in a silicon wafer factory.

He left the crematory and wandered into what appeared to be a storage area. Lining one shelf were heavy, foot-long boxes. Helen had labeled half of them with the names of veterinary clinics. Out of curiosity, he picked up a box identified only with a number and letters and shook it. Heavy, he thought. He opened the top and looked inside. It was filled with fine ash. He had no idea how much cremated remains for a dog weighed. Nothing was alarming about the unlabeled box. Could the ashes be Jerry Hoffman's remains? He pushed aside the thought. No one was in the building, and nothing had been disturbed. It impressed him how organized everything appeared to be.

It was so spic and span he smiled at the thought Melrose's new girlfriend, Lt. Marty Simpson, might be Briggs's organizational guru.

As he headed for the door, his eyes swept the room and he spotted the Have Paws—Will Travel van.

He walked over and stopped to look it over, then did a walk-around. It was huge. He wondered what was inside. Should he look? Was it an invasion of privacy? He didn't have a warrant. But no one had been accused of a crime. He was doing a security check for his friend Jim Briggs and his colleague, Helen Williams, Larson's girlfriend.

Larson opened the side door and surveyed the interior. It looked like a doctor's procedure room with an examination table, surgical gloves, a box on the wall for used syringes, a supply cabinet with bandages, a locked glass-front refrigerator with drugs, and a large metal storage bin, over six feet long, attached to the wall on the passenger side.

He opened the metal bin. It was clean and cool with an odor of disinfectant, like you might find in a hospital. He knew it was where Briggs and Williams put dog corpses.

Could a human body fit in the space?

He stopped himself from going there, making himself crazy over the case of the missing homeless.

Did he think Helen and Briggs were killing homeless people, transporting him to Heavenly Considerations and cremating them, then dumping their remains?

He tried to push his mind away from the chilling thought. Larson was about to close the door when he spotted a faint outline of tiny paw prints on a three-foot-long patch of dark green carpet just inside the sliding side door.

Should he take a sample? Probably not, but decided to, anyway. He would never get another chance to get an up-close look at Briggs' operation without a warrant.

He went out to his car, opened the trunk, and pulled out a pair of sterile gloves, and a plastic baggie to hold the sample, then returned to the van.

He pulled out his Swiss Army Knife, which included a pair of scissors, and trimmed off a tiny piece of carpet fiber, and then scraped some dark material into the collection bag, along with the fiber.

Larson put the sample in his pocket, walked out the front door, and locked it, double-checking to make sure it was secure.

On his way into the office, he put a rush on the DNA sample. This time, he would do it first and ask permission later. If Melrose didn't like it, he could dock Larson's pay.

Once and for all, Larson hoped, he could rule out Briggs and Williams as suspects.

CHAPTER THIRTY-ONE

August 3, 2019

At the end of a 10-hour day for both of them, Briggs and Jansen met at his townhouse for a date. Unlike their lunch quickies and long weekends under the covers, there was no rush to the bedroom. Neither had the energy to do more than lift a beer and talk about the day. Instead, they flopped down on Briggs' sofa, shoulders rubbing. The evening news was playing in the background. Top news items of the day: a new virus was spreading in China and the stock market was hitting new highs. Briggs put the TV on mute and put his arm around Jansen, pulling her in for a hug.

"Babe, how was your day?"

Kim plunged into a discussion, from a cop's perspective, about city woes. She also listened intently to Briggs's day, which was mostly routine, like hers, but with occasionally interesting dog stories to share. The remote still in Briggs' hand, he switched off the television and ordered Siri to play some chill music. "Turn around and look at me," she said.

The mood was just right for the tense conversation about to take place.

"How long have we been together, Briggs?" Kim's bright blue eyes pierced him like a spear of ice. Impaled, he could not look away. She was not smiling, just searching his face, watching his eyes for signs of lying—her police training.

"Is this a test?"

"Just answer the question, Briggs."

You screwed up again, Jimbo. Like your mom used to say, "You can do better."

"Better than what?" Briggs thought.

Briggs drew back a few inches as Kim's gaze intensified. She continued watching for telltale signs of evasion, like blinking, narrowing of the irises, squirming, hand wringing, or fidgeting. She saw none.

"You know the answer to that," Briggs challenged.

"You're evading the question, Dr. Briggs."

When Kim was serious, she referred to him as Dr. Briggs, by his last name, like she would a suspect.

"Kim, this feels like an interrogation. Don't you think I know the answer?"

"It's Sergeant Jansen to you. I'm serious. You're stalling."

"Kimmy dear, you're my best friend and soul mate. We've hardly been apart since we met. How could I not know the answer to that question?"

Kim raised her eyebrows, waiting for an answer.

"Okay, Sergeant, I give up," Briggs said and recited the stats she wanted.

"We met April 1 at the meltdown of Maxine Reid, and we have been together 115 days and… let me calculate… 12 hours and 18 minutes. Today is July 24, a week shy of our four-month anniversary."

"That's wasn't so hard, was it, Dr. Briggs?" Kim said, a big smile on her face. "You haven't lost your savant ability to calculate, Jimmy." In an instant, her cop face morphed into her admiring-girlfriend face. Then Kim let loose as if she were a suspect pouring out a confession.

"I have some news to share. I'm pregnant. You're the father. It's a girl. Based on our genetic pool, she'll be a blue-eyed blond or redhead with fair skin. She'll be at least 6 feet tall when she reaches her teens. Her name will be Lily Kimberly Briggs. She will follow in his dad's big footsteps, off to medical or veterinarian school. She'll be discouraged from being a second-generation cop."

"You've thought a lot about this, haven't you?" Briggs responded. Overwhelmed by the news, he asked, "how long have you been pregnant?"

"I'm eight weeks along," she said. This early, she could only guess the gender.

"Why did it take so long to tell me?"

"Because I wasn't sure I wanted the baby. Not because I don't love you, but motherhood has never been one of my life goals. And, miscarriages are common, I learned from talking to my mother."

"Great news, Kimmy. I love you, too. Like you, parenthood wasn't high on my list, but I'm ready for the responsibility. We can do this."

"Kim Mary Jansen, my best friend and love of my life, will you marry me?"

"Don't fuck around Briggs. This is serious. Plus, you've only known me for four months."

"And you're carrying our baby," he countered.

Kim stood up and walked a few feet away. She crossed her arms, frowned, and said, "I'm not some pity case. Poor pregnant girl with no place to go."

"I'm dead serious," said Briggs.

He stood up and walked toward her. "Come here, let me hug you. I'm not doing this out of pity. I'm doing it out of love." He kissed her and her anger melted away.

"I've been thinking about it from the first time I met you. I want you to be my wife."

Kim smiled. She hadn't given marriage much thought, let alone motherhood. It wasn't as if her maternal instincts were kicking in, and she was desperate for a family. Cop life gave her plenty of other things to think about. But now she was sitting in front of her fiancé-to-be James Allen Briggs, all-around good guy, veterinarian, and humanitarian extraordinaire. The question about how long they had been together wasn't a test. She had been afraid to tell him about the baby given how he had cut off other relationships when they wanted to get serious. Still, she knew Briggs was the guy. The pregnancy was the spark that finally lit her fire for commitment.

"I accept."

"That's what I love about you, Kim. You know what you want, and you take it when you get the chance. No hemming or hawing. Okay, it's a deal. Would our four month-anniversary be too soon? That's this coming Saturday."

"I like it," said Kim. "Let's do a simple City Hall wedding with a few friends. How about a week after you accept the Covington Award?"

"Perfect," said Briggs. "But not City Hall. Let's do it at Multnomah Falls."

"Very romantic," Dr. Briggs. "Briggs, let's finish dinner, then go to the bedroom and celebrate."

"I don't know if that is a good idea," said Briggs. "You need to avoid bouncing the baby."

"Bullshit. The baby will be like me: she'll be tough. She'll be fine."

As Kim led him to the bedroom, Briggs made a mental note to call his lawyer to get his will revised. He would make sure he took care of Kim and their unborn daughter financially.

Given what he had done to Maxine, he likely would view his daughter for the first time through prison bars—if not through the thick glass window on Death Row. He had looked up capital punishment in Oregon. He first thought the liberal majority in the state had outlawed it. They had not. Thirty-four inmates were awaiting execution. Would he be number 35?

CHAPTER THIRTY-TWO

August 4, 2019

Larson arrived 10 minutes early for his meeting with Helen at Ovation, his favorite coffee shop. One of the few ninety degree days in Portland, he found a table outside shaded by surrounding condo buildings, next to The Fields Park, where he and Helen could talk. Passing traffic would mute their conversation.

***

Helen was 15 minutes late. After Larson had called the night before and said, "We need to talk. ASAP," she knew something was up. He was neither flirtatious nor friendly. He was 100 per cent deadly serious.

Before coming, she had called Briggs to alert him to the meeting but got his voicemail. Helen did not leave a message. She did not want to alarm him to the possibility that Mark might be closing in on them—or her—as suspects in his case.

When Helen arrived, she plopped heavily in the chair opposite Larson and looked at him. "Sorry, I'm late. I could make an excuse, but I was thinking of not coming. I talked to Jimmy last night, and he said he told you what happened with the three homeless men and the woman who hangs out with them. You're probably going to hate me for being drunk and stupid and putting myself in a danger and what followed." Helen could not get out the words "gang rape."

"Stand up, Helen," said Larson. The command jolted her. She knew he was about to arrest her. Instead of telling her to put her hands behind her back so he could handcuff her, Larson walked over and wrapped his arms around her.

"Briggs told me about Little Bobby's gang attack on you. I feel so bad that I didn't know; I feel like I might have been able to help. I don't know how. But maybe I could have done something."

Helen started sobbing. It was not what she expected. She had expected rejection, recrimination, and a stern warning: "Never call me again."

"Helen, I was drawn to you the first time we met. I'm sure it started as infatuation, but now I feel like we belong together. I know we've only been out a few times, but I also know I'm in love." Helen hugged him tightly and said, "I feel the same. I don't want to live without you." And then Larson began sobbing. They were attracting attention.

"Let's just sit down for a minute," said Larson. "I'll get us two Moroccan lattes, and we can relax and people-watch for a while. We don't have to talk about any of this. Today, we are going to enjoy each other's company, have our coffee, then find another time to talk about Briggs and my case." She wondered if Larson thought Briggs killed them all, as an act of revenge. Or was she the suspect, now? Would he allow himself to believe she had committed any crime, let alone mutilate Little Bobby? No, he would not. He was a cop, but he was in love and he was too nice for his own good. No way he would blame Helen for the disappearance of five people, including Maxine, without a trace. The fact that Maxine was among those missing more than likely put Briggs squarely in Larson's sights. Everyone knew Briggs was on a quest to find a home for Maxine.

When Larson returned with the lattes, Helen's crying had stopped, and she had fixed her make-up. Still, it could not hide her red eyes.

"Maybe we should talk about it today," said Helen.

"No way," he said, backing off the push for an interview after Helen said she loved him. "Next week will be soon enough. My case will probably end up in a cold case box for several years the way things are going."

Larson wanted the whole thing to go away, despite discovering Helen had a powerful motive for killing the missing men. Larson could tell Melrose everything checked out; he found nothing to substantiate a murder charge against Helen or Briggs. Would Melrose buy it? Probably not, despite his eagerness to move onto more important investigations. Larson would try.

Helen suddenly realized she had gotten a reprieve. She would not need to confess anything.

"Will I see you at Jim's Covington Award presentation?" Helen asked.

"I wouldn't miss it," said Larson. "It's a big day for Jim." Just then, Larson's phone lit up. "This is Larson, what's up, Chief?". He listened for a minute, then hung up. "Melrose wants me back in the office for a meeting. I need to go." Helen and Larson stood up. They hugged each other again tightly. "It's all going to be okay," he said.

"Thanks," she said, but wondered how anything could be okay ever again, especially if additional evidence turned up linking her and Briggs to the missing homeless. How could he make it just go away? They waved goodbye and walked in opposite directions to their cars.

***

Larson's brain was screaming for a future with Helen, while theories about her helping kill homeless men pierced his heart. He was about to climb into the car and head to the station when his stomach convulsed. He ran to a nearby bush and threw up his lunch and his latte. His universe was collapsing.

***

When Helen finished her meeting with Larson, she headed back to Heavenly Considerations.

She was shaking, her stomach burning as she pulled into the Have Paws—Will Travel office. She spotted Briggs at his desk.

"Jimmy, we need to talk," Helen said, then started crying. "I just met with Mark. He wanted to discuss his case. I think I'm in trouble. I think we are both in trouble."

"I saw you tried to call. What happened?"

"I didn't tell him anything as we agreed," she said. "When he called to set up the meeting, he sounded stressed. When I got there, he let me know he knew about the rape and just hugged me. He told me he loved me. He said we would talk another time. We agreed to meet at your Covington Award ceremony tomorrow. He had mentioned on the phone DNA results had come through. We didn't discuss it. I have to be honest. When Mark called and talked about an interview, it sounded like he wanted me to come down to the station to make it official. Then he changed his mind and moved our meeting to Ovation. Being lovers is impeding his investigation. Making matters worse, this is his first investigation as a homicide detective."

"Helen, I'm sorry I violated your trust by telling Mark about the rape. I know it was your truth to tell or not. But I didn't want him to zero in on you. I figured with Maxine now missing, I would become his target. Doesn't matter if I killed one or all of them. Guilt on one count of first-degree murder would put me on

Death Row or keep me in jail for life. Doesn't matter if I got one life sentence or five. Life is life."

"I'm the one who did it for revenge," Helen pushed back. "You were performing a humanitarian act."

"Doesn't matter because I am now the prime suspect," said Briggs. "The first time I thought about the homeless as strays, like stray dogs—and how veterinarians euthanize more than a million dogs each year—it horrified me. I could not understand how I could harbor such a dark thought. The more I worked with these people, the more I became convinced that a majority of them were going to die horrible deaths on Portland's streets; that euthanasia was a humane way to put them out of their misery. Then I learned about Little Bobby's gang and what they did to you. Something snapped. My hesitation to put Maxine out of her misery began to evaporate."

"Little Bobby and the others got what they deserved," Helen said.

"Yes, they did," Briggs confirmed. "Big Betty should thank you. The addition of Propofol to sedate her was a genuine act of mercy."

"Given what they did to you and others," Briggs added. "I think you were very humane." "Does Kim know what I did?" said Helen.

"No. And she never will. Besides, I just found out she's pregnant, and we are expecting a little girl. And we are getting married this week. A little surprise. You are the first to know. And you're invited. We are still pinning down the date and time."

"Congratulations," said Helen, and hugged Briggs. Her head was suddenly pounding. She missed her chance of having a baby. Rod was dead and Briggs, a man she still loved and had once imagined marrying, would have a wife and baby of his own. He would be locked up for the rest of her life—until the state reauthorized executions.

"Everything has changed for me overnight," said Briggs. "More than ever, I want to be around to take care of my family. So, I want you to listen to me closely: based on what we know about how much circumstantial evidence Mark might have, there is nothing to incriminate us. No witnesses. No bodies. Motive and opportunity, probably. Still, I think a grand jury would consider all the facts and be unable to move the case forward. Even if the ashes had been a clue, Mark would need corroborating evidence. It doesn't exist. The investigation will never find evidence to connect us. The ashes are in the Columbia River on their way out to sea. But even if he ties everything together, I'm the one going down for this, not you. I hope that doesn't happen."

"Briggs, you're all over the map. First you say you're going to take the hit for the team, then you say there is no way you will let it happen because there is no evidence."

"Call it wishful thinking," Briggs said. "Or hope."

"We need to dispose of the dog collars in the pet cemetery," Helen reminded him.

"I will, but they aren't likely to be found anytime soon," said Briggs.

"Now, there is one more thing," admitted Briggs. "Mark said a DNA match came back on a pair of expensive underwear found in Jerry Hoffman's tent. The DNA matched a family in a genealogy database: the O'Donnell Family. And Mark has traced that to you."

"Oh my god," said Helen. "He didn't mention that when we met. He must have held it back. So, he does consider me a suspect. That bastard Hoffman must have kept my underwear as a trophy."

"It's evidence of nothing," said Briggs, except you were Jerry Hoffman's victim. Everything is going to be fine. Just relax. I gotta go. Tomorrow is a big day for Kim and me."

A nice pep talk, Jimbo, but Helen's goose is cooked. Both of you are dead ducks.

"No way," said Briggs. He was having none of DIME's fatalistic pronouncements. Helen would be okay. Briggs was certain everything would turn out well for both of them.

"Goodnight, Jimmy," Helen said as he headed out. "See you tomorrow."

"Helen, it will be okay. Just follow our plan. Say nothing. Admit nothing.

She knew better. Mark now knew she had the means, motive, and opportunity to kill the missing homeless.

"I see only one ending to this case," Helen thought. "It is the final solution."

CHAPTER THIRTY-THREE

August 7, 2019

Richard Rodman, President of the James P. Covington Foundation for Canine Care, stood at the podium shuffling his notes. He looked out at the filled auditorium, waiting for the chatter to subside. As silence filled the room, he thanked attendees for supporting the foundation, then made the expected announcement. "It is my pleasure to introduce our honoree this year for the James P. Covington Companion Animal Care Award, Veterinarian James Allen Briggs." Applause erupted with a standing ovation.

When they settled back in their seats, Rodman began his tribute. "Our Covington Award evaluation panel observed, 'Dr. Briggs is the very definition of compassion, tirelessly caring for the dogs of our city's unsheltered citizens as a free service to the community.' This isn't a lifetime award because Jim Briggs at 34 is still a young man. He has a long life ahead of him and will no doubt continue to distinguish himself with his good works."

With over 200 people observing his reaction, Briggs smiled and nodded his appreciation of Rodman's praise. At the back of the room was Briggs' support network: Mark, Kim, and Helen. UrbanStreet PDX blogger Chuck Grayson was also attending.

"Dr. Briggs' humanity is an example for all of us," Rodman continued. "He has cared for dozens of Portland's homeless companion animals, patching them up, keeping them healthy with vaccinations and food. He has given so much and asked nothing in return. Dr. Briggs is a hero."

A moment later, Briggs stood up, all eyes on him as he rose for his acceptance speech. Between the dais and his 6-feet-6 height, he appeared to be 10-feet tall. The audience of dog care providers and homeless advocates gave him a second standing ovation. "It is a great honor to receive this award. I am happy that I can play a small part in two noble community-wide efforts, caring for homeless animals and assisting the homeless human community.

Thank you so much."

Briggs appreciated the praise but did not for a moment think of himself as a humanitarian. He helped here and there, but was not sure he deserved an award. Still, he gratefully accepted the plaque with a simple photo engraving of dog paws and human footprints, side by side, on a beach. The words "Walk with a Friend" appeared below. It was a beautiful image.

As the meeting broke up, about two dozen members of the audience surrounded Briggs to shake hands and thank him. He spoke to each one and then watched as the auditorium cleared out except for his friends.

Kim Jansen walked across the room and asked, "You're not getting cold feet, are you?"

"Not on your life," he whispered back. "Tomorrow we'll officially be the Jansen-Briggs Family." Kim smiled at the thought of marriage and a baby.

Mark Larson gave Briggs a fist bump and said, "Marriage and a kid on the way. I'm proud of you, buddy. Wish I could hang out with you this afternoon, but I have a pile of paperwork to wrap up so I can take the day off for your wedding. And don't worry, I won't forget the ring."

Williams gave Briggs and Mark a hug and said, "I'm heading back to Heavenly Considerations. I've got three sets of cremated remains to deliver to veterinarians this afternoon. See you at the falls." Briggs and Jansen had chosen to marry on a bridge spanning Multnomah Falls, which towered above the Columbia River Gorge, 40 miles east of Portland.

Chuck Grayson also prepared to leave. He turned to Detective Larson and said, "I wanted to let you know you and I can still share information even though you're out of patrol and now a hotshot detective. You know I protect my sources."

"Sounds good, Chuck. Thanks."

"Why are you here?" asked Larson. "I know, it's a story for your blog."

"That and the fact that Briggs' dad was my best friend. I thought I would be a stand-in for his dad and mother since they couldn't be here for his big day."

"That's thoughtful," said Larson. "I had no idea you and Briggs had a family connection."

"Gotta go," said Grayson. "I have a story to post."

"Me, too," said Larson, who said goodbye to Kim and Jim and headed back to the police bureau.

"I'm heading out to Multnomah Falls to meet with the lodge restaurant manager about food for our reception after the wedding," said Briggs "First, I am going to make a quick stop at the condo and pick up a few things. I will meet you in White Salmon."

"Drive carefully, Kimmy. You've got a baby on board," he added.

"Come on, Briggs," she said. "We have talked about this. You will have plenty of time to fawn over Mary Kimberly when she arrives. No babying me."

Briggs smiled. "Yes, Sergeant Jansen. Anything you say."

After Larson and Jansen left, Briggs found himself alone in the middle of the empty atrium on the second floor of the Montgomery Park building, once a central warehouse for Montgomery Wards.

He wondered how he could he marry this woman—the love of his life and a police officer—after the crimes he had committed. Should he tell her? Would his confession drive Kim away or put him in prison? Could she push aside all her instincts and experience as a cop and keep it all a secret?

Jimbo, too late for second or third thoughts. Maxine and the others are in a better place. We just need to let sleeping dogs lie.

Maybe DIME was right, Briggs thought.

Just then, a tap on his shoulder made him jump. "Sorry, Dr. Briggs," said Richard Rodman. "You left your award at the table. I didn't mean to startle you."

"No problem," said Briggs. "I didn't see you coming. I was daydreaming, I guess. And again, thanks for the award and the praise. I appreciate it."

"You're welcome," said Rodman, who shook Briggs' hand, then headed out the door.

Briggs waited a minute and then stepped onto the escalator to the first floor, looking through enormous glass windows at a massive cloud formation in a clear blue sky. A beautiful day. So serene.

Despite what he had said to Rodman, his daydream was more like a nightmare. As his mind filled with visions of a crumbling future—despite his assurances to Helen that they would escape prosecution—a wave of nausea struck, making him bend over a planter box. After a minute, the feeling passed. He straightened up and headed to his van, and climbed in. He looked around and the queasiness returned. The van had been the scene of so much death.

Briggs took a deep breath, let it out, then pulled onto the street as he headed to the condo and then east to his White Salmon, Washington retreat. Maybe he could sit, look across the Columbia River with a beer in hand, and figure out what to do next. He had little time before his marriage to Kim the next day. Maybe he should disappear. Or tell her what happened and offer to turn himself in. Or just keep the whole thing a secret. Did he need to tell her anything? Didn't husbands and wives keep secrets from each other all the time?

CHAPTER THIRTY-FOUR

August 7, 2019

With the evidence now pointing to Helen or Briggs or both, Larson drove back to the Portland Police Bureau for one more look at the case file and paged through the evidence, including a witness report, a DNA match, and photos. Would he show up at the wedding and arrest Briggs before or after he sealed the deal with Kim?

After reviewing the file, he saw an email alert pop up on his screen. He had set it up so anything from Parabon NanoLabs identifying the DNA on the panties would send up a red flag. He opened the email, scanned the attached document and felt like lightning had struck him. His chest tightened. He heart race as he gasped for breath. The DNA on the panties belonged to Helen O'Donnell, maiden name of Helen Williams: his girlfriend and lover.

Larson had learned about the attack on Helen and now had evidence that Jerry Hoffman had taken her panties as a trophy. Poor Helen. The vision of her with Hoffman and a needle in her hand seared his brain.

Larson didn't want to put Helen in jeopardy. However, the puzzle pieces were falling into place: all the missing were Briggs's homeless clients. He did not want to think of Helen as a suspect. If it were his choice—and it came down to choosing someone to prosecute for the crimes—he hoped it was Briggs rather than Helen who would be guilty of killing five people. Larson closed the file and looked at his inbox. A sealed envelope was sitting on top. This was it. This was the report he had been waiting for that he had ordered without Melrose's knowledge or approval.

The envelope was from the Multnomah County Crime Lab. Inside the envelope would be the key to his entire case: an analysis of the blood from paw prints found in the Have Paws—Will Travel van.

If it turned up canine blood, he could discount the other evidence as a coincidence. Traces of human blood would change everything.

Larson began grinding his teeth and running his hands over his hair and face. He would like nothing more than a glass of Scotch to numb the pain he was feeling.

He stood up from the desk, took a huge gasp of air, and walked over to the Keurig coffee maker and put in a French Roast pod. A minute later, he took the filled cup back to his desk. Larson pulled a letter opener from his drawer, inserted it under the flap, and ripped it open. He reached in, pulled out a single sheet of paper, and put it face down on the desk. He threw the envelope in the trash and put the letter opener back in the drawer, sat up in his chair, and took a deep breath.

He turned the sheet face up, grabbed it with both hands, and read the findings.

"Oh, dear God, no. It can't be. God help me."

Larson slammed his fists on the desk, then twisted and tore the report, trying to destroy it. Make it go away. Finally, he wadded the shredded remains and threw them in the trash before sinking into his chair. The results were his worst nightmare. The blood matched DNA on the fiber taken from the Have Paws — Will Travel van floor: Robert McWhorter. He had found the smoking gun, and it had just sentenced the one or both of the most important people in his life to life in prison or worse.

Larson decided he would drive to White Salmon and confront Briggs and Helen. Kim would be there to witness it. He needed to find out and find out now. He ran out the door, got into his car, and checked out with the dispatcher. The probabilities were rolling around in his head as he drove over the speed limit along Highway 84 toward Hood River. He was 10 minutes from Briggs's get-away to help celebrate his award when Larson's phone beeped.

It was Jim Briggs texting a 9-1-1: "Helen just texted and said goodbye. She said there is no other way out. I tried to talk her down. Kim and I pulling into the driveway. You need to come ASAP."

Traffic ahead of him was forced to slow down and pay a toll to cross the bridge linking Hood River, Oregon, and White Salmon, Washington.

Larson opened his window, slammed his emergency light on top of his car, turned on his siren, and blew through the traffic. The steel ruts on the bridge caused his car to slip and slide, forcing him to slow down.

Two miles from the house, he pressed the accelerator to the floor and flew down the hill, barely in control as he hit 80 miles per hour on the narrow rural road.

Moments later, he pulled into Briggs' driveway, threw open the car door, and raced toward the house.

CHAPTER THIRTY-FIVE

August 7, 2019

Helen Williams had driven straight from the Covington Award ceremony in Portland to Briggs' getaway in White Salmon. During the drive, her thoughts jumped back to her college days with Briggs. Why couldn't she be the one having Briggs' child and heading off into the sunset? When she pulled into the driveway of Briggs' place, she turned off the motor and texted Briggs, apologizing for not being able to attend the upcoming wedding. Williams said something urgent had come up. She said she looked forward to greeting the new bride and groom.

Helen had something else in mind. Even if there was no DNA evidence of the bodies of the missing, there was circumstantial evidence for a prosecutor to win a first-degree murder verdict. The fact the so-called missing victims had either raped her or allowed it to happen was damning. She had motive, means, and opportunity. Helen had no way to get around that. No jury, no matter how sympathetic they might be to the assault, would exonerate her. Sadly, she and Mark could never be together. Briggs would go off on his new life, leaving little for her except a jail cell and decades of appeals.

Helen got out of her car and walked around the cottage to the front garden overlooking the Columbia River. She was quickly lost in a daydream as she watched windsurfers skipping carefree across the water. Then she sat down at Briggs' picnic table with a fat black marker and wrote six words, "I'm sorry. I love you guys" on a one-foot square of cardboard, the kind Portland's homeless flash at passersby looking for handouts. They would be her last words.

Helen picked up the cardboard and took it over to one of two Adirondack chairs. These were the same ones she and Briggs sat in a week before, drinking beer and talking about old times—talk that had led to the bedroom. What a sweet memory. They were living in the past and the reality of cheating on Mark with Briggs was far from her thoughts. She texted Jim and said there was only one way out of the mess she had created.

From her pocket, she removed a preloaded syringe. It would be a onetime experiment: since she could not give herself two shots simultaneously, she had combined the numbing pain-killing anesthetic propofol with a killing dose of barbiturate. She hoped that when she injected herself, she would get a little of the deadening effect of the sedating drug and less of the excruciating pain of the heart-stopping, brain-killing barbiturate. Just as she had inserted the needle into the intravenous line, Briggs and Jansen came around the corner of the house and froze. Briggs had shared Helen's text about missing the wedding knew something was amiss. They both understood what was going to happen and raced to Briggs' place in White Salmon.

"Don't come any closer," said Helen.

"Helen, stop!" Briggs commanded. He knew exactly what was about to happen. Then quieter, less threatening: "Just hold on one more second."

"Why wait?" asked Helen. "I killed those all those people. I'm going to be on Death Row within a year—or in jail forever."

"We talked about this," said Briggs. "No physical evidence exists, just the dog collars in the pet cemetery. The collars are evidence we found them wandering around, lost after their owners disappeared. Mark is just about to close the case. This is all about to go away."

Kim looked at Briggs, dumbfounded at the conversation, and Helen's ground-shaking admission that she was the killer Mark has been stalking. His feelings for Helen had blocked some innate sense that police detectives claim to have about guilt or innocence. He never saw this coming: his life was about to become a train wreck, and there is nothing anyone can do to stop it.

"Briggs, as usual, you're not making sense," said Helen. "You're standing right next to your fiancé, who is a cop, and I've just confessed. It's over."

"Helen," said Kim. "I heard what you said, and Briggs confessed last night about Maxine. The whole thing makes me numb. But I don't give a fuck. If I lose my job over this, so be it. I'm pregnant with Jim's baby, and I'm not raising her alone. As for Little Bobby's gang, they got what they deserved. 'Speak no evil, hear no evil, see no evil.'"

"It will not work for Mark," said Helen, relaxing her thumb on the syringe plunger. "He says he loves me but will have no alternative but to turn me in."

"Why don't you wait for a few minutes. I just talked to him. He is on his way. You could ask him."

"I care too much to put him in a position to choose me over his future. How could he possibly get involved with a serial killer?" Helen had killed four human beings—predators or not—who were not stray animals a veterinarian could legally euthanize. Briggs had been complicit, even cheered her on. He believed those killed deserved every drop of painful death they got. He had suffered from his own psychosis: DIME pushing him to help clear away Portland homeless strays. Was that a legal defense for Briggs? Yes, the homeless were going to die on the street. Still, Briggs understood that one cannot just kill people, and yet he took that step — pushed by a dark impulse and Helen's pain.

Kim had figured it out when she started reviewing Briggs' laptop files to help Mark. She had launched the PupFinder app and saw five points of light on the screen. They appeared to be in White Salmon at Briggs' getaway. At first, it puzzled her that all the points could converge on White Salmon. Then a light went on: they were the dogs of the missing. All had been wearing GPS collars. How could that be?

When she confronted Briggs, he did not deny it. He confessed everything. He said he would never lie to her. Keeping that kind of secret from her any longer would be acid to their relationship and future.

At first, Kim wanted to scream and yell at Briggs, even hit him. But her pregnancy had changed everything. Instead of reporting it to Mark, she deleted the app and the points of light, and all Briggs's homeless client information. Of course, the files had been backed up and would remain in the cloud for months or years. Eventually, they would be deleted, along with all references to the missing homeless.

As the drama unfolded, with Helen holding the syringe stuck into her arm, Mark was suddenly standing inside Briggs' home, in front of a large plate-glass window looking down on the unfolding scene. Kim and Briggs raced into the house to tell Mark what was happening. As he listened, never taking his eyes off Helen, she mouthed, "Sorry. I love you."

Larson, Jansen, and Briggs stood behind a picture window, bunched together like witnesses at the lethal injection of a death row inmate. Time seemed to stand still. They could not process the information fast enough to react. Death was coming for Helen like a freight train on full speed with no engineer onboard. As the thoughts raced through their minds, Helen pushed in syringe contents before they could get to her.

A slight grimace of pain crossed her face, a sign that her attempt to put the sedative and barbiturate into some combination to eliminate the pain of suffocation was only partially successful. A moment later, her eyes closed, and her head dropped into her lap. She was dead.

Larson, Jansen, and Briggs' faces were blank. They were stunned.

The first thing that came to Larson's mind before the horror of losing Helen hit him full force: "Case closed."

***

Mark, trailed by Kim and Briggs walked outside, kissed Helen on her still-warm lips, covered her with a blanket, and picked up an envelope on a table next to her body. In the chair next to Helen, he sank in the chair. Mark's name was on the front. He turned it over in his hand, delaying the truth he knew he would find—the shocking truth suicide victims told loved ones after the fact. He finally, pulled out the note and read it.

Dearest Mark,

How do I explain this to you—someone I loved, the man with whom I could have shared a future? For the past year, I have suffered incredible pain. I lost my baby, Rod died, then Little Bobby's gang savaged me. The only way to deal with that pain was to eliminate the threat I felt from these men—Briggs's clients—every time I went on the street to help the homeless.

I confessed to Briggs what I had been doing, and I begged Briggs to keep it a secret. Otherwise, he had nothing to do with any of it. He was on a humanitarian mission to help the homeless.

In the end, it damaged me beyond repair. I was that broken toy you get on Christmas that you had been shaking for a week, trying to figure out what it was. That's me, a broken person. I'm the defective gift you will be thankful you never need to open.

With Love Always,

Helen

Briggs, holding hands with Kim, turned to Mark who was now staring at the river below, like he was in a trance.

"Mark, I've already confessed to Kim. I'm ready to accept the punishment—for what I did and for not reporting Helen's crimes." Larson slumped in the chair opposite Briggs and Jansen, the picture of defeat. Briggs explained how he had euthanized Maxine Dorothy Reid, after desperately searching for a family to take her in. "You and Kim were there the day that Maxine screamed for God to take her. Her cries for help shook me. A dark impulse infected me, told me to help her find a way out."

"You're not God," Larson said coldly, looking up at Briggs, who frowned. He realized he could not expect a warm "that's okay, pal" response from his friend.

"After I got Maxine and her mother's sister on the phone together, I thought I had made a match," said Briggs. "I felt so good that my genealogy research and months working with Maxine would have a happy ending. I think if you could ask her, she would say the ending she got was peaceful. She escaped her addiction, fear of other homeless, and the brutal life on the street that would make her a coroner's statistic."

Larson did not need to tell Briggs that veterinarians are not doctors and prohibited from providing an assisted suicide prescription or helping humans die.

"Mark," Jansen said, drawing his attention away from Briggs. She and Larson had been police partners and she had saved his life when he was pinned down in a fire-fight with a bank robber. She wounded the bandit and pulled Mark out of the line of fire. Now, she needed a favor.

"I can't tell you how pissed I am at Briggs," she offered. "He jeopardized the future of our unborn daughter and betrayed your friendship and mine. Add to that, our friend Helen's pain and death, and I'm beyond emotion. I feel flat. I also know I'm not raising my child alone. I won't help put Jim in jail. I will do anything to prevent that from happening."

Larson and Jansen looked into his other's eyes. They had a connection from their years as partners that only another cop could understand. Some invisible code passed between them. Larson looked away and said, "I have a lot to think about, Kim. Right now, I need to take care of Helen's body and then figure out how to wrap up this case. I will not make any promises." Then he walked away.

CHAPTER THIRTY-SIX

August 19, 2019

Michael Melrose sat behind his gleaming desk, rubbing his hands over the surface, admiring the shine he had applied. He was like the captain of an aircraft carrier, satisfied that every crack and crevice had been spit and shined.

Melrose had neatly stacked case files in a black rack on the corner of the desk. Each slot in the file holder was color-coded by type of crime and status. Red signaled ongoing investigations with time pressure to solve them, while blue signaled cold case files headed for the basement storage area. Those would be digitized for future investigations. Once a paper hoarder, Melrose had acquired a new malady: obsessive-compulsive disorder. Along with an arrow-straight girlfriend, who was reorganizing his post-divorce life.

Larson pulled his gold detective shield off his belt and laid it down in the middle of Melrose's desk. Without looking up, Melrose picked it up, opened a drawer, and tossed it in. "I've learned a lot from Marty, I mean Lt. Simpson," Melrose said absently, moving his hand in a continuous circular motion, buffing his desktop to a soft sheen.

"I'll bet you have," Larson snapped. His tension was on full display.

"Do you have a problem, Larson?" Melrose said, looking angry as he put away his bottle of cleaner and buffing cloth. I'm trying to be more Zen, but you're not helping."

"Yes I do have a problem. And yes, we all are happy that you have someone new in your life."

That Melrose had been closing his door for private meetings with Lt. Marty Simpson for an hour, twice a week over the past month, was evidence that a romance was budding. You did not need to be a detective to see what they were up to.

Melrose also did not need his keen detective instincts to see that Larson was devastated. His girlfriend, Helen Williams, had turned out to be his suspect, a serial killer who took her own life. He had been sleeping with her for months and noticed nothing amiss. Watching her kill herself left him in shock.

"I've failed as a detective. My investigative skills are poor, and I have too much empathy to be good at this job. Street cop is a better fit. Or maybe another career altogether."

"Larson, being a good detective is all about learning from your mistakes. We all screw up. Our failures may mean that a parent who has lost a child to violence never gets justice because we missed a clue. A million things can happen. Yes, we apply some investigative tools we have learned. We also put our heart and soul into it, which complicates the investigative process. Heart and soul can help solve crimes, too. We look at what went wrong and what went right, and we move on."

"I can't do that," said Larson.

"Larson, I am putting you on unpaid administrative leave for the next six months. I'm locking your shield in my drawer. Go get a job as a night watchman or security guard. Or barrista. Whatever will give you a break and some peace of mind. When you're ready, your shield will be here. Now go, I've got a mess to clean up." Melrose was seeing a mess where there was none. Had his mountain of paper become so much a part of him, he was experiencing phantom pain like an amputee? Melrose pulled out his spray bottle and cloth and went back to buffing his desk. Larson shook his head and walked out.

***

A few hours later, Larson sat down with Chuck Grayson for over two hours, explaining what had happened. He left nothing out, including Briggs' role. He asked Grayson for no favors, nor did he try to influence how Grayson would cover the story.

In the end, Grayson reported Helen's death as a suicide, the result of the loss of her husband and a gang rape. There was no mention of Briggs' involvement, no doubt Chuck's favor to Briggs' dad, his best friend.

September 1, 2019

Larson picked up the phone and called Jim Briggs. They had not talked since the day Helen killed herself.

"Let's tie one on tonight," said Larson, "assuming your baby mama will let you out."

Briggs was surprised to get a call from Larson. Why now, he wondered, after he had called Larson and had left a half dozen messages over the past few weeks and got either no response or a curt, 'Can't make it' text. Briggs had reached out, attempting to soothe angry feelings over the loss of Helen and his own involvement and coverup of the death of five homeless people.

"Let me check with Kim about going out tonight," said Briggs, ignoring Larson's poke, then turned to Kim.

"Mark wants me to meet for a beer. He says he is celebrating the end of his detective career."

Kim shook her head and rolled her eyes.

She signaled for Briggs to hold his hand over the phone.

"You should go. Make sure you get Mark's ass in an Uber afterward. We want nothing happening to him. Same for you."

"Yes, Sergeant Jansen. By the way, I think I'm see a baby bump."

"Get the heck out of here before I give you a bump," she said playfully.

Jimbo, glad to see you're so happy. Still, you can do better than Jansen, don't you think? Isn't that what your mother would say?

"No, my mother would say she was proud of me."

***

Kim called Briggs the moment she got a copy of Larson's final report on the missing homeless. Maxine's status was undetermined. Briggs knew then he was safe; he had a new life ahead of him. He would not be living on Death Row.

CHAPTER THIRTY-SEVEN

September 15, 2019

Mike Melrose called Patrol Sergeant Kim Jansen into his office. When she arrived, she stood at the door, waiting for Captain Melrose to invite her in. He was not a warm and fuzzy guy, but gave her a big smile. "How long has it been since you took the detective exam?" Melrose asked.

"I don't know, a year or more," she said. "Why?"

"We need a competent, hard-working officer to fill a detective opening. Do you think that person is you?"

Too stunned to talk, Kim said nothing, while reaching down and touching her growing belly with both hands. Melrose opened his drawer and pulled out a detective shield and placed it on his gleaning desk. It was like a 24-carat, diamond-studded necklace in a display case at Tiffany's. It appeared almost too precious to touch. A thing of beauty. And Melrose was offering it to her.

"Don't be shy, Jansen. Take it before I change my mind. And don't worry, you'll get plenty maternity time off. Whatever our union benefit allows and more."

"She picked up the shield, clipped it to her belt, nodded at Melrose, and walked out."

"No need to thank me," he called after Jansen.

"Thanks, Captain," he heard as her footsteps faded down the hall.

"It's about time," she thought.

Jansen opened the door leading to the back lot where police vehicles were parked. She was so happy she wanted to jump up and down and scream. Instead, she tried to maintain her dignity as she walked slowly to her car.

She needed to call Briggs and meet for a little celebration.

CHAPTER THIRTY-EIGHT

Wounded Portland Police Detective Stabbed, Fights for her Life and the Life of Her Unborn Child

By Chuck Grayson

September 23, 2019—PORTLAND—The City is holding its collective breath tonight as Kim Mary Jansen, a Portland Police Bureau detective, fights for her life and the life of her unborn child. Jansen, a bureau veteran with seven years of experience, she had been a detective only a week.

A man wanted for an armed robbery stabbed Jansen in the abdomen moments after she arrived on the scene to back up Patrol Officer Bill Brayman.

The suspect, Arnold Ray Deerfield III, a man with a long criminal record who allegedly committed a robbery just days after being released from prison, was shot and killed by Officer Brayman.

According to a police spokesperson, Brayman saw Deerfield run a red light and pulled him over. Brayman ran Deerfield's license number and discovered the outstanding warrant that warned officers the man should be considered armed and dangerous. Before exiting his car, Brayman radioed for help. Jansen, the officer closest to the scene, responded to the call.

With the two officers approaching, Deerfield got out of the car with his hands up. As Detective Jansen moved within a few feet ready to handcuff the man, he swung around with a hunting knife in hand and plunged it into the detective, an inch below her protective vest.

Officer Brayman, his gun drawn, ordered Deerfield to drop the knife.

Instead, according to the police report, Deerfield advanced on the officer until Brayman shot him. They pronounced Deerfield dead at the scene.

At the hospital, officers have been standing vigil along with Detective Jansen's husband, Veterinarian James Allen Briggs. Briggs, who is the owner of the mobile canine care service, Have Paws—Will Travel. When I publish this story, Jansen will have been in surgery for over six hours. I'm told that obstetricians and trauma surgeons have teamed up to save the baby and the detective. According to Briggs, the baby has a name: Mary Kimberly Briggs. Prayers to the Briggs Family.

Watch this blog for updates.

***

Police Detective Will Survive While Efforts Fail to Save her Unborn Child

By Chuck Grayson

October 1, 2019—I am sad to report this morning that doctors failed to save the unborn child of Detective Kim Mary Jansen. Detective Jansen, as I reported a few days ago, is the police officer stabbed Tuesday while assisting another officer with the arrest of a robbery suspect.

Robbery Suspect Arnold Ray Deerfield III was shot and killed following the attack.

Detective Jansen, doctors say, still is in grave condition. She suffered severe injuries when Deerfield plunged a hunting knife deep into her abdomen, mortally wounding the unborn baby.

"We have done our best to stabilize Detective Jansen, but she is in extremely critical condition."

"We will stay strong for our fallen comrade," said Captain Michael J. Melrose, chief of the detective bureau. "She is a fine officer and a promising detective. She is a fighter. We know she'll make it through this tragedy."

I will report updates on Detective Jansen's condition as I receive them.

***

When Mark Larson showed up in the critical care waiting-area and saw his friend, Jim Briggs, across the room, his eyes filled with tears.

Briggs walked over to Larson and said, "Come with me." Larson said nothing.

Briggs led him down the hall to a door with stained glass. A sign identified it as the hospital chapel. Larson and Briggs walked in and looked around. They were alone.

The two men looked at each other. Briggs walked over, hugged Larson, and they both burst into tears. Nothing they could say would bring back Kim's baby or change what had happened.

"I know Kim will make it," said Briggs, wiping tears on his sleeve.

"We can only hope," said Larson.

ABOUT THE AUTHOR

Photo by Dennis F. Freeze

Bruce Lewis was a crime reporter for several California daily newspapers, covering police and fire. His reporting earned six awards for best news and feature writing. He is the author of the Master Detective cover story, *Bloody Murder in Beautiful Downtown Burbank*, and the book *Tweet It! Great News Writing 140 Characters at a Time*. His work as a communications consultant earned more than 30 professional awards. He lives with his wife in Portland, Oregon.

NOTE FROM THE AUTHOR

Word-of-mouth is crucial for any author to succeed. If you enjoyed *Bloody Paws*, please leave a review online—anywhere you are able. Even if it's just a sentence or two. It would make all the difference and would be very much appreciated.

Thanks!
Bruce Lewis